The Twin

The Twin

Paul Folmsbee

TIMBUKTU BOOKS AND PUBLISHING
New York   London   New Delhi

ISBN: (XXXXXXXXXXXXX)

Thomas therefore, who is called Didymus, said to his fellow disciples, "Let us go, that we may die with him."

The Gospel of John, Chapter 11 Verse 16

Didymus: Greek word meaning twin

Tau'ma: Aramaic word meaning twin. Alternate spellings: thomas, tomas, t'oma.

"Now since it has been said that you are my twin and true companion."

Jesus speaking to Thomas as recorded in the Gospel of Thomas

Judas (not Iscariot) said to Him, Lord, what then has happened that You are not going to disclose Yourself to us, and not to the world?

The Gospel of John, Chapter 14 Verse 22

Now Thomas (also known as Didymus), one of the Twelve, was not with the disciples when Jesus came. So the other disciples told him, "We have seen the Lord!" But he said to them, "Unless I see the nail marks in his hands and put my finger where the nails were, and put my hand into his side, I will not believe." A week later his disciples were in the house again, and Thomas was with them. Though the doors were locked, Jesus came and stood among them and said, "Peace be with you!" Then he said to Thomas, "Put your finger here; see my hands. Reach out your hand and put it into my side. Stop doubting and believe." Thomas said to him, "My Lord and my God!" Then Jesus told him, "Because you have seen me, you have believed; blessed are those who have not seen and yet have believed."

The Gospel of John, Chapter 20 Verses 24–29

Jesus performed many other signs in the presence of his disciples, which are not recorded in this book. But these are written that you may believe that Jesus is the Messiah, the Son of God, and that by believing you may have life in his name.

The Gospel of John, Chapter 20 Verses 30–31

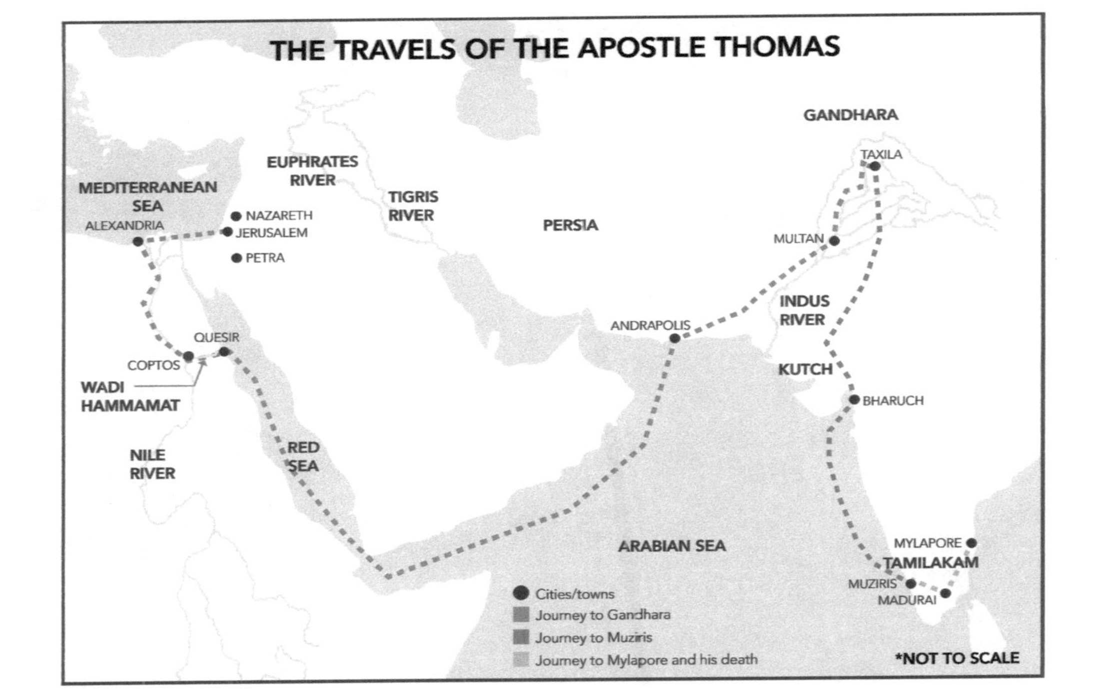

THE TRAVELS OF THE APOSTLE THOMAS
GANDHARA
TAXILA
EUPHRATES RIVER
TIGRIS RIVER
PERSIA
MEDITERRANEAN SEA
ALEXANDRIA
NAZARETH
JERUSALEM
PETRA
MULTAN
INDUS RIVER
ANDRAPOLIS
KUTCH
BHARUCH
QUESIR
COPTOS
WADI HAMMAMAT
NILE RIVER
RED SEA
ARABIAN SEA
MYLAPORE
TAMILAKAM
MUZIRIS
MADURAI
Cities/towns
Journey to Gandhara
Journey to Muziris
Journey to Mylapore and his death
*NOT TO SCALE

Prologue

Lieutenant Orna Kiretz heard the call coming in on the radio. Despite the static, she could still hear the emotion in the dispatcher's voice.

"Bombing at the Western Wall!" the voice said in Hebrew. The Israeli soldier picked up her radio and motioned for her squad to come near.

"Copy, Center," she responded. "We are not far from the site and will run over there as backup. Confirm location, please. The Western Wall? Where exactly?"

Damn, she thought. *Don't we have that place locked down? How did this happen again?*

"Roger, Rover," crackled the voice on the radio, acknowledging Orna's transmission. "Apparently, he detonated right at Wilson's Arch. Standing by for more. I will update further as we go."

"Copy that. Bombing at Wilson's Arch. My squad should be there in a few minutes."

Orna pronounced "Wilson's Arch" with a decidedly American accent in her otherwise fluent stream of Hebrew. The 2000-year-old arch on the plaza by the Western Wall was oddly named after British explorer Charles William Wilson in 1865.

It seemed like her squad had just stopped to take a break, and now they were moving again. Orna quickly began strapping her equipment back on. She turned to look at her team, all turned towards her, watching her expectantly.

"Time to go," she said decisively, putting her arm and index finger in the air and twirling it in a circular motion. "Eddy"—pointing at the young man—"you take point. We are just backup guys, but everyone stay alert! There should already be a heavy presence, there."

Her squad assembled, Orna led the way.

Chapter I

*Greetings! I was born in Bethlehem, in Judea, not far away.
I am traveling with my brother Judas, not Iscariot, son
of Joseph. We usually call my brother Judas "Thomas,"
which means "twin" in my language. The Greeks call him
Didymus, which also means twin. You may already know
him by that name. We call him twin so that we do not
confuse him with my other companion named Judas, the one
who betrayed me in the garden. Many of you have called
my twin "the doubter." True perhaps, but he is a man of
great courage, too, and braver than most. When I healed
Lazarus and my own people wanted to stone me, it was my
brother Thomas who said to the others, "Let us also go that
we may die with him." My twin has the strength and courage to travel to the east, to India, although he does not want
to. I will go with him for a while.*

—My name is Isa.

THOMAS WOKE WITH a start. He knew he had been dreaming, but he couldn't remember what. Something had frightened him. He was lying on his back, his slender frame stretched out on a woolen cloak on the earthen floor. Staring at the ceiling, he focused on the rough-carved and splintered beams above. The floor was hard-packed clay, a circumstance the Nazarene was accustomed to. A poor carpenter, he had spent his life sleeping on the ground.

As his consciousness slowly returned, he began to remember everything he had been dreaming about. All the events of the last few months sifted rapidly through his mind. How could he forget? Isa had been killed. He had died on the cross for all to see. He, Thomas, had watched in horror. The unthinkable had happened. Isa killed!

Thomas had touched his dead body. And then, like the others, he had run away. He had not run far. Where could he go? It was more like hiding, just enough to stay out of sight. The authorities, especially the religious leaders, were after them. Best to avoid Roman soldiers too, even now.

But with Peter guiding them, the disciples had come together. Slowly, even timidly at first, but they came. They began to find themselves. They found their courage.

And as they came together, a great miracle happened. Mary had come to the companions with an incredible story. Isa was alive! At first, he couldn't believe it. He needed to see Isa alive with his own eyes before he could believe. He told the others so. Thomas, lying on the floor, smiled as he remembered the moment. He would not believe unless he saw Isa. And then he did.

Thomas first saw his brother in that locked room. He had touched his hands, hands that had been nailed to the cross and had somehow miraculously healed. He had seen and touched the wound where the Roman soldier had thrust his spear into the side of Isa. He had seen him do it. Even now, Thomas again felt agony as he remembered the terrible sight. And yet, Isa was now back among them, never really staying long but appearing and then disappearing.

And now, here he was in Egypt with Isa. Thomas' mood quickly changed from nightmare to happiness as he considered the day. Isa was here with him in Alexandria. The great lighthouse, the monumental buildings, the library, the mighty city, spread out before him. Even Jerusalem lacked the spectacular beauty and setting of this city. Thomas rose and stepped out, seeking his brother.

Thomas could see that the Mediterranean reached into the very center of Alexandria, a very different city from the mighty Jerusalem he knew. The main commercial market was massive, beyond compare to any of the thousands of markets stretching from the Indus River in the east to the great markets of Rome herself. The market in Alexandria was bigger than any of them, with sections imaginatively organized, divided, and arranged by produce and products from the whole world: fish, vegetables, bread, clothing, leather goods, and on and on. Each boundary of every section of the market was negotiated and then renegotiated again and again by the guilds as seasons and produce changed, political and economic fortunes rose and fell, and the tides of the economy ebbed and flowed. Kings and emperors from all over the world sent their commercial emissaries to Alexandria to trade, purchase, and invest. When you lived in Alexandria, it seemed like you were at the center of the world.

In practical terms, the market was made up of hundreds and hundreds of vendors packed together in one corner of the teeming city. The border of each stall or vendor was marked out using an assortment of narrow beams, cluttered mud bricks, and even stone walls if the vendor could afford it. In some cases, less successful vendors only managed makeshift branches or worn-out fabric to delineate a border with their neighbor.

The sounds of the market produced a riotous din, made by both man and animal. Hundreds would shout out in one great cacophony to the city like a disorganized chorus: Onions! Bread! Mutton! Dates! Fresh spinach! Cattle would bellow. Adding to the cacophony, the voices would speak out not in one language but in the many languages of the place. Aramaic, Greek, and Coptic—the mother tongue—seemed to dominate, but the general clamor made it nearly impossible to distinguish what any single person was offering unless the ear was practiced.

Powerful, stocky men, naked, sweating, and straining, labored past the stalls and down narrow lanes and passages, carrying in and out heavy sacks filled with grains, lentils, and salt. Most of the stalls were occupied by women dressed in drab linen, arms impossibly filled with nursing babies, crying or laughing children, and merchandise and produce of all descriptions. Donkeys and street dogs dozed in every available piece of shade, with cattle chewing their cud nearby. Camels and horses remained hitched to posts on the edge of the market and mostly stayed clear of the bedlam, too large to be moving around in the cramped spaces unless their strength was absolutely necessary. The occasional angry camel could be heard and seen spitting or moaning at whoever foolishly disturbed its stupor in the heat.

Women squatted upon the ground in front of the stalls, careful not to actually touch the filthy earth that passed under their feet.

Each had spent a lifetime sitting on their haunches, a practice that was clean and comfortable in their poverty. For them, the world had little or no furniture on which to sit. Poorer vendors, such as the migrants and newer arrivals without a stall, unable to negotiate a place in the shade, laid their goods out on a tattered piece of woolen cloth, reed matting, or in some cases leaves, exposed to the harsh sun.

Abandoned children played on the edge of the market along with the most destitute of migrants. This segment of humanity was kept out by Roman soldiers, market officials, and hostile vendors. Entire families, destitute and lost, camped along the walls, waiting for handouts, work opportunities, slavery, or death. The numbers were smaller this year because harvests were good.

The market was punctuated with color in a sea of drab linen tunics. A few managed to purchase dyed clothing, blue being much preferred, although red, yellow, and other colors and designs were evident. Most of the garb consisted of simple linen fabric, although some coarse wool garments were present, usually indicating the wearer was from Judea or another land. Working men tended to be barebacked with not much more than a loincloth or simple skirt. Some slaves and their families were completely naked. Others were dressed in linen tunics, as were most of the women.

The men doing all the heavy work and lifting in the market were treated much like the domestic animals they worked with. No one gave them a second look. The laborers were men without history, and their faces revealed little emotion. They had been sold into slavery or indentured, most since childhood. It was a natural condition for most of them, although a few chafed at the lack of independence. In many cases, the men willingly sold themselves into bondage, viewing it as the only way to ensure protection and obtain food and shelter for their families in a world that was harsh and unforgiving. More than half of them, when they completed their indentured obligations, would sell themselves back into bondage, an acceptable social pact and contract.

A few distinguished men could be seen in the market too. Men who dressed better than all the rest, with bright colors, cleaner and newer looking clothing, and leather sandals on their feet. The most important of these men wore headbands or even a turban. The most exclusive of all would exhibit startlingly white, bleached tunics, marked by colorful scarfs and sashes, all pressed and clean looking. These men marked their place in society by the clothes they wore. A few of these were quite plump, showing off their health and wealth.

Isa, with Thomas just a few paces behind him, took note of these better-dressed men as they made their way through the market. He spoke Aramaic to most he encountered, asking for one such distinctively dressed man, a traveling merchant he was seeking.

"Sh'lam!" Thomas would hear his brother call out in greeting, a warm and inviting smile on his visage, as they met the eyes of each person they encountered. Isa's queries were always rewarded with understanding, although a few of the men Isa spoke to had strong foreign accents and clearly preferred another tongue.

Isa and Thomas were in the market looking for Abbanes, the merchant. Isa had first met Abbanes in Jerusalem at the Temple Mount, by the famous Great Arch, just a few weeks ago. Abbanes had gone there to the temple to pray. As he was leaving the complex, Abbanes found himself in conversation with Isa and was soon explaining the purpose of his journey. Curiously, Isa seemed to already know Abbanes and everything about him.

Isa and Abbanes had agreed to meet in Alexandria to seal a contract. For Isa, traveling with Thomas, the journey down to Alexandria from Jerusalem had been brief, almost pleasant. The majority of the population in Alexandria seemed to be Coptic, Greek, or even Hebrew, although Isa found representatives of the entire world living here, a condition he approved of. Alexandria also had colonies from Ethiopia, Persia, Taprobanes, India, as well as Roman soldiers, and even representatives from some of the Chinese empires. Thomas liked the city, and if times were different, he would have considered staying on to find work. But that was not an option, anymore. He was on a mission: The Great Commission and India were on his mind. Isa was directing him.

While both Hebrews loved the sights and sounds of the market, not everything delighted them. The market odors were like a living force: a humid, evil convergence, a black concoction of days-old rotting vegetables, butchered goat meat, human feces, and stagnant pools of fetid water. Thomas found the fish market to be the worst. Most of the ocean fish sold were dried and hard, the best way to preserve this vital source of protein. The drying fish were laid out all over the banks of the Nile, close in from the sea and leading right into the market, forcefully delivering an overwhelming saltwater stench.

Despite the smell, Alexandria, the city of the Mediterranean Sea, also had a special treat for those who could afford it: fresh river fish from the Nile. These were much more palatable and sweet than their sea cousins, particularly if cooked and eaten the same day they were caught. The only exception to the rule was during the rains when the Nile flooded and took on a muddy and cloudy look. Then the river fish absorbed the flavor of the mud and were best avoided.

The location of the market had been determined in part so that fishermen and traders could drag their boats close up on the land to the market to load and offload easily. All day, bounty from the sea but also imports of all kinds from many different Mediterranean lands constantly arrived or departed this way. And early each morning, fishermen would drag their fishing boats up the channel in the back of the market, loaded down with their catch, in some cases still alive in their watery holds. The freshest fish would be distributed in wooden tubs to each stall, graded and sold by size and quality. Few could afford more than a few pieces of one fish. At times during the day, a vendor would cut off the head of a fish and quickly impale it high up on a small stake for all to see, advertising the immediate sale of fresh fish. The eyes on the head of the fish would briefly continue to blink in the hot sun, gills straining for the oxygen it could not find: fresh fish from the Nile. The head was the signal for all close by that the stall would sell pieces, not just whole fish. The most expensive piece would be the head itself, prized both for stock and the delicate flesh it contained.

Both Thomas and Isa stood exactly 5 feet 6 inches tall, about the same height as most of the men around them and considerably taller than the women who operated and managed the bulk of the market stalls. Their eyes were deep brown, and their faces were lean and angular. Each kept a beard, their skin baked brown anywhere the tunic failed to cover. Both sported muscular arms, their hands strong and calloused from decades of building and carpentry work, travel, and fishing. Their tunics were light brown and made from simple wool, clean and neat. Not men of wealth, but hardworking men. Despite the remarkable similarities, Isa stood out with a very special smile, warm and caring, that seemed to brighten the day of everyone around him.

"Isa," called out Abbanes, cheerfully if not abruptly in greeting, as the men found each other in the shade of a fruit seller's stall. Isa turned around and walked towards his friend. It was a hot day, and Abbanes was already sweating in the tiny sliver of shade the small stall managed to create. Isa greeted Abbanes warmly in return, introducing Thomas.

Abbanes, a son of David like Isa, was a very different kind of man, both in bearing and in appearance. Three inches taller than Isa, he was heavier set but less muscled. His beard was full and neat and carefully trimmed. His clothing was made of the finest white linen, and Isa could see fine blue lines and designs in the tunic he had not noticed before when they had first met in Jerusalem by the Great Arch. On his hands were rings of gold and silver, and about his neck but tucked partly under his tunic, Isa could see what appeared to be a gold chain. As the two men talked, Isa noticed four more men standing back from Abbanes. These men maintained a respectful distance but clearly were with him. Two of these men visibly sported daggers and spears.

After a few moments of courtesies, Abbanes motioned to Isa and asked him to follow. The two men set out side by side, with the others following behind. They continued to speak lightly and cordially, mostly of their brief journey from Jerusalem. After a walk of a few minutes, they left the area of the market and came upon a section of town that sported high, clean walls. The men turned down a second street until they stopped in front of one grand entrance in a long wall. Massive wooden doors, framed in iron, barred entry to all comers. In front of the doors and in the street, four men, deeply black in skin and hair, stood in front of the gates with spears and shields at the ready. They had a hard, toned look with strong muscular torsos. Isa had seen few Africans in his life and greeted them warmly. The warriors, not used to even being noticed, politely nodded back.

Abbanes had spent most of his life in the lands far to the east, in India, in a country called Gandhara, in the service of King Gondophores. This young king was ambitious, intent on expanding his growing empire in all directions. Kingdoms from the south, west, north, and east were now sending emissaries to meet and consult with this mighty and rising king. Still others sent students and scholars to study at the growing Buddhist University and to learn more of the teachings of the Middle Path.

But it was not enough. Most of the buildings in the capital, Taxila, were great masonry works. They were impressive, but not impressive enough. As the empire expanded, Gondophores needed to impress visiting kings, princes, military commanders, allies, and even enemies who visited him from near and far.

The king desired builders who could bring something new to the city and region. He wanted something different. Carpentry was well-known and developed throughout the civilized world, but his friend and merchant Abbanes, a Jew originally from Jerusalem, often bragged about the great woodworkers, masons, and builders he encountered on his journeys to Judea, Egypt, and even distant Greece and Rome.

In the mind of the king, these cities were the great power centers of the world. He decided to send Abbanes on a trade mission to buy laborers, builders, architects, and artists and bring them back to Taxila. The king also needed fine furnishings for his new palace. The Jewish merchant was instructed to buy the finest furniture, chairs, tables, dishes, lamps, cloth, and even rare wood, if he could carry it. Parts and pieces of a great palace containing immense wealth and bearing treasures needed to showcase a rising empire.

Abbanes had first made for the cities of Egypt, a journey of great distances and no easy feat even for an experienced traveler. A successful trader, he used commerce to help pay for the voyage as he traveled and traded down the Indus and across the sea. He finally entered Egypt on a port on the Red Sea, where he began the overland route to the Nile River. Sailing up the Nile, he, at last, reached Alexandria. From there, he had branched out north to many cities, including Damascus and Jerusalem.

Once again, Abbanes had marveled at the beauty of Jerusalem, the city of his birth. It was there that he had chanced upon Isa the carpenter near the temple. They had stopped next to the famous Great Arch, the biggest near the temple and a favorite place for the trader. He had to come here every time he visited Jerusalem. It was like touching home for the Hebrew.

There was something special about Isa. In front of the Great Arch, the two men talked easily, as if they had been friends their entire lives. Abbanes was immediately taken with him and invited Isa to join him on his return journey to Taxila. Isa explained that he could not make the journey to India, but his brother Judas, whom he called Thomas, was an even better carpenter and builder. Isa told him that he would collect Thomas, and together they would travel from Jerusalem over to Alexandria to meet Abbanes there.

Abbanes was a contradiction. He was a hardened businessman but at times also a compassionate and intelligent man. He normally advanced his cause at all costs—even ruthlessly, if necessary—but he would help individuals who appealed to him and even show mercy at times. This deal simply appealed to him. He liked it even more that the terms were made in Jerusalem at the Great Arch. No money would change hands until Thomas first arrived in Alexandria ready to take passage to Gandhara. Isa readily agreed to the terms and guaranteed that Thomas would be there. He reassured Abbanes by telling him that he, Isa, would personally escort him there. Abbanes was using a store in Alexandria as his base of operations where he would consolidate all his purchases. The two men agreed to meet in the market in three weeks' time. And so it was that Isa and Thomas found Abbanes in Alexandria.

Abbanes escorted the two brothers through the great gate and into the residence. Sitting in the shade of a tree in the courtyard, the deed was signed, and the fee paid to Isa: three litrae of unstamped silver. It seemed a good deal, and Abbanes was more than pleased with his new acquisition. He kept thinking about the nature of this man, Isa, who seemed to have a calming effect on all those around him. Abbanes would normally have demanded more proof that Thomas was an accomplished builder. Yet, Isa conveyed a truthfulness and earnestness that was impossible to resist. Abbanes took Isa at his word and purchased Thomas' services.

As Isa walked away, he suddenly turned to Thomas and said, "You shall go with your price and always with my grace." He handed him the three pieces of unstamped silver.

Chapter 2

The devil whispers, "You cannot withstand the storm."
The lion replies, "I am the storm."

—Anonymous

THERE WAS ONLY one twin now, old and weak. It had not always been so. Once, there had been two strong and powerful Sher: great Persian lions. Each was more than three meters in length from nose to tail, with great claws, and teeth as long as daggers. They had formed an alliance at birth in the dry scrub brush that was their home. Their mother had hidden them from the beginning: two males and one female. At birth, they could not open their eyes. But as the days passed, they grew steadily, first on a diet of their mother's rich milk and later that of their mother's sisters. Still, later, they would feast on the protein-rich diet of the super pride kills provided by the many and fierce female Sher.

Their sister was killed in the brush before they even returned to the pride from their birthing. A passing family of hyenas found their hiding place and killed her. The twins were silent throughout, instinctively knowing that staying hidden was their best chance for survival. Their mother returned just in time to save them. The hyenas, not completely cowed by a single lioness, begrudgingly moved on, knowing that the super pride was nearby with many more lions willing and ready to defend their members. It was after the death of their sister, and one month after their birth, that the two brothers returned to the pride with their mother.

Pride life was exciting but dangerous. Most of the cubs would not survive. But the twins did. They noisily fought for their fair share of the scraps of flesh at each kill, being the offspring of a massive Persian sher and the swiftest and best lioness hunter of the pride. As they grew, their aging father mostly tolerated their presence, along with the two other companion males that guarded the super pride. All three males represented a serious threat to the twin cubs. A massive male with a huge black mane, the twin's father, along with the two other males, defended the pride area with brutal force.

When their father roared, the shock waves alone would make the acacia leaves seem to tremble. The cheetah family two miles away would stop and turn with alarm, and the very ground itself would seem to give way to the cavernous vibration. Men passing in the caravans just south of the river would momentarily halt, feeling a slight shiver run through their bodies, a primeval sense of danger and caution running through them. The roaring seemed impossibly loud, almost supernatural.

Pride life was not stable and changed constantly. The equilibrium of pride was often altered and affected by a singular event. In the case of the super pride, the change began with the kick from a lone buffalo that broke the jaw of the twins' father, a seemingly indestructible male. Now unable to eat and defend himself, he slowly starved to death and finally gave himself up to the harsh sun and the predators of the air.

But the kick of the buffalo heralded the first of many important changes in the life of the twin male cubs. They were nineteen months old now, formed by evolutionary biology into junior but growing apex predators, members of an elite species on the planet. The other two males, uncles to the twins, no longer tolerated their presence, and it was clear they would soon be driven from the pride. With the loss of the twins' father, the super pride territory was now only guarded by these two males. It was not enough to protect the super pride lionesses from the other nomadic males constantly searching for their chance to spread their genes and rule their pride area.

The transition happened quickly. Four apex predators—an alliance of young, strong Persian Sher, two brothers, and two male cousins—approached. They had been calling and roaring all night in the darkness. They came to the super pride from the east, scenting the bones left by the vultures of the twins' father, and catching the scent of the pride and the lionesses too. The scent of the females was strong, involuntarily causing the male lions to scrunch their noses and driving them on to action.

The twins' uncles listened as the four contenders approached. Instead of conserving their strength for the coming battle, they maintained a tense and exhausting vigil all night, angrily answering each challenge with a roar of their own. As the ranks closed, the two older male lions finally ran off in the direction of the four usurpers. At sunrise, the four younger males finally came upon the two aging kings. The twins' uncles were not easily cowed and had long experience chasing off younger suitors.

This time was different. The older sher were outmatched by numbers, strength, and the very youth of the usurpers. The battle was fierce and loud, as lion charged into lion, brush and branch thrust aside. And then it ended abruptly, with the two older males giving way to the younger, more powerful generation. Humiliated and weakened, the retiring kings disappeared into the bush and oblivion.

The four new males were the new masters of their domain. The new super pride had no place for two adolescent male lions not related to them. Although not yet fully accomplished hunters, the adolescent twin brothers were chased off to hunt on their own, unwelcome in the pride, unwelcome by the newcomers.

The young brothers assumed the life of nomads like their fathers before them. During the course of the first year, they nearly starved. But they soon found their pace and, working together, began to make bigger and bigger kills. Nomads in every sense, they wandered far and wide in the land, often encountering other males who would chase them off. As time passed, they became successful hunters and scavengers, using their dark manes to look twice as large as they really were, chasing off leopards, hyenas, and other predators from kills and seizing their prey as their own. By the age of five, the twins were magnificent specimens and nearly succeeded in chasing off a few males to seize females and a pride of their own. Each twin had surpassed their father in size.

And at the age of five, the two male lion brothers finally had a chance at their own pride, driving off a lone male who was vainly clinging to a pride of five lionesses. The old male was long past his prime and an easy target for the twins, suffering a rare mortal wound on his neck as he was unceremoniously chased off. The twins found and killed the remaining pride cubs and drove off one adolescent male. The lionesses were out on the hunt that day and not present, or they would have savagely defended their offspring. Not now. The females returned to find their cubs gone, their remains already consumed by predators with just a slight scent here and there recording what little remained of their brief existence. Within days, the lionesses came into estrus anew and soon welcomed the twins, killers of their own cubs, as their new mates, lovers, and companions.

For more than six years afterward, the Persian sher twins dominated their landscape, roaring out their primordial being in one great voice, marking the terrain with their pungent urine so that other predators would take special care and note their fearsome presence. For five years, they mated, hunted, slept with full bellies, and contributed to a new generation of predatory lions. They endured heat and dry spells, the indignities of cubs playing with their tails, and the death of two of their pride lionesses. And then, like before, the change in the status of the pride was abrupt and unexpected.

The twins were nearly twelve years old now. Their teeth were decaying, yellow, and broken, their bodies covered in scars from battles small and large. Their reactions were slower, their bellies bigger, and their manes black and thick. Frequently, rival partnerships of males could be heard roaring in the distance, sometimes nightly. Like before, there was one small mistake in judgment, and then everything changed.

One of the tributaries was swollen with flood waters, and the carcass of a wild ass, just at the edge of the water, was caught up on the edge of the embankment. One of the aging twins had jumped down to seize the animal, not perceiving that part of the shore was under a blanket of leaves that camouflaged a deep and impenetrable bog. His legs immediately became trapped in the dense mud as he landed. The frantic lion thrashed about, making his predicament even worse, his body slipping still deeper into the grip of the mud. The mud was like a vise, locking each leg like a cold, wet force but still exposing his hind side.

The mighty lion roared his frustration. His great distress drew the attention of a hyena clan close by, offspring of the very animals that had killed his cub sister years before. At first, the hyenas were cautious and careful, watching their ancient adversary from afar.

The rivalry between the two species was natural and deep. There was no hatred between them. Hatred is a human trait. Lions merely killed hyenas whenever the opportunity presented, instinctively recognizing them as a threat to their cubs and as competitors for their prey. The hyenas operated on much the same level, killing their competitor whenever the rare opportunity presented itself in reverse. Neither would generally feed on the remains of the other, although even that was not out of bounds.

Trapped in the mud, the lion tired quickly, his stamina gone, unable to defend himself while the hyenas cautiously approached him from the relative safety of the embankment to his rear. He could hear and even smell them coming, but he could not quite see them as he vainly thrust about, looking back, slashing at the air with his powerful jaws open. Still, they did not immediately rush in, not quite trusting the predicament the lion was in. Lighter and nimbler than the heavy male lion, the hyena clan, growing in numbers, managed to extract the ass carcass from the dense mud as the lion angrily watched.

Still, they waited as the lion vainly struggled to free himself, becoming weaker and weaker in the effort. The hyenas waited patiently, at first stealthily rushing in and out, taking small bites at the rear of the animal as he tired, watching as exhaustion took him. As the morning passed, the twin lion, panting heavily in the hot sun all afternoon, barely registered a moan as the hyenas moved in close to tear at his exposed flesh.

And yet, the lion clung to life as the day melted into the night. The clan was relentless, keeping up the attack until the twin lion, once mighty and powerful, could no longer stop the attack even close by his side. The matriarch of the clan, a particularly large female, finally succeeded in grasping the soft underbelly of the lion, tearing open his bowels, and exposing his flesh. The end approaching, the once fierce male suddenly reanimated, finding a brief reservoir of hidden strength. He inflicted a mortal wound on one of his tormentors, an unprepared adolescent who approached too close and lingered too long. For the lion twin, though, it was over. His renewed strength abandoned him almost as fast as it arose and just when he needed it most. He had nothing left.

The battle had drawn the attention of the river dwellers, too. As the hyenas backed off from the momentary surge of the lion, two massive crocodiles succeeded in seizing the lion from the riverside, nearly tearing off the two hind legs of the twin as they twisted for position in the water. Now seizing the carcass in their jaws, they finally pulled the once mighty male free from the mud and into the brown depths of the river.

And so, there was one twin, now. In days, it was his turn to be driven from the super pride and return to the life of a solitary nomad. One old twin lion was not enough. Three males chased him off with little fight. And this time, nomadic life was much harsher than before. His twin and life partner was with him no more. His once great speed was not fast enough. His eyesight was not clear. Time after time, he failed to make a kill, and now, too often, he would suffer the indignity of hyena families chasing him from a kill.

And so it was that the twin lion discovered easier prey. At this place was the crossroads of the great caravans. A steady procession of camels, horses, oxen, cattle of all kinds—asses, dogs, goats, and especially men—all passed by. At first, the old sher male remained cautious. An instinctive fear told him to be wary of men. But hunger consumed and tormented him. He tracked a caravan as it passed, staying hidden in the acacias that marked the passage, invisible to man, although camels and horses would nervously pick up his scent from time to time, and dogs would suddenly bark and bristle, their masters looking about and wondering why.

At times, the twin would lose sight of the caravan, sleeping in the heat of the mid-day sun, up on a hillock, and in the shade of a small tree. But other caravans would soon appear, and the old male finally stopped trekking, content to wait for them to pass his hillock. And finally, ravenous, driven almost mad by hunger, he attacked one night and killed a donkey on the edge of one caravan's camp. The hunt was easy, and the prey was almost defenseless.

Easy prey for an aging male lion. Success soon followed more success. Donkeys, goats, and even a dog once fell to his brief and easy charge. The twin stayed near the hillock, watching the caravans pass, ready to feed on this easy source of prey.

And he finally tasted the flesh of men too.

Chapter 3

*I have sold my brother Judas Didymus, you may call him
Thomas, to the merchant Abbanes for three pieces of
unstamped silver. Do not judge me too harshly. I do not do
this for money. Thomas is the bridge between east and west,
between that which is far and that which is near. Traveling
to distant lands filled with wild animals and danger fills
Thomas with paralyzing fear and doubt. He will not go of
his own accord and must have a companion and proof of
the way. My Father has sent Abbanes to me, a fine merchant from India to guide and protect him. With Abbanes'
help, Thomas will find the right path for those who need
him. I am the facilitator and path for men of free will.*

—I am Isa.

THOMAS SQUATTED IN front of the hearth, his brother next to him.
Both men were silent, still slowly waking and contemplating the day
before them. The nearby clay hearth was covered in soot, blackened
and dark. The world was quiet, just at that moment when most are
still asleep but waking is near. Silent.

The tiny house was about two kilometers from the Alexandria market, located in a densely settled area. The entire structure was made of dusty-colored mud bricks. Even the mortar was made of mud, so the walls had eventually fused into one large block of hardened earth, individual bricks being bound together with straw. The walls had been laid out so that there were two rooms. One room was for sleeping, and one slightly larger common room for cooking, meeting, and living. Thomas and Isa were only two of the seven men who slept the night there.

The street in front of the house was packed hard from centuries of constant traffic: carts, people, and pack animals of all kinds. Bullock carts left their marks in the dust but usually did not manage to carve their mark into the street, so hard-packed was the parched earth. Only the stone-paved streets nearer the city center had worn ruts marked right into the stone from constant use over the centuries.

The smell of wood smoke and mildly pungent burnt dung hung in the air, animal dung being an important fuel source. The blackened hearth in the common room was the central feature of the entire house. There was no furniture in the house at all. The people slept on the floor and squatted if they needed to sit. They ate out of a common clay pot or bowl they all shared. Another pot was often found bubbling on the fire, not infrequently with little but water in it.

The hearth also acted as an oven. Flat bread was pressed on its sides near the fire just inside the hearth and toasted. The hearth also doubled as a heater during cold weather. However, today, it was mostly a cook stove and a place to gather and talk the world away. If women had been present, if Isa or Thomas could have afforded them space, they would have portioned off part of the sleeping room with a woolen curtain. However, neither Isa nor Thomas had traveled with the women on this trip, unlike their earlier journeys in Judea, and found their absence a real hardship. It was the women who knew how to cook best, who could carry their weight in firewood, and who often sang on the long road and made life merry. It was the women who made the world go around.

Thomas was apprehensive. He had agreed to follow his brother Isa down to Alexandria, but he did not clearly know why they had journeyed there other than to escape the Roman soldiers again. Isa had said little since their last conversation in Jerusalem. The disciples had been commissioned to go out into all the world and tell the story of the Kingdom of God and Christ. Thomas had drawn the lot of India.

India? Well, I will not go, he had first thought, with a pang of anger and defiance seizing his very being as he contemplated such an endeavor.

He had told Isa so and not gently either. India was the land of wild animals, wild tribes, and wild souls. Thomas, barely literate, had learned that the mighty conqueror Alexander, the man who had founded the very city of Alexandria itself, had nearly been laid low in India and stopped his march on the banks of the Indus River. *Alexander himself! What could he do against such odds?* he wondered.

But Isa had suddenly turned and looked at him and smiled. He seemed to understand what was running through Thomas' mind again. He knew the pain and agony his brother was facing.

"Do not be afraid, my twin," said Isa reassuringly, smiling softly. "I send you to India, so go with good grace and my blessings. I will join you and travel with you at the beginning of the journey, but God's touch will soothe you on all your travels. Have faith, my brother. We will go tomorrow with the merchant Abbanes."

With those new words, Thomas felt his defiance weakening. Isa had a powerful way with people. His voice commanded attention and obedience but was also always gentle and reassuring. It was the way. All this despite the fact that Isa's hands still bore evidence of the terrible events of the last months. His side wound from the thrust of the Roman soldier was now completely healed. Only a scar remained. Thomas felt frustration, but there was nothing to be angry about.

He focused his mind on one part of Isa's statement: "I will be with you for the start of the journey." He ignored the possibility that Isa might not be with him for most of the journey, refusing to consider how little Isa might actually be with him. Traveling to India with Isa as a companion was a very different prospect than going there alone. *Maybe he would even expand his trip? Maybe he would see Isa regularly? How far was India, anyway?* Considering all this new information, Thomas felt much better when he contemplated the prospective journey. The task of bringing the truth to India was too great an undertaking for one man alone, he told himself. Isa understood that. Isa would not leave him. Thomas, the doubter, wishing and wanting not to go to India, finally resignedly accepted his new assignment. If Isa was going with him, what fear could he have? He would not look back. He would go to India and do as Isa asked. Thomas said nothing to Isa out loud, but the decision was made.

The sun rapidly rose up over the eastern lands in a fiery display of orange and red, as only the privileged inhabitants of Alexandria and indeed as only the inhabitants of all Egypt experience. The early morning was the best time of the day. The air was cooler, and the light was good. The body was not yet exhausted from the day's toil. The sounds of the day were still gentle and soft. Voices seemed to softly murmur. All sharp sounds were stilled.

Isa and Thomas walked just two doors down from their temporary home to the front of another home for travelers. Squatting with others in a circle outside, near the doorway, they acquired and tasted a piece of flatbread each. A young woman in a neat tunic tended the fire and prepared the meal. Her brown hair was mostly hidden by a head covering, her face revealing a cheerful, healthy smile. Most of the travelers said little, as they slowly and carefully chewed their food, savoring it and making each bit last, as they watched the woman skillfully tend the fire and cook the bread. It was the morning: time to eat and contemplate, and then to work and travel.

An hour later found both men at the city port, adjacent to the great market. Activity was everywhere as the city prepared for another day. Thomas could see Pharos, the mighty lighthouse and wonder of the world, a short distance away, reaching to the heavens. He thought that the structure seemed so great, it was as if man had made an attempt to reach God on their own terms. *How futile,* he thought. *How Egyptian and human in their thinking! God is greater still.*

Abbanes was waiting for them in front of one of the larger feluccas, already heavily loaded.

He greeted Isa warmly and then looked upon Thomas, surprise written upon his face.

"Twins!" The presence of both men together often evoked this reaction. Abbanes' head turned back and forth between the two Hebrews, as he studied them carefully. He had not fully appreciated

the tremendous physical similarity between the two men when he first met them. He had been drawn almost exclusively to the magnetism of Isa and had failed to study his brother's features carefully.

Now he understood the name "Twin." Thomas was not a first name or any name to the Hebrew. It was just an Aramaic word for twin. It would take some getting used to, calling this man "Twin." These two men were clearly brothers, if not actual identical twins, he realized. Both faces were angular, tanned, and leather-like, as those who had worked outside all their lives. The two brothers had powerful, slightly gnarled hands, as workers often do. Yet their hands showed delicate movement too. The hands of skilled carpenters and builders, Abbanes noticed optimistically. Their faces were still youthful, if not handsome. Abbanes knew then that his selection of Thomas as a builder was a wise choice.

Still, twins, he thought. *Remarkable.*

And it seemed that Isa would follow them, at least for a time. Abbanes viewed the addition of Isa to his journey, even if temporary, with pleasure.

Port laborers had been hard at work hours earlier, readying the feluccas for the journey, a trip that would take weeks sailing up the Nile. Abbanes' craft was nearly five meters long, with a large sail, and sported a single high mast with lateen rigging. The boat had no rudder, but instead had two large manned oars, one on each side primarily for steering. A half dozen skilled sailors would operate the vessel, veterans of repeated journeys up and down the Nile.

Each boat also carried a small contingent of men at arms. These were men who could help with the sailing, if needed, but were primarily along as a show of force, and capable of minor fighting, if needed. The convoy represented a tempting and lucrative target. An additional twelve boats stood at the ready with crews, some still larger than the one that would carry Abbanes. Yet, there was no doubt about who was in command. Abbanes stood upright and strong on the deck of his felucca, shouting clear commands to all, resplendent as the breeze gently whipped his flowing robes. His voice was clear and crisp.

The journey from Alexandria and up the Nile would be accomplished in the widest stretches, as the boats would crib into the wind and try to pick up greater speed, always sailing against the current. Each craft carried oars, and at times some paddling was needed, but the oars were mostly used for steering, being relatively ineffective as a means of propulsion against the strength of the river. The return journey to the north would be much easier, helped by the direction of the Nile itself.

Each boat had cedar flooring in places and little else for the passengers and their baggage. Abbanes had leased a fleet of thirteen vessels of various descriptions, now all heavily loaded for the journey. Thirteen was seen as an auspicious number and in any case, had to suffice. Abbanes had little gold left with which to make purchases. He needed what remained to pay for the long journey home.

He had procured well for his king. Isa and Thomas said little, as they stared with amazement at all the goods, timber, carvings, and pots and baskets stuffed with all kinds of products being tied down in each craft. Sailors called out to each other in coarse talk, most laughing or singing as they worked. The banter was generally friendly but also crude at times, the universal language of men who work the seas.

There was only a little uniformity among the craft. All thirteen feluccas had large sails so they could travel south, but some were better outfitted for rowers and steering. Still others were much larger at the gunwales, and one even sported two masts, an unhelpful complication in the eyes of most of the sailors who preferred the simplicity of one.

Thomas and Isa were directed to a place near the back of Abbanes' boat. The two men found a comfortable position and squatted down next to each other. By midday, the travelers were off, cribbing into the current. The journey to the passage to the sea had at last begun.

Any journey to Yam Suph from Alexandria was expensive. The leased fleet would only take the party as far as Coptos, at the head of Wadi Hammamat. From there, Abbanes would have to negotiate with Nabatean traders on a fair price for a massive camel train that would take the goods down the Wadi Hammamat and to the Yam Suph port of Quseir. The Nabateans were not political rulers in Egypt, but they controlled most of the commerce on the Yam Suph and destinations east. Wise traders, they made friends and allies with all. The mighty city of Petra was their capital not far to the north.

The prospect of traveling down the Wadi Hammamat held great meaning and emotion for the two men. All their lives, they had heard and read of the great exodus from Egypt. It was said that Moses had taken this path to the Yam Suph, known by some as the Red Sea, because of the red and colorful plankton that bloomed in its waters each year. Visiting this famous highway, the Wadi Hammamat, was nothing short of a holy pilgrimage for the two men. Isa already knew the route, though not well. As for Thomas, this was the first time he had experienced anything like this.

Abbanes was concerned by the tone of some of the traders as they left Alexandria and was worried that a few might try to steal his goods or even extort money. An observant man and always on the lookout for trouble, he watched several traders eyeing his purchases and the convoy with great interest. Too much interest.

He quietly shared his apprehensions with Isa but said nothing else to anyone, a nervous tic in his eye the only real evidence of the concern he felt. Isa did his best to assure him. The journey to India was ordained by God he told him. Nonetheless, Abbanes exhorted the men to be observant and to watch the comings and goings of all.

The journey up the Nile was long and hot with frequent stops along the way to take on fresh water. On one such break, the party visited a small village. Thomas looked down the river and was startled to see a large pod of hippos snorting and grunting in the water.

"These are water horses," explained Isa, looking at him with a smile. "I am surprised they come so close to the village."

Thomas looked on in wonder. Neither man had seen the animals before, although they had heard of them. The calls were distinctive and loud. Abbanes looked at his two visitors with amusement.

"They will likely move, I think. I am sure these river horses will run when the village men start hunting them." Abbanes pointed out several men clearly preparing for just such an endeavor. One river horse could keep the entire village in high quality meat for months. "They must have moved downriver too far during the night. They come up on land at night and sometimes travel great distances."

In a matter of weeks, they could finally make out the town of Coptos. As they neared the shore, smaller reed boats, common everywhere along the banks of the Nile, rapidly approached the small fleet, manned by young boys and older women, offering everything from dried fish and fruit to crude linen cloth for sale. Coming from Alexandria, the sailors took little notice of the vendors and made for shore. The travelers were delighted to put their feet back on dry land and to feel that this first part of their long journey was now behind them.

Coptos was a surprisingly beautiful city whose colors and charm seemed to explode on the otherwise brown and drab world surrounding it. The city was the start and trailhead for the Wadi Hammamat, the dry riverbed and highway to the Red Sea for all of Egypt. Through the centuries, armies, traders, and travelers of all kinds sought passage here.

Commerce was so great along the trail that toll stations had been erected along the highway to extort money from passing caravans. Like many other cosmopolitan places of the world, Coptos existed with many names to match the many languages spoken by traders as they passed through the town. Many of the local population continued to call their city Gebtu, not fully accepting the Greek variation that had overtaken their world. Roman soldiers policed the route, but here the power and glory of Rome waned, and the Nabateans found more favor. It would be the Nabateans that Abbanes would have to deal with as he journeyed across the sea and eventually on to the port at Andrapolis.

Unloading the thirteen feluccas and repacking everything on camels, carts, donkeys, and horses was a huge task and would take the better part of a week. Before any of the work could be carried out, the crews of the boats secured their crafts and then hurried off to the shrine to give thanks to Min and Horus. Abbanes watched them go. He knew that once the gods were properly thanked for safe passage, the sailors would return with renewed energy, eager and ready to take their craft back down the Nile, an easier journey with favorable currents.

Both Isa and Thomas were feeling cramped and constrained from the tight quarters of the felucca. Like the sailors, they eagerly stepped over the gunwale and jumped down onto the beach. Thomas surveyed the town laid out before him. In moments, both men drew a group of children, hawkers, and some destitute orphans. They were soon all laughing with great delight as Isa greeted each one and talked to them. Thomas watched his brother as he spoke, marveling at both his command of this language as well as the easy way he seemed to connect with people.

During the slow week of unloading and repacking, Thomas and Isa had little to do. Most of the caravan managers did not want the help of the two men. They preferred to be paid for their labors by Abbanes and regarded the two men as spies and critics provided by Abbanes. Seeing this, Abbanes sent Isa, Thomas, and four guards ahead to the western road to establish a base camp at the entrance into the wadi.

The two men were carpenters but working with stone was not unfamiliar to them. The walls of the wadi were alive with marks from the past, graffiti of long-forgotten travelers. Each had a story to tell but the meaning of many of the marks was lost in time. Each man examined the inscriptions with interest, Isa seemingly understanding all, while Thomas and the guards accompanying them understanding much less.

The establishment of a base camp at the trailhead was quickly accomplished, leaving the guards and Thomas little to do. The apostle took out a new hammer and a worn chisel. He sat down in the shade before one of the great rocks. Over the next days, he slowly and carefully carved his message while Isa spent his days in meditation and prayer. At times, Isa would seem to wander off and just disappear, leaving Thomas alone. The guards too, with little to do, were often wandering in the area, looking for better shade and fresh water.

On one such occasion, when Thomas was alone, he encountered a Roman soldier who had strayed from his encampment.

"Hello, there!" the armed man cried out in a commanding tone, approaching Thomas with authority. "You can't work there!"

He was walking directly towards Thomas and then looking past him and upon the message Thomas had intently been working on: the symbol of Isa. As he stopped in front of Thomas, he stooped down and examined his stonework. Nearly illiterate, the Roman nonetheless noted the skill and talent of the man. His demeanor changed. While in no real position of authority, a small extortion was not out of the question.

"You have to pay for this," said the Roman, smiling at Thomas, a mischievous glint in his eyes. "Not just anyone can carve on the walls, here. You need my permission. What do you have?" he added a bit too eagerly.

Thomas felt intimidated by this strange man who had such a strong accent that he could not think of an adequate response. His practice in Judea was to avoid Roman soldiers at all costs. Here, far from the powers of Rome, where most Roman soldiers were forced to live on military encampments and few strayed alone, the single presence of this man was unsettling to Thomas. Before he could answer, he turned to see Abbanes rapidly walking towards him.

"Ave, ave," said Abbanes, an easy smile on his face, greeting the Roman in his native language. The soldier stopped and turned towards Abbanes, immediately taking in his fine robes and royal bearing. Before he could say much in response, Abbanes pressed a small unstamped coin in his palm and sent him on his way.

"We are ready for our journey," Abbanes said. Thomas looked past Abbanes and could see the great caravan moving up behind him. He could not see Isa. And so at last and with no additional fanfare, the caravan struck out for the city of Quesir and the Red Sea.

Chapter 4

"I have been a stranger in a strange land."

—*Moses as recorded in Exodus Chapter 2 Verse 22*

THE JOURNEY THROUGH Wadi Hammamat was hot, dry, and rocky. Shade could often be found along the treed embankments of the dry riverbeds lining the passage. In a few areas, small pockets of heavy growth, undoubtedly marking water close by, added to the effect. The caravan deliberately moved to the shaded side whenever it was on offer. Thomas would often see antelopes and other animals in the distance. On one occasion, he saw a leopard sitting in the brush, carefully watching the party pass by. It was a reminder to stay close.

Somewhere along the way, he realized that Isa was no longer walking with the caravan. Thomas backtracked his steps a few times but could not find him. Sitting by the fire at night, he constantly hoped to see his brother suddenly appear, perhaps walking up to him out of the darkness. He would imagine him sitting down by his side. But Isa did not return.

The apostle did not worry for the safety of his brother, fully confident in his ability to take care of himself, despite the dangers posed by wild animals or worse people. Had not Isa defied death? He remembered what Isa had told him. "This Great Commission I have given you is yours alone, my twin. Go to India and carry with you the new message of salvation. Teach them the pathway to the Kingdom of God. There is great need in all the world, including India." Despite the confidence and words of his brother, Thomas still missed him. Isa always knew what to do next. He always knew what was right.

Caravans that moved along the Wadi Hammamat were well organized and productive and generally found the pathway safe and secure, despite the heat and dry conditions. Abbanes' caravan was no exception. Commerce was profitable for most and especially for the Nabateans, who controlled the passage. During the short journey through the wadi, Thomas even found himself riding on a camel for a short time. The beast was one of many in the train, and a kindly, well-meaning handler had insisted on the ride. To the great amusement of all, Thomas was clearly uncomfortable on the animal and made it clear that he thought he might actually fall off. Eventually, the constant jarring and the loud moans and groans from the camel convinced him to take his place alongside the creature, but not before providing quite a bit of comic relief to the traveling party.

The arrival at Myos Hormos on the coast of Yam Suph, what others called the Red Sea, was a welcome break. Thomas enjoyed the cooling sea breeze. It was a balm for the weary travelers. They pitched their encampment in a shaded grove, while Abbanes occupied a great house nearby. Once again, another massive effort was underway, as Abbanes organized the workers and supervised the unloading and then reloading of his cargo and supplies. This time, the load was being transferred into larger, seaworthy craft. As before, Abbanes could be seen marching about the port, one moment issuing short commands, and the next moment bargaining astutely, a broad smile on his face as officials of every level came forward to demand payment or attempt to sell something to the experienced trader.

Abbanes was an extraordinary linguist who seemed to understand everyone's mother tongue—often better than the native speakers. He provided a fine and noble sight to all. Despite the days at sea, his robes were always neatly pressed, his hair groomed, his demeanor direct and forceful but somehow always polite. There was a hint of laughter just hiding within his face whenever he spoke. He understood the importance of greetings and banter and kept a smile for all who came to see him.

In short order, the entire caravan was back at sea and heading for mainland Asia and Gandhara. The wadi and the great river of Egypt were rapidly becoming a brief memory on the long journey. The sea was the force to reckon with, now.

Thomas was feeling ill. The young man from Nazareth shuddered involuntarily and looked about. The sea rolled before him in a seemingly endless cycle of pitching waves topped with small white caps. For the experienced seamen on the craft, this sea was nothing more than a light rolling chop. The carpenter, however, was only accustomed to relatively brief journeys on modest lakes and rivers in Judea, and recently the relatively flat Nile. The constant rolling and bobbing in the open sea was a new experience for him.

An acute wave of nausea took hold of him again. He bravely tried to smile and looked forward. His face held a gray tint, an almost impossible color against his browned, sun-hardened skin. A light, cooling breeze pushed along, giving Thomas only the slightest sense of relief from his misery. If it were not for the rolling chop, the day would have been quite pleasant. Land was not far off, evidenced by the increasing number of gulls darting in and out of the waves as they hunted their aquatic prey.

It wasn't just the weather and the long sea voyage that were making Thomas feel ill. As they drew upon the port city of Andrapolis, Thomas felt a disquieting chill rise inside him. With each kilometer traveled, he felt that the air, the weather, and the people were changing. The changes unsettled him. In his heart of hearts, he still did not want to make this journey, but he did so out of love for his brother Isa.

Despite his apparent bluster and confidence, Abbanes was feeling unsettled too. He had considered a number of ports of call as he made his journey back to the kingdom, never quite trusting the friends and allies he would encounter along the way. He still remembered the careful and studied looks that some traders gave his cargo as they left Alexandria. He knew they were noting the immense wealth of goods that he had accumulated for his king. Even here, far from the land of the pharaohs, Egyptian traders could still plot to steal his treasures.

He had considered going on to Bharuch or even another port further up the coast on the Asian mainland. From there, he could join one of the larger kingdom caravans. His cargo was bulky, and he knew many traders in Bharuch who he could trust to help him. Yet, he also knew that some of the Egyptian traders who had watched his departure so closely expected him to do that and likely anticipated his journey on that route. It was even possible that word of his holdings had already been sent ahead. The wise Hebrew trader knew that it was often best to consider the unexpected and take a different path.

Andrapolis was closer than Bharuch and close to, but not on, the Indus River. It was smaller and would not normally be his anticipated stop. Navigating the Indus River when traveling north was no easy task. Navigating south from Taxila with the flow of the river to the sea was easier. But Abbanes needed to travel north, in the opposite direction of the flow. He calculated that he could march straight north from Andrapolis for ten days and then rejoin the highway along the river. He mused he would avoid a lot of problems if he took that road. He reckoned his caravan would essentially disappear for a short while as he marched towards Taxila out of sight of prying eyes. Andrapolis it is, he decided.

Most of the residents of Andrapolis, including the satrap, would be nominally friendly to King Gondophores. Yet, Abbanes could never fully trust anyone. The closer he got to Gandhara, the safer he would be. The entire party was tired from the long journey and ready to get on shore, anxious to start the long road into the interior and home. In Andrapolis, Abbanes would once again have to outfit a new baggage train to carry all his goods. He would be buying camels, slaves, and horses for the long trek.

Striking white buildings slowly came into sight as the craft neared its destination, and the coast came into view. Andrapolis! Thomas had never even imagined such a beautiful small city. While it was modest in size, it made up for it with its clean lines of organization and its gleaming whitewashed buildings. The apostle was taken with the sense that order must prevail there.

Thomas surveyed the town from the side of the boat. He shielded his eyes with his palms as he took in the place. Despite not wanting to make the journey and his unease at the thought of carrying out his mission, it was hard not to feel safe with Abbanes in command. His limitless supply of confidence was a clear mark that he left with all whom he spoke. His manner reassured Thomas and helped pull him out of the near depression he sometimes felt. Thomas knew the world was a dangerous place, but perhaps with Abbanes, it was safely navigable. Perhaps that was something his brother had recognized about Abbanes.

Thomas could also see that Andrapolis was a bustling, vibrant port. As the boat drew near land, he studied the buildings in the background and recognized the function of some. In the middle of town, he could see a great temple structure, not unlike some of the Greek and Roman temples he recognized in Egypt. He also saw several other structures he did not recognize. A great round pagoda stood out, freshly painted white. It was modest in size compared to the central temple, but it still stood out. It was not clear what function or purpose it had to the less experienced travelers, unfamiliar with the path of the Lord Buddha. Drawing closer, Thomas could see what appeared to be a carved stone statute of a seated figure and still more bell-shaped structures scattered around one side of the city, all painted in white.

"The stupa of their god," said Abbanes suddenly, noticing Thomas' interest, gesturing with his hand towards the larger of the stupas. As Thomas looked towards the structure, he could see several figures in the distance clad in light saffron-colored robes.

"We are not in my kingdom yet, but most of the people here are friendly and know my country, my country Gandhara," Abbanes explained. "Many people worship the Lord Buddha. They also worship Mithra and other gods. You will soon learn their many names. These supposed 'gods' are less."

Abbanes was unable to hide the contempt in his voice when he referred to "gods". He turned and smiled at Thomas, as he considered how much his Hebrew friend had to learn. Yet, Thomas did not answer. The fact that other gods were less needed no explanation.

"Some of our own people live here to trade and to find passage to the outside world," continued Abbanes, this time referring to their fellow Hebrews. "Most of Andrapolis does not know our one true God, whose very name we cannot utter. In my kingdom, in our country, most of the residents, most of the people, are followers of the Lord Gautam Buddha."

Abbanes purposely repeated the name Buddha several times in his conversations to make sure Thomas was learning it.

"The stupa that you see holds parts of the body of that foreign god himself. Can you imagine?" He shook his head in disdain. "At least that is what these bhikkhus, their priests, teach all the people here."

Abbanes' voiced trailed off when he said these last words, increasingly unable to hide his dislike for what he considered to be heathen beliefs.

Thomas continued to look out at the unfamiliar structure of the stupa but did not respond, lost in his own thoughts. *This is my mission,* he thought. *God brought me here to minister to these people. Isa brought me here.*

Both men continued to study the shore in the distance.

"The people here are poorly educated and have not heard of the one true God that you and I must obey," Abbanes continued, now with a slightly paternalistic tone. "Still, King Gondophores is my king. I think you will find him to be a generous and wise king. He is a follower of the Lord Buddha, but he is also tolerant of others and their beliefs. You will see. Like here, there are followers of many different gods in our kingdom. King Gondophores believes we must protect all of them. By accepting all, we become bigger ourselves. We will become a nation of nations," he added with a big smile on his face. There was nationalist pride in his tone. Despite his Jewish identity, Abbanes was still a man from Gandhara.

"Maybe one day, we can challenge even Persia or Rome," he added with emphasis, boasting slightly. There was a glint in his eye. "But for now, we remain poor men of God only," his tone returning to a humbler level. He moved his hands in a supplicating motion as if to highlight the point.

Whenever wealthy caravans and merchants arrived at Andrapolis, like most ports along the coast, all activity changed, and all attention was redirected to the new arrivals. The arriving boats meant there would be trading to do, things to sell, stockpiles to purchase, and news to be heard, all adding excitement to what otherwise was a generally boring existence.

As the craft approached the shore, Abbanes' attention grew, as he studied the approaching land. The Hebrew was quick to observe anything out of the ordinary, a skill and trait that sometimes meant the difference between life and death. His eyes strained to make out all the banners fluttering in the wind. These were banners he had not expected to see in Andrapolis. He realized that there was more happening here on the shore and so was immediately on guard. This was more than just excitement over his arrival. Much more. In addition to the satrap's guard, he detected the banners of a great prince visiting the city.

As the boat moved closer to shore, Abbanes pointed out the difference between government officials of Andrapolis, the guards of the satrap, as well as foreign soldiers and other officials coming into view. He was still not sure exactly what kingdom was visiting and if this portended good or bad news for his business. It was already too late to turn around. He studied the banners as they moved closer to the port.

"See here," said Abbanes, gesturing towards several beautifully saddled horses in the company of some immaculately dressed men along the shore. "That indeed must be an official delegation from one of the western provinces and followers of their lord God Mithra . . . " Abbanes voice trailed off as he spoke, attempting to decipher who the visitors were. "See how they wear their blue robes thus?" He pulled his robe in tighter, making a sash as he spoke.

Then Abbanes relaxed. He could see the soldiers on shore were at ease.

"This is probably a great day for Andrapolis," he continued, realizing that whoever the visitors were, they were not in Andrapolis to make war. "If one of the great Persian kings has sent one of his sons, a prince perhaps, to take the daughter of the satrap for marriage—what a great honor!" he exclaimed with enthusiasm, his mood quickly switching from somber to happy.

Indeed, this princess must be a woman of great beauty, he thought. He could see the satrapy standards flying high as well as that of the visiting force. It was increasingly apparent that a holiday sense of excitement was washing over the town. There was a festive and happy air in everything that one did even at the port.

Chapter 5

"I have come into the city of Andrapolis to see that my brother makes good progress on his journey to India. This is the last stage of my travels with him, although he does not know. He must find his own path from here. My brother will grow in wisdom from his experiences, as all do. His new companion and friend Abbanes is a man of wondrous talent and ability. He is a man of God. I love my brother dearly."

—I am Isa.

AFTER SEVERAL HOURS of negotiations, counting, and still more negotiations, followed by exchanges of flowers and even food, Abbanes and some of his party including Thomas were finally led off into the town and to their quarters by the satrap's own man.

It was abundantly clear to Thomas that Abbanes was well-known and welcomed jubilantly by many in the town. Those who did not know him in person knew him by reputation. Andrapolis was not often his primary port of choice, especially with such a large shipment, and this added to the enthusiasm. For some, his very presence meant opportunity and profit.

The satrap's man led the party to an inn not far from the center of town with high mud-stucco walls. In the center of the quarters was a broad courtyard onto which most of the rooms opened. At one end of the courtyard stood a great tree, and in the center a dried-up fountain and an unused firepit.

There was a beehive of activity in some of the rooms, and Thomas could see smoke billowing out of one—clearly the kitchen. He was guided through the courtyard to the backside of the inn. Facing a wall and to the rear, there was a room with a mat and a place to put his things and to sleep. The day was hot, but the Hebrew was accustomed to the heat and feared more the cold that might come later in the year.

Temporary quarters were at a premium with a great prince in town. However, the travelers were closer to home now, where Abbanes' rank as an important emissary of Gondophores had to be taken into account. While Thomas' room was modest, the inn itself was well-equipped with smart tile floors, and some rooms had embroidered cushions and carpets to soften the effect. Thomas was startled by the luxury, among the finest furnishings he had ever seen, with tables and even carved chairs. A humble carpenter, he was not fully comfortable staying in a house with such value.

Abbanes was tired but realized that his tasks were far from over that day. Before returning to his work, he lay down on the cushions before him in the common room. Servants, including several uncovered women, served a prepared meal of spiced goat meat and flatbread. Thomas sat on the floor near Abbanes, not quite able to luxuriate himself on the carpets and cushions that Abbanes clearly appreciated. The apostle stared disapprovingly at the uncovered heads and faces of the women but ate his meal ravenously. He knew Isa had readily accepted the presence of women, even seemed to enjoy their company, something that made Thomas uncomfortable. If there had been one weakness of his brother, Thomas privately thought, it was that he was too generous in his acceptance and tolerance of women.

The whereabouts of Isa was a topic that was coming up more and more between the two men. Abbanes was just beginning to understand the unique beliefs of his new indentured servant. Thomas was fast becoming a friend and companion and less like a servant to the trader. As the two men conversed over their meal, Thomas began by discussing his mission and the great message of Isa. The conversation drifted, and soon the two men were discussing Isa again.

"He left us somewhere in Egypt," Abbanes commented. "Somewhere in the wadi, it must have been."

"I know," Thomas answered softly, trying to keep the sadness out of his voice. "I know this is my journey to make, but I was still hoping he would travel further with us."

"I am certain that was his intent," Abbanes responded. The elder Hebrew was mildly frustrated that he had to have this conversation more than once with the apostle. "I don't know Isa well, but from what I can tell, he is an honorable man and brother." Abbanes emphasized the word brother for Thomas' benefit. "He will join us again if he can. He is very resourceful, and I still think he intended to travel to Asia. That was my understanding of what he intended to do." Thomas nodded his head gratefully, appreciating Abbanes' mildly optimistic assessment of the situation.

During his earlier travels to Jerusalem, the trader had heard of Isa and some of the stories surrounding him and his followers; however, he was initially inclined to dismiss them. Had he not met Isa, who some called the Christ? Had he not conducted business with him? Those were not the actions of a great prophet. What more could he be? To the follower of Yahweh, the thought of worshipping any man was idolatrous, and fakery quickly came to his mind. Yes, the world was filled with apostates, he thought. He listened politely, as Thomas changed direction in the conversation, moving from Isa to the intellectual topic of the Kingdom of God.

Scarcely rested, Abbanes rose once the meal was over and returned to the port and his cargo, continuing to manage and plan the next phase of their journey. He had provisions and stores to protect and to account for, and he only had a small number of key people he could rely upon.

Abbanes remained at the port for several more hours before he again found his way back to the inn. At the inn, he seated himself in the shade of the tree at the end of the courtyard. He called for the apostle to join him, motioning him to sit next to bundles of provisions while he continuously met with still more contacts. Thomas watched as businessmen and emissaries of all kinds came and went through the door into the courtyard, some of whom Abbanes clearly did not want to meet with. The trader finally posted two armed guards to help him control access.

These two men were rather severe looking, well chosen for their task, scowling at most who came. Many visitors were not completely cowed by these two, but the pace slowed. Most of the visitors visiting the inn were clearly interested in selling Abbanes something, but a few were also emissaries of the satrap and the government. One such visitor was from the satrap's immediate family and instantly commanded respect from the entire household. The guards recognized the man as he entered, and they stepped back with a bow. The young man was finely cloaked and had a strong, confident air about him, not lost by his otherwise slightly portly frame.

Abbanes greeted him with great happiness, embracing the young man and calling him a brother before God, kissing him on both cheeks. After briefly introducing Thomas, Abbanes and the young man talked for over an hour, sipping small cups of chai steeped with herbs, clearly enjoying each other's company.

The language spoken between the two men was foreign to Thomas, and he followed nothing of the conversation. However, it was clear that both men were enjoying the moment and frequently laughing. After a few hours, Abbanes walked the young man and friend out into the street, his face seemingly happy the whole time, skillfully concealing any anxiety he initially felt from the unexpected presence of a foreign prince and military entourage.

"The satrap is marrying his daughter to one of the Nabatean princes tonight," he said, walking back into the courtyard and addressing Thomas directly. He spoke in Aramaic, easily slipping back into that language. "I had thought he would connect with one of the Persian Princes or even one from Gandhara," he explained somewhat pensively. "However, this alliance will help expand our trade, and our king will be pleased."

"The satrap's son has just invited me to join in the celebrations," he continued, referring to his visitor just departed. "There is much happiness in the city right now. Our coming was most fortuitous. Tonight, there is a great banquet, and we have been asked to be seated there." Turning to Thomas, he beamed, "We have been asked," he said with renewed emphasis. "You are coming with me!"

There was an almost joyous tone in Abbanes' voice. He was clearly delighted that things were going well at this stop. It was not always so. But his mood shifted again almost immediately, his face taking on a worried, furrowed look.

"I suppose I will have to come up with an appropriate gift for the satrap."

There was resignation and an almost weary tone in his voice when he said this. Abbanes had just spent the better part of a day doling out favors and gifts. There seemed to be no end to the requests and requirements at this stop.

"I am sure the satrap sees our arrival as fortuitous." He said these last words rather wryly, shaking his head. "But there is little gold left," he added, voice betraying fatigue.

It was not clear to Thomas how much an honor the invitation was until night came. Abbanes was decked out in his finest robe and had slaves perfume him in the courtyard. He also sent new robes to Thomas with the admonishment that they were only being lent for the evening. Abbanes had a price for everything, and there was always a purpose to what he did.

"I can't have you looking as impoverished as you actually are, tonight," Abbanes explained, with an amused glint in his eye. He tossed Thomas a scarf from Judea, the land of their birth. He clearly wanted to show off his prize: a builder purchased from a distant part of the Roman Empire and now arriving in mighty Gandhara and Asia. The scarf would be an exotic marker, a sign of distant places and faraway lands to all who saw them. Abbanes was sporting one of these scarves too.

The elder Hebrew was increasingly fond of Thomas and enjoyed his conversations with the younger man, though still unsure about the religious dogma the apostle would sometimes preach. Yet, Abbanes could have taken any one of the others to the dinner, and he chose Thomas. Thomas cleaned up nicely, much better than others in the traveling party, the trader considered carefully. *Dressed in his new robe and now freshly bathed, he is quite presentable. He has an almost noble bearing*, he decided, as he studied his younger friend carefully.

The walk up to the palace was long, but the stone passage was clear. The guards had chased most of the townspeople off the streets, making way for the guests of the satrap. Thomas had seen parts of the building and structures from the port at a distance. As he walked among them, the edifices seemed to have grown tenfold in size—powerful, gray, and ancient. Equally intimidating were the guards they encountered as they walked. Thomas realized he was terrified that some might stop and accost him, certain that some mistake had been made and that he was not actually supposed to be there. However, they all seemed to know their business and let them pass.

The two Hebrews walked on worn cobblestone streets through several grand stone archways. Torches on the wall lit the way, with a few watchmen holding up lanterns in a few places. At each passage, there were men at attention, finely cloaked but with helmets and long pikes at the ready. At last, they arrived at the entrance to the building itself.

Lamps that hung round the exterior of the great hall partially illuminated the enormous stone structure. The roof alone was over twelve meters in height, with great arches and carvings in the shadows. At the doorway, Thomas saw light coming from within. Such a huge amount of light was indeed a show of extravagance, wealth, and power that he had only heard of and imagined. Night and darkness seemed to have been beaten back, and here was a magical, lighted world before him. Candles and lamps of all kinds created a sense of enchantment.

Almost as soon as he walked through the archway and into the hall, he saw her. She was seated on the floor next to a column, playing the flute. Her lithe figure, gentle against the stone, was youthful and stunning. She was wearing a light cotton robe that failed to fully hide her beauty and form. Thomas was enchanted at her sighting and for a moment found that he could not look away. He could not have imagined a more delicately beautiful woman. She was a girl who had recently become a woman but still did not know her power.

He felt the blood rushing to his head and a sense of joy and desire in his being, as he watched her every move. Her skin had a delicate white tone, and her face gave off an aura of health and strength that further complimented her features. She had a radiant smile on her face and a look of joy about her, as she played the flute. Her hair was raven black, shining and sparkling in the lamp light, a stunning contrast that highlighted her beauty. Despite her great beauty, the manner in her seating and dress also told Thomas that she was a slave. Still, there was something magical about her. Thomas could not take his eyes off her.

As he surveyed the room about him, he realized that the woman held the attention of many other men in the room too. A pang of intense jealousy and anger coursed through his body. How could he feel jealousy for a woman he had not even met before, he immediately wondered. The sharp feeling of anger and sheer emotion startled and unsettled him.

The great hall was recessed, but on the far side, he could see a raised platform and dais. Clearly, that was where the satrap would sit, attended by many others. The platform was empty, indicating that the satrap had not yet arrived. There were few tables or chairs in the room, and so at the edges of the room, many squatted or stood. He could make out sections with cushions along the recesses, and it was to one of these that Abbanes was directed, while Thomas was shown a lesser place on the floor by the entrance. Still, for Thomas, at first, the seating seemed a perfect vantage point from which to watch the young girl as she played. He could see straight down the aisle and look upon her form. As he settled down against the wall and a cushion, he listened to her play.

He began to make out more and more people in the room. Servants were carrying in food and drink of all kinds, and Thomas soon found himself being offered a cup of strong wine, which he declined.

Thomas turned and set his gaze once more on the young woman playing the flute. More guests were arriving, and as they did, they started to block his view of her. He stood up to improve his view. Her cloak was cut in a familiar pattern to his, and he found himself studying her every feature. It suddenly hit him to his great astonishment: She was a Hebrew! A Hebrew slave girl, here in this distant land!

Thomas realized there were eyes upon him as he stood. Abbanes was watching him from a distance, carefully noting his reactions with great amusement. Thomas blushed and looked away.

"Yes, our people are here," Abbanes mouthed the words as he caught Thomas' eye. In a breach of protocol, Abbanes stood and walked over to Thomas. "Our people were enslaved by the great Persian Empire and only saved by our Queen Esther. I was also a slave once, but now I am a free man. I choose to serve my king. This girl, her name is Sarida. As you can see, she is a slave."

As Thomas and Abbanes were talking, Thomas made eye contact with the beautiful Sarida. A look of surprise instantly came over the girl's face. Thomas felt embarrassed and looked away. For Sarida, her instant realization was that both Abbanes and Thomas were Hebrews.

As Thomas watched Sarida play, he also noted another young man who was constantly watching Sarida too. Between songs, this young man, Natan, went to Sarida and gave her water to drink. Thomas watched the two engage in a brief conversation. The girl was cool to the server but thanked him for the drink, even giving him a slight smile. The young man was clearly taken by the young woman, unable to take his eyes off her.

A pang of jealously crept into Thomas' being again. What must it be like to know her? To talk to her? The mere thought of talking to her excited him.

He realized that Natan must have an interest in the young Hebrew woman too. He watched him walk away and noted that his gaze was constantly moving back to Sarida as he went about his duties.

Natan in turn had taken note of the look Sarida had given Thomas, and it alarmed him. Like Sarida, Natan was an indentured servant, and tonight he was serving the wine in the hall. It was Natan who had initially tried to serve Thomas and while doing so followed Thomas' gaze to Sarida. Not unlike others in the room, Natan harbored a secret hope that one day he might be the man of Sarida's choosing. It was troubling for the young man to see Thomas, in the company of the powerful Abbanes, finely dressed and worldly, enchanted by Sarida as well. Natan had a serious competitor.

Before Natan could continue with his dark thoughts, the mighty Satrap Tai, the son of the great Queen Mei Kalochi, made his entrance. For a moment, Thomas completely lost sight of Sarida, as the entourage surrounding Tai moved down the center aisle and passed to the dais.

Tai was resplendent in a robe with embroidered gold and silver motifs and a great turban on his head. Thomas noted that most heads bowed in respect as the royal moved past, but surprisingly not all. *This was not the king, after all,* he thought. Tai took his seat, as others of the family took their places nearby. With little fanfare, Tai gestured that the music should continue, looking directly at Sarida, clearly a favorite. The room was now crowded, with every possible place taken.

Thomas momentarily sat down again as the music continued. Immediately realizing he could not see Sarida if he sat, he tried to stand up again. As he did so, he came into direct contact with Natan walking past him at that very moment. Natan, seeing his competitor suddenly rise up before him, jealousy already burning inside of him, bumped into Thomas hard as if by accident. It was much harder than he meant to, sending Thomas to the floor.

"You oaf!" cursed Natan, pretending it was Thomas who had made the contact. Natan righted himself as he spoke, somehow not dropping the tray he was carrying at the same time. He tried to sound somewhat indignant, although the tone of his voice revealed more anger than it should have.

It was now Thomas' turn to be angry. For a moment, he forgot his station, and a flash of raw, irrational anger coursed through him. He cursed the man harshly. "In this life, may your bones be dragged by the dogs," he spat back. Feeling like he overstated his anger, he added only slightly more softly, "Only God will forgive you in the life to come."

Thomas' words almost sounded like a curse. Natan immediately turned his back on Thomas and walked away. Several watched the incident with slight amusement, although some also noted that Thomas' curse was delivered as though a prophecy.

The meal was magnificent, served on a leaf laid out before each guest. Roast and spiced meats of all kinds were served along with vegetables and fruits, some of which Thomas did not recognize. Thomas would have normally eaten his fill and more, but the incident with Natan still unnerved him, and he picked at the food.

When the meal was over, Thomas looked around for Sarida. She was no longer at her station. As he prepared to stand and find her, to his astonishment, Sarida appeared before him and neatly sat down next to him. In the distance, he did not see Abbanes smiling, for it was Abbanes who instructed the girl to sit with Thomas.

For Sarida, the very idea of associating with powerful Hebrew men could only mean possible salvation and connection to her people. She gladly acquiesced, becoming emboldened even and sitting close to Thomas, with the room being so crowded.

Thomas was stunned and at a loss for words. He was also secretly delighted. Forgetting his mission, forgetting his solemn pledges to Isa, he greeted her in Aramaic, pleased to see she retained her fluency in their common language. Quickly getting over his surprise, the two began to exchange stories, excitement in their voices.

Sarida was surprised to learn that Thomas was an indentured servant too, despite the fine robes that he wore, not realizing that Abbanes had loaned them to him. Thomas now appreciated that the people of Yahweh were scattered about the earth, mostly a result of past military incursions into Judea, especially from Persia.

In the corner, candlelight flickering across his anguished face, Natan watched as the two fellow Hebrews connected. His heart sank as he watched the two in close conversation, jealousy overtaking his being.

Chapter 6

*"The groom lifted up the curtain of the bride chamber
to bring the bride to himself. And he saw the Lord Jesus
bearing the likeness of Judas Thomas and speaking with
the bride."*

—*The Acts of Thomas, Chapter 11*

THE NEXT DAYS were filled with great festivities for the townspeople, though not for Abbanes, who remained hard at work preparing his caravan for the final push to Gandhara in the interior. His time was spent organizing the caravan, paying expenses, bargaining over terms with camel and donkey herders and horsemen, and generally avoiding paying as much as he could. Whenever a wealthy trader passed through town, few could pass on the opportunity to make a profit of some kind, and thus most attempted to seek him out.

In the evenings, Abbanes would take a respite from his labors. The two Hebrews would sit near the fire in the central courtyard of the inn, spending their time sipping spiced chai and talking. It was during these moments that Thomas again found the opportunity to explain the new revelation of Christ and how he must share this message with the world.

Abbanes always listened to his friend politely when he talked about this path and was careful not to comment too much. Some of what Thomas said made sense to him. Many fundamental teachings he recognized from Judaism, the mother religion to his mind, such as keeping the commandments and honoring those in authority over you. However, this extreme devotion to Isa and to God, even to the point where one might consider forsaking interpersonal relationships, was too much. It sounded unnatural to the trader.

The apostle frequently explained that one's relationship to God could be likened to the relationship between a man and a woman. All were married to God. For Abbanes, this whole concept upset the natural order of things. When he had visited Jerusalem, he did not recall anyone ever explaining such a doctrine and then attributing it to the teaching of Isa. What Thomas was teaching was new to him.

The senior Hebrew recognized that Thomas, a young man, had much to learn in the world and would profit from hearing the message of the many other religions he would encounter in the Kingdom of Gandhara, not the least the practices of dharma, of Buddha and the Middle Path. Learning from others, as Abbanes had, was one path to wisdom.

Perhaps Thomas might even be able to share his very devout but tolerant form of Judaism, Abbanes mused. But he would need to grow in wisdom first. That was clear to him. Could he talk to him? Soften his words? His message of exclusivity? Would Thomas listen? So far, he had only encountered a man who was quick to speak his own truth. A man who did not easily listen to others. Still, there was something special about Thomas, and Isa too. There were stories of great power coming out of Judea surrounding these two. Stories of how Isa and his brother had miraculously healed people, even raised some from the dead.

Abbanes had initially dismissed all those stories; however, he recognized that there was something unique about the pair. It was remarkable how many believed these stories or even claimed to have witnessed them. There could be something to it, after all. He pondered the possibilities.

Abbanes continued to be attentive to Thomas outwardly but actively continued to be lost in his own thoughts as he stared into the fire. Then the thought came to Abbanes suddenly. A blessing! Thomas could perform a special Hebrew blessing for the wedding of the satrap's daughter and her prince. Perhaps as a final offering to the satrap? He could have Thomas officiate over a special Hebrew blessing for the satrap's daughter and her new prince?

Which family did this Nabatean prince come from? he pondered.

⋆▸▬◉ ◉▬◂⋆

The new day dawned and with it the sound of a herald riding fast through the streets and alleys of the town. As in many towns, the herald played an important role in the life of Andrapolis. Residents would often stand outside their homes anxiously waiting for the herald to pass just to hear the news. Sometimes, the herald brought terrible word such as a warning of an approaching army. Today, the herald brought joyful news, announcing that the celebration of the great marriage was nearly complete. Soon, the young Nabatean prince would be off with his prize.

On this, the fifth day of the caravan preparations, Abbanes was still in the port, seeing the last of his cargo move off the boats and properly prepared for loading. At last, the caravan was staged and ready for the journey inland. It had all come together faster than he expected. He gave instructions for the massive train to move to the trailhead and prepare for departure in the next day or possibly two. He still had matters to resolve in town and set out to complete those tasks.

He had scarcely walked half a kilometer in the direction of the inn before he encountered a large crowd quietly sitting before a teacher—a fakir of some kind, Abbanes assumed—speaking to the assembly. As he came closer, much to his surprise, he realized that the speaker was Thomas!

He recognized the shape and form of the man from a distance. Adjusting his stride and moving still closer for a better vantage point, Abbanes was able to gaze directly upon the speaker. It seemed to be Thomas indeed, but his cloak was different, and his bearing more serene. Having not seen Isa since the beginning of their journey on the Red Sea, Abbanes assumed that Isa would not be near. This had to be Thomas, the twin.

The audience was riveted to the speaker, who seemed to be teaching a great parable. Abbanes marveled at the man. He was speaking to the crowd in their own language. How was this possible? He was quite certain Thomas did not know any of the dialects of Persia and was only now learning Gandhari. He had already witnessed his stumbling attempts. The seated assembly was paying close attention to this man, hanging on every word.

Abbanes had pressing matters to attend to and decided to investigate this remarkable event later. He turned and continued on in the direction of the inn. Soon thereafter, he entered the courtyard.

He was stunned to see Thomas sitting in the corner, with the slave girl Sarida serving him! His surprise at seeing Thomas here left him speechless. As he greeted Thomas, ready to ask how it was that he was in two places at once, the satrap's son walked into the courtyard and greeted him.

The momentary distraction left Abbanes no choice but to turn and greet the man in return. The arrival of the satrap's son left no doubt in Abbanes' mind as to why he came. It was clearly time to give the satrap a gift, both in recognition of the great wedding and new union—an important trade union—but also simply as a form of courtesy for passing through his territory. While lesser to the great king, Gondophores, the relationship with Satrap Tai was not fully settled, and it was generally best to keep as many allies as possible. Loyalties changed constantly.

"Greetings, my Lord Abbanes," said the young man, smiling and addressing Abbanes with more of a title than he actually commanded. Abbanes graciously greeted the man back, motioning him to sit with him. The first time the two men had sat down to enjoy chai, there had been joyful friendly banter between them. No more. This was a business meeting, and both men understood that. As the men reclined, Abbanes made eye contact with his senior servant and nodded. The man needed no other instruction and soon brought forth a specially engraved box.

"Please accept this gift, a gift for the great Tai, son of Queen Mei, as my humble contribution," said Abbanes, formally handing it to him. His tone was friendly. Abbanes genuinely liked the satrap's son and imagined the day would come when he would need to work closely with him. Servants brought refreshments and the two men continued to speak lightly. Still, the possible presence of Isa in Andrapolis and the miraculous stories surrounding both Isa and Thomas were on his mind.

Pointing out to Apostle Thomas in the courtyard to his guest, Abbanes explained some of the stories surrounding him and of the great healing powers both he and Isa were said to command. "Both men are skilled at attracting large crowds of followers," continued Abbanes. "I witnessed one forming near the port."

As Abbanes continued with his story, he offered to have Thomas prepare a blessing for the union of the visiting Nabatean prince and his new princess bride. Abbanes was thinking the satrap would not be impressed and made the offer as more of a courtesy. To his surprise, the satrap's son liked the idea.

"The satrap has also heard of the Hebrew prophet speaking in the city," said the young man, nodding his head and not understanding there might be two. "I am confident my father would approve of the idea of receiving a blessing from him."

Unspoken in the man's mind was that it would not only be a blessing but also an acknowledgment of the divine power of the nobility and the right of rulers to govern over the ruled, whatever the religion. By accepting the blessing, the satrap would be perceived as maintaining power over this new religious figure too.

Abbanes found himself agreeing to bring forth Thomas to bless the union, outwardly showing enthusiasm for the idea but privately less certain the more he considered it. He hoped the blessing would go well and perhaps help make up for the modest gift Abbanes proffered to the satrap. He would have preferred to offer a more extravagant gift, but he was running out of gold. He knew he would need to explain to Thomas the commitment he had just made, a blessing upon the prince and his new princess, unsure what his reaction would be.

That evening, the slave girl Sarida was gone. Abbanes had been surprised to see Thomas with her but quickly put it out of his mind as he approached his charge.

"Has Isa returned?" inquired Abbanes as he approached. His sentence served as a greeting and an inquiry. Thomas turned to gaze at him.

"Why do you ask?" replied Thomas.

Abbanes then proceeded to explain how he had seen someone who he thought was Thomas speaking to a large crowd and then how he found Thomas here. "It must have been Isa," finished Abbanes. "Who else could it have been?"

At this news, Thomas was animated, ready to be off to find his brother Isa. Yet, Abbanes would have none of it, physically restraining Thomas by the arm.

"All in good time, my friend," he told the excited man. "Before you go seeking out Isa, I need you to come with me to bless the satrap and his family. Perhaps his mother Queen Mei herself will be there. This alliance is important," finished Abbanes. The trader spoke these last words in an uncompromising tone.

"Bless the satrap and his family!" exclaimed Thomas. "It is Isa who should be blessing them, not me. I am the lesser, he is the greater."

Abbanes was exasperated. "You are not the lesser of your brother," intoned the elder, firmly. "Come, let us present a blessing in the name of the unspoken to the satrap. With this blessing, we can continue our journey in peace, and you can be free to track down Isa. This blessing will meet our obligation." Abbanes was appealing to their shared religious identity.

With these words, Thomas' resistance to the idea ended. It seemed a simple matter. Go forth and bless this family. He had seen Isa do many things like this before. Surely, he could utter a blessing here. He could then go about his business and find Isa. Reluctantly, he agreed to Abbanes' demands.

Abbanes instructed that the finest cloaks should be brought out, indeed the very same cloaks the men wore on their first night at the palace. As before, both men were perfumed in the courtyard by the slaves, and again the men repeated their journey up to the great hall.

This time, the great hall was set up very differently than it had been for the wedding banquet. The satrap sat on the dais with his courtiers about him. No women were in attendance, not even the bride—a big surprise to Thomas. Queen Mei was either not home or not interested in this event. In their place were religious men of all sorts: Buddhists, Brahmins, and others Thomas did not recognize.

The young Nabatean prince sat to the right of the satrap. The air was filled with smoke from burning incense. Abbanes and Thomas were seated to one side of the dais and waited as the preparations continued. He understood the chanting of the Buddhist monks and bhikkhus not at all. The chanting sounded high-pitched but melodic. The monks were solemn in expression, but also friendly, seemingly unthreatened by this strange man of God who had come among them. When they stopped chanting, the young prince stood, and clasping his hands together, he bowed to them. The senior monk acknowledged the gesture and then turned to Abbanes and Thomas and smiled, indicating it was their turn. The monks and bhikkhus seated themselves and turned their full attention on Thomas, watching him expectantly.

Thomas stepped forward and motioned to the young prince to do likewise. The young man, still somewhat unsure of himself in this foreign place with foreign customs, unquestioningly did as he was asked and presented himself before Thomas. The young prince was no more than fifteen, still finding his way in the world of men. Bringing home this bride and cementing this alliance was one of the first tasks he had been assigned by his father. He was determined to make it all happen smoothly.

Thomas was not unhappy that no women were present. Perhaps the distraction of women at this special blessing would not be appropriate. It was right that they should be left out of the room, he thought. All were beholden to God alone.

Inexperienced in offering a blessing in any language, Thomas knew how to say some of the correct words and was confident he could parrot the words of Isa and indeed of many of the rabbis he had listened to over the years.

"Birkhot ha-ha'ah," began Thomas, words that were used for virtually all Hebrew blessings. Here, these words sounded strange, even exotic to the audience.

"Blessed are you, Lord our God, King of the Universe," he continued in a loud voice for all to hear. He spoke in Aramaic, his native tongue. The satrap and a few other couriers understood enough of the words to follow generally. While not unknown in these lands, Aramaic was not spoken by most and added to the sense that a special rite was being carried out. Thomas' grand Hebrew robes added to the effect.

"He who has granted us all life," he cried out. "He who has sustained us. He who has enabled us to witness this great union of families." Thomas voice was strong and commanding. Like his brother, he realized speaking to a crowd was a special talent and he had that talent. It was in his being.

He continued for another five minutes, reciting virtually every phrase he could think of that might seem relevant to the occasion. The satrap appeared to be delighted by the blessing, choosing to interpret all the references to God, to King of the Universe, and more as references to himself.

Finally, Thomas turned to the bowing groom before him. He was surprised by the man's youth and apparent inexperience. He was not accustomed to seeing satraps and princes, and so he immediately realized that his expectations were too great.

These royals were just men, he thought as he continued. Here before him was a boy. A youthful and attractive young man. Thomas thought the bride lucky. Perhaps she had not even seen her prince yet.

He placed oil upon the young man's head and upon his brow and repeated the blessing, again and again, chanting as best he could.

His task complete, he could tell the satrap was pleased, his face beaming. Excited and perhaps a bit out of protocol, the satrap suddenly leaped from his throne and ran off, his courtiers in hot pursuit.

The satrap wanted to be the first to tell his daughter of all the special blessings she had received that day, including that of Apostle Thomas. She was the apple of his eye, and so far, he was delighted that the wedding had proceeded so well. The Nabatean was young and barely a man, but he seemed like a fair and generous man. He thought he would be good to his daughter. The Nabateans had shown their trust in him by sending someone young but important. They trusted him, and the partnership would last a long time.

The satrap burst through the door to his daughter's quarters, joy on his face. To his complete astonishment, there was his daughter in her bedroom, speaking to Isa! And her head and face were uncovered!

"Abomination!" he cried. "How did this happen? How did this intruder get past the guards?"

As fast as he entered, he ran out of the room, calling for the guards to come immediately. The men rushed into the room, only to find the satrap's daughter now alone, terrified by the arrival of the guards, weapons drawn. Isa was no longer there, apparently making his exit as fast as his appearance.

Satrap Tai, confused and not understanding that there might even be two Nazarenes in his midst, turned to the guards. Thinking Isa was Thomas, he was at a loss for words as to how Thomas managed to enter his daughter's bedroom when he had just been in the audience chamber. He sent the guards back to the great room with instructions to find and arrest Thomas and detain Abbanes. The guards quickly returned, reporting that Thomas and Abbanes were no longer there.

As the satrap ordered the immediate arrest of Thomas and indeed even of Abbanes, his son entered the room. Recognizing the emotional state his father was in, he quickly engaged him in conversation, his tone calming and soothing, effectively slowing all hasty actions.

"Arresting Abbanes would be tantamount to a declaration of war on Gandhara, a war that the satrapy does not need!" he said emphatically, his voice firm but calm.

The satrap initially would not hear of anything short of all-out war, but reason slowly returned to the older man. He listened to the wisdom of his son's words and began to consider his options more carefully. He stopped speaking so forcefully as reason overpowered his anger. He finally turned his attention to his daughter, worried that her reputation risked being sullied, but quickly assessed that his intervention had prevented anything from happening. At least nothing outwardly so.

"Let them go," he finally said to the guard, his words heavy. "Hinder them not but tell them they must leave Andrapolis now!" His words were a command.

Chapter 7

Jesus said, "Blessed is the lion which becomes man when consumed by man; and cursed is the man whom the lion consumes, and the lion becomes man."

—The Coptic Gospel of Thomas Verse 7

ABBANES HEARD THE commotion in the hallways and immediately realized that something was terribly wrong. A veteran of nuanced and dangerous situations, he instinctively grabbed Thomas by the arm and immediately exited the palace. He did not know precisely what was happening, but he sensed that it was better not to be there. He soon heard cries in the distance, some shouting for Abbanes and others for Thomas the Hebrew. There was no time to wait.

The two men hurried down the hill and immediately moved in the direction of his assembled caravan, now camped at the trailhead nearly two hours' march outside of town. He knew that if he could reach his encampment, he would be in a stronger position, with more fighting men if needed.

Additional guards of Abbanes' escort met them a short kilometer from the palace with horses at the ready. Thomas was no horseman and elected to walk on to the camp, a condition which Abbanes reluctantly agreed to. He was in a great hurry to begin preparations and knew that Thomas would slow him down. He needed to get to his encampment quickly.

The trailhead was a short distance inland from the coast, a small village marking the place, its economic lifeblood based on the many travelers who passed through. Men on horseback could close the distance quickly. Thomas would continue on the trail on foot along with four others who knew the road.

The roadway to the camp was forested and hilly in some places. At night, it was not always a safe place to walk, especially alone. The occasional laugh of a hyena or close-by cough of a leopard could regularly be heard. And occasionally, even a mighty sher, one of the great lions of Persia, would roar in the distance. Usually, it was simply males attempting to establish and protect their domain from other encroaching lions. As frightening as the sound was, experienced travelers knew that the roaring sher was not a threat. The threat was lions on the hunt in the dark. And they were silent.

Abbanes, riding quickly with his guards, reached the tiny village near the trailhead and from there was guided to his encampment. He immediately roused all with instructions that the entire caravan was to prepare for a forced march within a few hours. His own guards, in contact with the palace guards, informed him that Thomas was discovered in the bedroom of the princess. Abbanes knew this was not possible. Thomas had been with him the whole time. Still, he understood the danger. The palace guards told Abbanes and his men to just leave. If they just left, all would be sorted later.

As the commotion surrounding the discovery of a man in the bedroom of the princess overtook the palace, one young man seized a different opportunity. Natan could hardly sleep, so fearful he was of losing Sarida. Ever since the arrival of the Hebrew, his very being was overcome with pangs of jealousy. His constant agony was the thought that Sarida might even now be locked in the arms of the strange Hebrew. Earlier that day, he had watched Sarida walk out of the palace, following a small party heading for the trailhead. She carried on her head a small bundle consisting of clothing and other possessions. He could only guess she was going to meet Thomas and that she planned to run away and join the caravan to Gandhara. She planned to leave Andrapolis permanently. The thought infuriated him. She planned to leave him permanently!

His thoughts tormented him as he considered all his hopes and desires were being taken from him. If these two Hebrews had not arrived, Sarida would be his. Unmitigated hatred burned in his soul. He would follow the caravan, follow Thomas, and if need be, find a way to kill the Nazarene.

Lacking even the low status of a slave girl and musician, Natan's status being that of a slave and server, the young man was forced to sneak out of the palace grounds. With all the commotion going on surrounding Thomas and the presence of a stranger in the princess' bedroom, Natan's departure went unnoticed. Armed with nothing more than his walking stick, he took off down the road, a lonely, unnoticed, and insignificant figure, marching towards the trailhead, knowing approximately where Abbanes' caravan must be.

And so it was that at last, the aging sher heard the sounds of human prey making its way through the forest towards him. The sher did not roar. He did not make a sound. He had been lying patiently for hours, waiting for just such a moment. All his senses keyed to the approaching man, his tail erect but camouflaged in the tall grass and darkness.

A puny, defenseless man approached. The only sound the sher would make would be when he charged full out upon his prey. A massive lion bearing down, accompanied by a deafening cavernous roar, often induced paralysis. The end often came quickly.

In the dark, Thomas and his companions moved silently through the forest. Thomas could make out the other four forms just ahead of him, each visible in the pale moonlight. As the march continued, Thomas eyes grew more and more accustomed to the darkness, and his visibility steadily improved. The men, except for Thomas, were seasoned travelers, warriors, and hunters, able to call on either skill set, depending on what the occasion required. They moved in silence, accustomed to traveling by night, their eyes more easily adjusting to the moonlight.

Suddenly, the leader froze and raised his hand. All the companions obediently stopped. At this point, the trail turned west and gradually descended towards a small creek, giving Thomas and his companions a view, however slight, of the trail ahead.

The leader pointed forward, down, and to the left, but said nothing. At first, Thomas could not make out much but then he detected slight movement. Studying further, he detected the outlines of a large cat in the brush. The huge erect tail was moving ever so slightly, revealing the balance of the body of an enormous lion. Thomas felt secure with his armed, battle-tested companions, but still, he trembled slightly as he looked upon the fearsome predator.

At that same moment, Natan walked into view. The man was traveling alone, ahead of them, quietly unaware of the eyes upon him. Thomas was surprised that Natan would be out on the road like this at night. Although he had only seen Natan a few times, he was sure it was the man he already hated, the man who seemed to be in love with Sarida too. And he was about to walk past the lion waiting in tall grass.

The headman looked back at Thomas inquiringly. It was plain that he was asking for permission to take action, to warn this man of his impending doom. The hunters could save the man and drive the sher away. It would not be the first lion the hunters had killed. But to do so could also put them at risk and might reveal their presence to others seeking them out. Still trembling, Thomas watched the situation unfold. He looked back at the headman and shook his head. He realized that the headman would assume from his response that stealth was important to the journey and that it would be best to remain quiet, almost invisible. They would not intervene. Thomas would allow Natan to be attacked.

In his heart, he knew that concealment was not his real motive. A momentary surreal sense of joy invaded his thinking. The man who would be his competitor would be killed. Joy!

At that moment, the great sher, not sensing the presence of the other men, suddenly charged upon Natan. His fury unleashed, his roar sent a flock of birds to a shrieking flight from a nearby tree. Natan turned and had little time to feel fear or even react at all. Sher was on him. Sher killed him.

Thomas' momentary joy immediately dissipated as the absolute horror of what was transpiring enfolded before him. The enormous lion had killed Natan almost instantly, seizing him by the neck and biting right through, simultaneously breaking his neck and nearly decapitating the man with the force of the bite. He then picked up the lifeless body in his mouth, his teeth buried deep into his shoulder. Natan's head flopped loosely, barely attached to his corpse, as Sher ran off with him into the brush. Mighty Sher carried his prey as easily as a house cat carried a mouse.

The headman held his arm up again with a clear message: Everyone stay still and silent. A male lion might be alone, but the headman was not sure and wanted to proceed with caution. He stayed still for another few minutes, and then along with another of his team, began a process of carefully moving forward, stopping, studying, and listening to the forest around them and then silently moving.

With hand motions and extreme silence, the party crept past the place of the attack. The five men could distinctly hear the sounds of bones crushing as the lion feasted on the remains of the man not far away. At one point, they could hear the great cat growl, as though he had picked up their scent but elected to not abandon his feast. The party kept moving.

The headman knew that the attack and kill would attract still more predators, and so he was anxious to keep walking away from this place. They moved slowly at first and then picked up the pace as they got further and further away from sher.

Thomas was numb. Remorse was now flooding his consciousness. He could think of nothing else. *How could I have let that happen? I should have warned Natan. Why didn't I?*

As he wrestled with these thoughts, he again came to the startling conclusion: The consequences of the needs of man were sin.

His vision had been clouded by his desire to be with Sarida. These thoughts reaffirmed to him once again that the only path forward in life was to be in an exclusive union with the one God. This is what Isa had been teaching. Union between a man and a woman impeded the connection between man and the divine. The lesson was clear. This thought would stay with Thomas always.

Sher had carried the lifeless body of Natan into a thicket not more than thirty meters from the roadway. Easily capable of devouring the man entirely, he soon found himself fending off a pack of wild dogs who wanted a share of the spoils too. While savagely defending his kill, several pieces of his prize were successfully snatched away, including an arm and a foot. The dogs, scavengers who lived on the edge of the village at the trailhead, would leave behind grizzly mementos of the night's feast for the trailhead villagers to find in the morning, a grim reminder of the risks of taking the trail at night, but also a fulfillment of the curse Thomas had laid upon the cupbearer. Some in the village, like Natan, servers to the king, would forever remember the words of Thomas.

An hour later, Thomas and his party arrived in the encampment, finding the entire caravan a beehive of activity as everyone prepared for an early departure. Still shaking from his ordeal with the lion, he immediately sought out Abbanes, who as usual was the center of everything, issuing orders, answering questions, and encouraging everyone to try harder, to do more. He was a leader of men.

The man has amazing energy, thought Thomas, as he watched Abbanes conducting his business, realizing that it was best not to engage him at the moment. Fires burned all around the encampment, and Thomas made his way to one of them. He greeted those around him as he walked up to the fire blazing brightly. He squatted at first, and then fatigue overcoming him, he took his cloak and lay down to sleep. There was nothing for him to do.

Drifting into a light slumber, he dreamed of the terrible attack on Natan over and over. He should have prevented it. He did not. He could have saved the man. He did not. The conclusion of such a terrible event clear in his mind: the only real path forward for a man on this earth was celibacy. The earthly delights of women were a distraction, a sin. Thomas stumbled upon the same conclusion that would drive his companion Peter and the Christian church for the next two millenniums and require celibacy of its priests. That thinking would become a founding tenet of the Church of Isa.

Thomas had not laid down for more than an hour when the fire he was sleeping next to was unceremoniously stamped out. The caravan was in the final stage of preparing for a hard day of forced marching. The activity wakened the apostle. As his senses slowly returned, he realized that someone was cuddled up next to him. Touching him, even. Sensually touching him, caressing him, waking him gently. The sensation was pleasant, calming. Hands were reaching under his cloak and touching his body. He sensed an early stirring in his loins. Thomas, now fully awake, sat up. There, lying beside him, was the beautiful Sarida smiling up at him. She sat up too.

"Good morning," she said to Thomas softly. She was expecting a face of joy and happiness for her presence. She was intending to join the caravan and go off to Gandhara with Thomas and Abbanes.

Thomas' mind was instantly overloaded. The events of watching Natan being killed so recently and now the arrival of Sarida sent him into distress. He had been dreaming all night of the terrible wages resulting from desire and lust. The presence of Sarida was too much for him.

"No!" cried Thomas, standing and stepping back from the startled young woman. "No," he cried out again, this time with even more conviction. "You cannot be here. You cannot travel with me."

His tone was emphatic and anguished.

Sarida, at a loss for words, could hear the anguish in his voice. This was not the reaction that she expected.

"You cannot be here with me. You must leave," implored Thomas, only slightly more gently.

"Thomas, I am offering myself to you. Take me with you. Protect me. I am as you are, a believer in the God who cannot be named." Sarida was unable to hide the growing anguish and emotional pain in her own voice now. In her mind was confusion. She was certain that the two Hebrews had entered her life to bring her out of bondage. This was her chance.

Thomas, shaking with emotion, looked back at her. His terror had turned into determination. He knew what he had to do. He understood his mission. "Leave me," he commanded. His voice sounded harsh. The tone surprised him. "You cannot be a companion of mine. Satan has placed you before me as an obstacle." All desire for Sarida was gone. His face was hard.

Sarida knew her chance was lost. She could see it written on his countenance. She realized she did not know this man. Even if she somehow managed to find another companion to travel with her, she now also understood the irrationality of Thomas. She must move on. Tears came to her eyes. She covered her face and walked away from the fire and back towards the village. In daylight, she would join a procession of villagers walking to Andrapolis, and then she would return to the palace. Her heart was broken.

Thomas watched her go and then turned away. From that moment forward, he knew he must be celibate. He could never love a woman again. Ever.

Chapter 8

*"Let one not neglect one's own welfare for the sake of
another, however great. Clearly understanding one's own
welfare, let one be intent upon the good."*

—The Lord Buddha in the Dhammapada Verse 166

MASTER RINPOCHE AROSE before the daylight began to pierce the still darkness surrounding the city. A highly disciplined man, he allowed a slight yawn to escape as he sat up. Normally, he would spend some time alone in meditation before the day began. Today, he would need to proceed directly to the assembly.

A tall man but slight of posture, the Buddhist priest carefully donned his black robe and walked the short distance to the vihara. Entering the great hall next to the Dharamarajika Stupa, he sat down in the front of the room on a small dais. The images of the Buddha and his life were beautifully carved in stone and lined the walls of the chamber. Before him, members of the sangha continued to enter and prepare for the day. Rinpoche sat cross-legged, his back straight, his mind clear, and his body frozen but also somehow amazingly supple and relaxed, the consequence of a lifetime of mindful posture and stretching. The sangha revered their leader, Master Rinpoche, seeing him as an example of an arhat, that is one who has achieved nirvana but has not achieved the status of a Buddha.

The assembled priests, bhikkhus, novices, and ambitiously self-declared bodhisattvas spread out before him and began to chant. Buddhist world diversity was much in evidence in the hall. Students from around the world sought out Taxila, the "City of Cut Stone," and a center of learning and trade known throughout Asia. As Rinpoche looked upon the assembly, he could see bhikkhus who had come from the Persian states, from all over India, from distant Taprobane—the island kingdom south of India—and even from as far away as China to the east and Greece to the west.

Several of the novices were unmistakably from his own native Tibet, the epicanthic fold in their eyes betraying their lineage. Completing the picture were several different-colored robes worn by the assembled senior bhikkhus, the most unusual being black, with saffron and blue hues being more common.

Most had been sent by their communities from far and wide to learn and study under Master Rinpoche, wanting their priest to be linked to an actual arhat. This diversity at Taxila was only a brief marker in time. At other times, conflict and war would break out between various sects, visually pitting robe color versus another robe color, or on a larger scale, Buddhist versus Hindu. Each side might eventually find the words for a "just" war, ordained by their God. But not today. Today, tolerance ruled the world, and peace and prosperity followed. Master Rinpoche was firm on this point.

Rinpoche surveyed the room with a certain sense of pride. *Surely, this diversity is the world imagined by the Buddha,* he mused. *Has not the Buddha taught us to question all, even the Buddha himself? Isn't this diversity a wondrous proof of that?* A man of little emotion, he found himself suppressing a slight smile that threatened to creep into his otherwise stern visage.

Rinpoche continued the ceremony for several hours before resting and taking a small breakfast in his room served by a samanera no more than seven years old. He greeted the youth warmly and thanked him for the food. As he spoke, the senior priest's voice was hoarse from a lifetime of chanting in smoke and incense-filled rooms. Master Rinpoche was in excellent health with the exception perhaps of his throat, a common problem for many of the priests.

The balance of his day was filled with teaching, consulting, and managing the university. Rinpoche was a strong proponent of the Middle Path, the right way to understand the path of Buddha and the role of the bodhisattva in this world. Clinging to an older tradition, a Hinayana priest was going to be visiting him later that day in the afternoon to debate the growing "idolatry" that he associated with Rinpoche and his Dharmaguptaka school. The Hinayana were growing angry at the changes they were seeing in the university's teaching in reference to the enlightened path. Rinpoche welcomed and encouraged debate among all his priests, students, and visitors and attempted to model that behavior by regularly seeking out a diversity of views himself.

Taxila's distinctive architecture of cut stone stood out in the region. Laid out before the vihara and university, it sat on the Great Trunk Road linking China to the Western world. All the world known to the Gandharans passed through their city in all directions. The city was Buddhist in orientation and dominance, but

King Gondophores was tolerant. Taxila also harbored houses of worship for those following Ahura Mazda, Jainism, Hinduism, and even a tiny synagogue, mostly serving Jewish refugees fleeing from Persian persecution.

Later that day, in the great hall, Rinpoche greeted Shigao, his Hinayana friend, with a smile. The men knew each other well, clasping their hands in the prayer pose as they tilted their heads towards each other in deference and respect.

The differences in their religious perspectives and dogma were mirrored in the color of their robes and even in the state of their health. Shigao had taken a vow of extreme poverty and regularly could be seen on the side of the road with his begging bowl and little else. His simple robe was a faded saffron cloth sown together from rags. His body reflected the physical effects of long years of extreme food deprivation and poor nutrition.

Rinpoche was also modestly dressed, but his black robe did display some evidence of tailoring. While he was lean like Shigao, his body displayed greater muscle development, and his skin radiated health, the only noticeable physical defect being the rasping sound of his voice. The men exchanged pleasantries, clearly enjoying each other's presence.

On other days, Rinpoche would entertain followers of Mahavira, a contemporary of Lord Buddha, Hindu sages, or even followers of Mithra. Yet, Shigao always held a special place of honor with Rinpoche, and he frequently met with him. Rinpoche always looked forward to the talks, recognizing that despite their differing views on some matters, Shigao was a great priest and teacher in his own right.

To the mind of Rinpoche, some of the beliefs of these other religions and the Hinayana Buddhists were almost on the right track, but some went too far in denying the practicality of life's needs. In taking these extreme positions, they missed the entire point and value of self-denial.

Still, Rinpoche learned a lot by debating with these different representatives and eagerly sought out new perspectives. These debates strengthened his own understanding of the Buddha's teachings and reaffirmed to him the absolute "Right Thinking" and wisdom of the Buddha. The Buddha understood the importance of self-denial and how the suppression of self could help lead to enlightenment. But extreme denial, such as that of his friend and fellow Buddhist Shigao, would lead nowhere. To deny one's physical body would simply be to starve the body. The Buddha, on his path to enlightenment, had understood this. The Buddha had once literally starved himself—and to what effect? Likewise, one could study the opposite extreme: The Lord Buddha, as Prince Siddhartha, had once indulged in all worldly needs and desires. Again, what had that accomplished? Nothing. Not all could be a Bodhisattva. That was the core disagreement between the two friends. Master Rinpoche considered all these issues as he anticipated the meeting.

But today, he sensed that the debate was going to be different. For one thing, Shigao had asked that they meet to talk in the great hall, a departure from where they usually met: the quarters of Master Rinpoche. Shigao had told him that he was increasingly uncomfortable with the direction the sangha was taking, although he did not clearly explain his point when proposing the meeting. Rinpoche had noted that his friend's tone and attitude betrayed a growing anger over something. *Perhaps this has to do with his usual complaints about imagery,* considered Rinpoche. *Thus, he wanted to meet in the great hall.* The Hinayana priest often insisted on the older belief that any imagery of the Lord Buddha was a desecration of the path to enlightenment.

Both men were seated in the front of the room, facing each other. Wasting little time, Shigao made the first general declaration, an attempt to frame what was on his mind.

"Buddha did not declare himself to be a god," he began firmly. His tone was only slightly confrontational. "The Buddha's goal was to arrest the cycle of rebirth that all living things are trapped in," he reminded Master Rinpoche. "Beings are trapped in this cycle because they crave illusory needs and comforts. By denying the self, the bodhisattva can interrupt this cycle. The Buddha even took a vow of poverty to put himself on that road. The Buddha followed this path to nirvana. He taught a path for all men." His tone was firm and clear.

Rinpoche smiled back at this friend. Many of their debates started out like this, reaffirming the common beliefs of both. He knew that the Hinayana priest was just setting him up for a more direct confrontation on a different matter. He was just affirming what they both could mostly agree upon. It was a starting place.

Master Rinpoche took the bait. "Are we all to become bodhisattva, then? Are we all to seek enlightenment at the level of Buddha? Who will grow food? Even in your poverty, mustn't you eat something sometimes?" Rinpoche's statement was a gentle question too. He had privately noted the declining health of his friend but chose to say nothing.

"Don't we depend on everyone's contribution to support life? Even here today, I sit sheltered from the sun, as do you, because of the valued labor of craftsmen. This vihara is just one example set for the people to live a good and lawful life. The Buddha instructed us to do that also," Rinpoche reminded Shigao.

Shigao nodded his head as his friend continued, setting the stage for the real issue. "When the Buddha preached his first sermon after achieving enlightenment to the five ascetics, many originally did not recognize the wisdom because he had chosen the Middle Path."

Master Rinpoche felt the need to repeat and emphasize one basic point. "How can we all be sangha? We cannot all be priests. We must seek the Middle Path," he intoned with firmness, yet smiling back on his friend. Rinpoche knew this was the biggest problem with Shigao's view.

Shigao sighed and bowed slightly, recognizing the point, knowing the two men could go around and around on this. The fundamental point would never be fully resolved between them. Shigao would normally respond, but not today. There were other things on his mind. This opening discussion was framing the more important conversation coming. Both men knew it.

Shigao returned to his opening statement. "We know that the Lord Buddha said repeatedly that he was not a god. Yet this vihara, this group of sangha, is promoting that very idea with all these carvings and structures. Master Rinpoche," Shigao continued using a respectful tone, "surely you cannot justify all this idolatry here." He paused for a moment for effect. He used the title "Master" to soften his words slightly.

Shigao was moving the conversation to what was really on his mind. As he spoke, he gestured disapprovingly at the many fine carvings of the Buddha's life in the room. He pointed at one set of stone carvings that detailed the famous story of when a king attempted to dissuade Prince Siddhartha from becoming a teacher by tempting him with young beauties from all over the kingdom. The story was laid out in the stone in great detail for all to see. The bare breasts of carved stone maidens were now blackened and discolored from the many thousands of mostly young male hands that had caressed these realistic but cold breasts over the years. Here was Shigao's point today.

Rinpoche had initially anticipated that Shigao was going to launch into a discussion about the dangerous pathways of imagery. He was prepared for that. He now understood that Shigao was not troubled by the simple idolatry so much as by the fact that many of the young priests were clearly distracted by these specific images in the room. Shigao did not approve of and would continue to speak against all imagery. Yet, his point was the obvious deviant behavior of some of these young acolytes and students. Their misbehavior was undeniably evidenced by the discoloration in the stone. These young men did not have their minds in a disciplined place. Unable to suppress their desires, they would not grow as sangha. They would remain in a state of desire that would block their growth and development as priests.

He has a point, observed Rinpoche as he looked more carefully at the carving across the room. The blackened and discolored breasts told an undeniable story. He would need to say something to a few of the senior bhikkhus and made a mental note to do so. Today's debate could be short. He would do something amazing and concede the point to his friend.

Master Rinpoche threw up both of his hands in a gesture of surrender. "You are not wrong, my friend," gesturing towards the maidens as he spoke. He continued, "I will need to address the issue with our students."

The two men continued to discuss and then reaffirm the problem and the very real danger the carvings represented to the impressionable young minds in the entire region. The students would be unable to grow. Rinpoche was unwilling, however, to entertain the idea that he needed to take the statues down. He elected to tackle that point now.

"One cannot insulate the youth from the world," he told Shigao. "Temptation has always existed at many levels. Temptation will be with them always, creating suffering. And it will not be just the temptation by maidens. Temptation and therefore impediment can be food, riches, or many other material things. Every person has to learn to reject these things on their own. The Lord Buddha as Prince Siddhartha left the palace to experience the real world," he continued. "Our students must do the same. We cannot hide beautiful maidens from them. That is what is truly important, my friend."

Shigao felt he had made his point and elected not to say more on the matter. Master Rinpoche further reminded his friend of the value of the Buddhist statues. "The carvings and in fact all of the imagery in the room are simply teaching tools that help us spread the wisdom of the Buddha. They are particularly important to laymen. In the case of the story of the beautiful maidens, the Buddha himself recounted the story. How can we make an exception for that one story? They are indeed imperfect representations. But as part of the Middle Path and Right Thinking, they are powerful aids. We would be imperfect in our ability to tell these stories without them. We tell our story with greater accuracy and clarity with them."

Rinpoche was firm on this point, reanimating Shigao. The two men continued their unresolvable debate for another hour until the bhikkhus and others began to assemble in the room for evening prayers and meditation.

Chapter 9

"Oh Lord Surya, Ruler of the Universe, you are the
remover of all diseases, the repository of peace. I bow to
you and please bless your devotees with long life, health, and
wealth."

—*Mantra of Lord Surya, the Sun God*

AND SO THOMAS and Abbanes began the long overland journey to Gandhara and its capital, Taxila. Abbanes explained to Thomas that the road might be difficult in places and could take at least forty days, and longer if weather or other conditions slowed their progress. The initial part of the journey was hurried, but as they moved further and further away from Andrapolis, the tension all had been feeling evaporated. Mountains, hills, and rivers blocked their passage and needed attention. Villagers along the way helped the caravan at certain strategic river crossings with boats and labor, but always at a cost.

Thomas watched the terrain change as they moved further and further north. The road wound through hills, with rocks and dry scrub in abundance. In the distance, he could sometimes see what appeared to be high mountain ranges. At other times, he realized that massive and distant cloud formations masquerading as mountain ranges seemed to disappear as the caravan drew closer.

As they marched upon the road, Abbanes and Thomas often had long hours when they could talk, with the apostle seizing the opportunity to explain again and again the great mission of Isa and the importance of becoming one with God. The conversations helped Thomas clarify his own thinking, increasingly realizing that self-denial was an important element on the pathway to the Kingdom of God. His strongly passionate beliefs came through to Abbanes, who did not realize that part of that passion came from Thomas' experience with Natan, the lion and Sarida.

Abbanes was also struck by the near miraculous appearance of Isa at Andrapolis, as well as remembering all the stories he had heard in Judea. The Jewish trader was starting to believe that there was indeed some kind of deified power surrounding Thomas and his twin. He silently shook his head every time he thought about it. The two Hebrews spoke in Aramaic as they walked, and even as they occasionally rode together on horses, Abbanes' preferred method of transportation.

As Thomas interacted more and more with members of the caravan, he began to develop fluency in basic Gandhari, the language of the kingdom. Other than when speaking to Abbanes, all others were speaking Gandhari as well as an assortment of other languages that Thomas did not understand.

Unable to contribute effectively to caravan operations, the apostle provided what amounted to entertainment for the herders each evening when the caravan called a halt to the march. The entire caravan looked forward to the stop each day, seizing the opportunity to rest and eat. Putting together even a day camp was challenging, and most were content to sleep by a night fire on a cloak.

These rest stops gave Thomas a ready audience. He often began each evening with a tale or sermon he had learned from Isa. Soon, there were more and more men listening, as Thomas explained a particularly interesting or entertaining story or miracle. While Thomas tried hard to drive home a point in these talks, the herders were often tired after a day's labor and were simply content to listen to the strange Hebrew speak. Thomas initially spoke in Aramaic, which limited his following. However, he was soon fluent enough to deliver his message in Gandhari, and his followers grew in numbers. As he gained experience preaching, his sermons rapidly improved, understanding what would cause the crowd to react to his words. He cut a fine figure by the fire, a robust if not handsome man, His stories demanded attention, often revealing his passion and conviction.

But preaching sermons caused the apostle to carry out some self-reflection too. Having to articulate what he believed and what Isa had taught caused him to think through much of the meaning of what he was saying. When he was just listening to Isa, he could take the message at face value. Now he had to really believe in what he was saying. How could he do otherwise? How could he otherwise defend his message and the pathway to the Kingdom of God? His experience with the flute player Sarida, along with the role that he had played in the death of Natan, were constantly on his mind.

In addition to winding through rocky hillsides, the caravan needed to cross the great Indus river tributaries on several occasions.

These stops often created long delays and gave Thomas additional time to preach the word of God, while the caravan laborers and handlers waited to cross.

After nearly one month's march, the party finally arrived at the great city of Multan. Most in the caravan were unable to suppress their excitement at arriving at such a major city after the long road. Even the spirit and morale of the slaves seemed to perk up as they entered the city.

Recognizing the need for rest by all, Abbanes, weary himself and increasingly relieved that their journey was almost over, agreed to a three-day rest stop. Multan was allied with Gandhara. and the satrap here was a friend of the king and known to Abbanes. After establishing an encampment and tending to the animals, many of the herdsmen were released, and they rapidly made their way to the great Sun Temple and shrine to Surya. A few armed men and boys were required to stay behind and watch the animals and cargo, freeing up most of the herdsmen to leave.

Abbanes immediately departed the encampment with his usual cohort to pay his respects to the satrap, leaving Thomas free to wander. He observed the city with great interest. He was startled that the herdsmen, after hearing his nightly sermons, so readily dropped all knowledge of what he had said and took off to the Sun Temple. *Clearly, I need to find other ways to reach these men,* he thought. The pathway to the temple itself was clear; the entire party seemed to know where it was and made a straight line for it.

The apostle observed this behavior with growing disquiet and elected to walk to the Sun Temple to see for himself what this worship of the god Surya was all about. As he walked, he observed several minor temples along the way. The passage took him right into the market of Multan itself. Not unlike the market in Alexandria, although on a much smaller scale, the market was adjacent to the Chenab River and bustling with activity. He could see all manner of economic activity, from fish sellers to fine shops selling garments and goods of all kinds. Birds and other animals in cages were sold for both food and sacrifice in the surrounding temples.

While the Sun Temple was the most famous in Multan, it was not the only famous temple. There were important temples dedicated to Lord Buddha, to various Hindu deities, and to Mithra. To Thomas, much of this seemed an abomination. As he walked long, he encountered a few stand-alone statues, idols in the eyes of the apostle, with devotees praying before them. Thomas shook his head and struggled not to intervene or preach to these people. He saw again the terrible consequences of man focused on his primal needs first and not aligned with the one true God. They created abominations, statues to false gods.

A caravan of three chariots suddenly burst through the crowd, forcing all to jump to the side to escape being run over. Thomas himself narrowly avoided the chariots.

"Thomas!" someone yelled at him. He turned to see Adika, one of the herdsmen, motioning him to the other side of the road after the chariots had passed. Knowing Thomas was a foreigner and someone who had never seen the great Temple of the Sun before, Adika decided it was his chance to introduce him to the wonders of the complex.

The two men chatted and walked together down the road to the temple. Adika had attended many of Thomas' sermons and, while not a convert, seemed to understand and to be open to what Thomas preached.

As they approached the Temple of the Sun, the apostle could see all manner of activities occurring inside dimly lit doorways lining the road leading to the temple. Bells were being rung, incense was burning, and he could see people bowed in prayer before various shrines inside some of the rooms. Off to one side of the temple, he observed several young women dancing and nearly naked, gaudily dressed and waving at them. Thomas stopped for a moment to stare back.

"Temple girls," chimed Adika, nodding his head towards the girls, amused at Thomas' widening eyes. "They will bless you in very special ways for the right price."

Thomas turned his head. The men continued to walk on up the steps of the great structure. The two travelers were wearing leather sandals and removed them as they entered the temple. A young boy sat on the steps to "guard the sandals" for all wealthy visitors. Many did not wear sandals to the temple and often left them at home rather than risk theft, choosing instead to walk barefoot, even in the cold.

The entrance of the structure housed many carved stone deities, including representations of the god Shiva as well as others of the Hindu pantheon. Precious and semi-precious stones lined some of the carvings. To Thomas, the deities looked like visions of Satan. Walking further into the dimly lit interior, Thomas could hear unintelligible chanting. Incense filled the room with a sweet pungent smoke.

All around the top of the room, there were narrow windows that allowed in light and let out smoke. One such opening lit up a dais at the top of the room. Underneath the dais were seven seated priests, each chanting and praying but close enough to tend the eternal burning fire. The two priests closest to the fire kept a cloth over their mouths and noses so that their very breath would not pollute the purity of the fire. Devotees of the Temple of the Sun represented one version of Hinduism but kept many of the tenets of Mithra too.

Upon the dais, the incoming light illuminated the Sun God Surya. Surya was a wondrous sight for all to behold. A human figurine at least one meter in height and struck in solid gold. Red ruby eyes sparkled in the sunlight and cast a powerful image to the worshipers.

Adika nudged Thomas. "Catch the eye of the idol," he told him excitedly. "He sees you. We go forward respectfully to the priests for a blessing," motioning forward with his arm.

Adika displayed a tiny unmarked and broken coin in his hand. Bowing respectfully, Adika entered a line off to the side of the dais, moving forward as devotees slowly stepped forward, their hands in prayer pose. He placed his tiny offering in front of a carved phallic stone on a plate with other coins and bits of coins, where it joined the offerings of hundreds of other devotees. Most of the offerings consisted of fruits, grains, flowers, and even vegetables, all scattered about the plate and around the stone. Only a few were able to offer an actual coin, a prized donation.

Once directly in front of the dais and the Sun God Surya, priests acknowledged Adika's presence and said a blessing upon him. They had carefully noted the coin offering, clearly something special and worthy of an extra blessing for this devotee.

Unbeknown to Thomas, Adika was seeking healing for his young family in the village near Andrapolis. The healing powers of the Sun God were well known and famous. Adika had been planning this auspicious moment for some time.

The Temple of the Sun and the idolatry were too much for the Hebrew. Sacrilege! Idolatry! Indignation raced through his mind. He was reminded of the story in the Torah of Baal and how the Hebrews had once created a false god, a golden calf to worship.

This must have been what it was like, he thought. *Had not Isa even gone into the temple in Jerusalem and chased out the money changers and heathen?*

Thomas turned his back on the priests and ran out of the temple. He briefly considered attempting to chase everyone out of the Temple, as Isa had once done in the Temple in Jerusalem, but soon thought better of it. For the Hebrew, this was no place of worship for the one true God, the God so holy one could not even speak his name. A visit to one temple was enough for him. He had seen all he needed to see. He walked back directly to the encampment.

Late that night, Thomas recounted his temple experience to Abbanes. Abbanes listened gravely and again explained to Thomas the reality of the world they were entering.

"This is a land of strange and broken gods, Thomas," he said, speaking in Gandhari and forcing Thomas to gain fluency in the language. He inserted Aramaic words only when he realized that his friend would not understand the point in his elementary Gandhari language skills. "We must tolerate some of what we see here, even though it is not the right path," he emphasized."

Abbanes realized he needed to help Thomas connect to these people on terms that he might understand and relate to. The elder

Hebrew proceeded to explain how the grandson of Noah had founded the town of Multan and that there was a time when the people of Multan were indeed followers of the one true God. He hoped that the story of Noah might reassure the Nazarene, now traveled so far from home and in a distant land.

"Now most of the people here are lost. They have forgotten our great story of Noah," he lamented wistfully. As the two men spoke, a young Hindu boy tending the fire nearby listened to the two foreigners. He shook his head but said nothing at the mention of Noah, a story beyond belief. Everyone knew the great Hindu sage Kashyapa had founded Multan.

⊷⊷⊷◉ ◉⊶⊶⊶

Three days passed quickly, and soon the caravan was back on the road to Taxila. The caravan passed through more and more villages as it approached the capital. In some towns, great structures dominated, carved from stone, or built from substantial materials like brick and mortar. Finally, a few great white stupas could be seen from the road, some said to be holding the funerary objects of the Buddha himself. The point was lost on the apostle as he listened to the herdsmen and looked with wonder on the buildings. *Funerary objects of the Buddha*, he pondered. *Frail physical evidence of the Lord of Hosts? My God is greater!* he thought fiercely.

The herdsmen had all seen these structures before, but they could not cease to be amazed by them each time they passed. It gave them a sense of pride and even a sense of reassurance that the world could be controlled like that, that great buildings could be built. It was absolute proof of the divine.

In addition to the stupas, Thomas regularly observed great brick kilns with tall chimneys breaking the profile of the land. Formations of soldiers crossed paths with the caravan twice. Each time, the officer in charge greeted Abbanes as a friend and brother, warmly embracing the trader. Thomas watched the exchanges, recognizing that Abbanes was increasingly relaxed and sure of himself as they approached the capital.

And finally, the gates of Taxila appeared. Soldiers, customs officials, and palace guards soon greeted the massive caravan with great fanfare and joy. It was almost like a holiday for the townspeople, who came out of their doors to greet the caravan as it passed by, cheering the arrival of potentially new commerce. King Gondophores was a popular and benevolent ruler. What great and wonderful things had he now brought to Gandhara?

It was suddenly obvious to Thomas that Abbanes, the man and leader whom he had come to rely on for so long, was no longer in charge of the caravan. Several other men, finely dressed and somewhat haughty in demeanor, took control of the entire party and its goods. Abbanes, with two of his senior clerks in tow, disappeared into the doorway of one building with several of these men and was gone for a few hours. There was nothing to do but wait. By early afternoon Abbanes returned, beaming, and embraced Thomas.

"Come," he said. "Your time is finally approaching. It is time to meet King Gondophores and start your work and mission."

While Abbanes' mood was still jubilant from his safe return to Taxila after the massive journey, he spoke these last few words hesitatingly. He had gone to Jerusalem and other cities to the west to hire builders and purchase supplies. Abbanes had purchased the services of Thomas for that very purpose. However, as he observed Thomas on the journey and especially on the overland route to Taxila, he was increasingly unsure if the apostle was really committed to building a palace for King Gondophores. He seemed much more interested in preaching.

"Should we not dress properly for the king?" asked Thomas. He also was suddenly not sure of his commitment and was feeling a small amount of tension at the thought that he would now have to account for his own work and no longer be merely baggage on a voyage. Thomas had become a messenger of the one God and was no longer a builder in his heart.

"No," replied Abbanes firmly. "The king will not wait. He is anxious to see what his three pieces of unstamped silver has purchased!" Abbanes said these last words with a smile, despite the slight disquieting sense he felt in his heart.

Before Thomas could say more, horses and a large, covered chariot were brought before the men. Thomas was motioned into the chariot with Abbanes. There was no seating. The Hebrews were instructed to hold on to the side rests within the chariot itself. Six other mounted royal guardsmen escorted the chariot as they trotted off to the palace. Thomas saw that everything was being scripted. The Royal Chariot ride to the palace told the townspeople that the two men were being sent to the palace for an audience with the king.

After a short ride, the chariot stopped inside the palace. The travelers were instructed to wait, the guardsmen motioning them to stay standing on the chariot. After fifteen minutes, the men were assisted off the chariot and met by a well-dressed, balding courtier, who politely but soberly informed them to follow him. As Thomas stepped out of the chariot, he finally witnessed the full glory and grandeur of Taxila. In the chariot ride, he had been concentrating on holding on and thus only caught glimpses of the city itself. He now looked up and all about. He found himself in a massive walled compound where statues of the Buddha in various meditative states lined one side. Some of the images of the Buddha were in teaching poses, and still others illustrated the Buddha sleeping, meditating, and even in death. Great stone doors dominated the other side of the compound.

The two Hebrews entered one of the doors and were led down a hallway, light filtering in through windows. They were ushered into a small holding room where they were instructed to remain. The room had several cushions on the floor, but the visitors elected to remain standing. After a few moments, the courtier returned and asked the two men to come forward again. The two Hebrews finally entered the chamber of King Gondophores, supreme ruler of Gandhara.

Chapter 10

And he sent for the merchant who brought him, and for the apostle and said to him, "Have you built the palace?" And he said, "Yes, I have built it." The king said, "When shall we go to inspect it?" And he answered and said, "Now you cannot see it, but you shall see it when you depart this life."

—*The Acts of Thomas, Chapter 21*

KING GONDOPHORES, DRESSED in flowing robes of black and red, was a magnificent sight. On his head was a tall headpiece covered with precious stones. A large and regal-looking man, he sat on a finely carved and jeweled throne surrounded by his court. His queen and consorts sat together on a lower platform. The king's younger brother, Prince Gad, and the other princes sat closest to the king but still at a respectful distance. A fire burned on two sides of the great hall, this time to create heat. The fire did not seem to have a ceremonial purpose. Unlike the temple, the smoke from the fires was vented to the outside. Windows allowed light in from all four sides of the building.

There was no formal announcement of Abbanes. While Abbanes was highly respected and admired, he was only a merchant and once had been an indentured servant of the king himself. Still, the king put great trust in Abbanes and did not hesitate to send him on important missions such as to purchase furnishings for his palace from distant lands.

The Hebrew took two short steps forward and then dropped to his knees. He bowed low before the great king, his forehead touching the fine carpet on the floor of the chamber. As he did so, he reached his hand back towards Thomas, motioning him to do the same, realizing that Thomas did not know or understand the protocol and might not respect it. The two Hebrews remained bowed for several moments until the king finally bid them rise. Abbanes sat up but remained on his knees, sitting back on his haunches. Thomas, observing Abbanes, did likewise.

Gondophores greeted his servant Abbanes with obvious pleasure. "My friend Abbanes. How are you? Has the journey been hard?" The king's tone was earnest and warm.

"I am well, my king," Abbanes responded. His tone was happy, but all could hear fatigue in his voice too. "I have indeed had a long and hard journey, but I bring you many great things for the palace that will bring you joy—and for the queen too," he added quickly, turning to her. The queen smiled back and nodded her head.

"Your pleasure is my compensation," Abbanes continued. "The stores will give you the inventory and details of the many great treasures I have purchased this time: rare hardwoods, carvings, amazing pottery, carpets, and other furnishings. But the greatest treasure I have brought you is here by my side. Allow me to introduce Thomas, a builder from Judea, still ruled by the Romans." Abbanes could not resist frowning slightly when he said Romans. "Thomas will build your palace in the style of my mighty city, of mighty Jerusalem. You will have the palace of your dreams, my king. No one will have the equal in our world." The king nodded his approval and briefly turned his eyes upon Thomas.

"The king is pleased, Abbanes, and not the least because you are safe and strong. I am sure that the stores will give me a long and boring list, but please let me know more about what you bring. Tell me of the best treasures that you carry."

In response, Abbanes laid out in greater detail many of the materials that he brought with him, including fine cedar planks and wood carvings that he knew the king would take special interest in. Gondophores loved the smell and feel of hard-grained woods, carefully prepared by master carpenters. Although the new palace would be primarily constructed of stone, fine woods would be an important highlight.

The king was pleased, and his face beamed. At last, he turned his full attention to Thomas. "Abbanes tells me you can build from wood and from stone. Can you do that for me? The Kingdom of Gandhara is growing. I need a great hall and buildings to show the world."

Thomas, uncertainty creeping into his being, responded positively, always mindful that Isa had sold his services for this very purpose.

"In wood, I can build plows, yokes, goads, pulleys, boats, oars, and masters." He said these words timidly, almost reflexively. More confidently, he continued, "In stone, I can build pillars, temples, and yes, even court houses for kings." Thomas' confidence rose as he spoke these last words. *In Christ, I can do all things,* he suddenly thought. Isa did not send him to India to fail. Abbanes turned to look at Thomas as he spoke, astonished that his charge had suddenly found his voice.

This last answer delighted King Gondophores. "Can you build me a palace?" he asked excitedly.

"Yes, I can build and furnish you a palace, great king, for I as a carpenter have come to do this very work," responded Thomas with more confidence.

The king was pleased with the answer and was unable to contain his enthusiasm, ignoring Thomas' apparent exclusive carpentry credentials for the promises and potential of a new and interesting builder. This Hebrew builder could build him a palace like no other. He had come from far away Judea and the Roman Empire. The king continued to describe the project and share his vision with Thomas. Thomas, fully engaged, reassured the king that he could do great works for him.

As the conversation ended, plans were made for the king and Thomas to walk the city and identify the very best location for the new palace. Word of the new initiative quickly spread all around the town and into the countryside. Merchants and other builders soon began to consider the project and the wealth and work it might bring them.

The next day, Thomas and the king, surrounded by a dozen courtiers and still more soldiers, were soon on foot walking about the palace grounds and then the city itself. Although the king was initially determined to have the palace built closer to his great hall, Thomas eventually convinced the monarch to build his palace on a small, forested hillock, further out from the city center.

Such was the king's enthusiasm that along with his brother Prince Gad, he made several trips to the hillock where Thomas began the work, discussing the exact location of the main palace building, even staking out on the earth where doors and other structures could be built as his excitement for the project led him. He also brought forth a dozen of his best builders, and along with their work crews, put them under the charge of Apostle Thomas.

Most of the finer goods that Abbanes had brought with him from Egypt and Judea were going to be used in the furnishings of the palace itself, not the actual construction of the building. The initial work was to cut down trees, to quarry rock and stone, and to dig foundations. The king gave Thomas money, gold, and other valuable goods to pay for this work, along with food of all kinds to feed the laborers and tradesmen.

Not wasting any time, Thomas got right to work. He organized the workmen and soon had them clearing the forest and preparing the land to dig the foundations and footers for the buildings to come. While he had great skill as a carpenter, he welcomed the men with expertise the king had given him, particularly the tradesman who knew best to carry out the needed earthen works. A camp sprang up to support the workmen, complete with support staff and kitchen and food preparation operations, all funded by King Gondophores.

As the work slowly progressed, Thomas discovered that the camp and laborers represented a ready audience for his mission and message. He soon established a custom of ending each day's labor by preaching to the assembly, very much just like he had done during the overland journey to Taxila. Like his former traveling companions, the workers were only too happy to sit in the shade of a tree in the cool hours of the day and be entertained. Most gladly listened, some with amusement. Thomas took full advantage of the audience, often preaching against the heathen Buddhist beliefs that so many seemed to follow.

"The Kingdom of God is at hand," he would announce to the assembly spread out upon the hill. An outcropping of granite jutted out and presented a small platform from which he could preach. Women would sit, holding restless children, while the men, most sitting on their haunches, carefully watched and listened to the apostle as he spoke.

"Every man shall find his place and his palace in heaven. Deny yourself human needs, even marriage to a woman, and instead join in union with the one God." That rather strange message often caused some men in the audience to look quizzically at each other. They said nothing in response, having no intention of stopping physical union with the women in their lives.

As Thomas preached to the laborers, his understanding of the nature of God had begun to change. The older Hebrew concept describing the Lord of Hosts as an omnipotent God who was so holy one could not say his name was not right. Thomas finally understood Isa was preaching about a personal God. Thomas had a name for this God: the Christ. He had originally struggled with this concept—*was Isa not his brother?* However he was speaking to real people with real problems. Christ was the model.

Abbanes initially stayed with Thomas, helping him set up the construction operation. As time went by, he found himself increasingly forced to return to his trader responsibilities and to abandon the building project. He did try to return to the construction site when possible, increasingly worried that Thomas was losing his way. Abbanes could see that the religious views that his friend was advocating seemed to be evolving. Thomas' tone, passion, and emotions were becoming more and more pronounced during each sermon. His advocacy of a life of asceticism and restriction seemed to be getting stronger and stronger. To many of the local population, encountering religious teachings of asceticism was not new. Many bhikkhu's had similar messages.

The workers were delighted that Thomas was a gifted storyteller, and he often held their rapt attention. Most were happy to ignore the rather impractical or complex religious implications of the teachings. The stories were exotic and interesting. The speaker was magnetic and entertaining. As a consequence, the size of Thomas' audience on the hilltop slowly continued to grow. Soon, the crowd was more than just builders, workers, slaves, and their families. Others from the community were coming to hear this man of God too. It was known that the apostle was able to perform miracles and even to heal the sick.

Thomas, looking out upon his flock each evening, saw great pain and suffering. He saw widows with no income, orphans, and the diseased. Remembering the great compassion of his brother Isa, he offered food and other necessities to the people, all from the stores that the king provided to build the palace. Using all the powers he had, he would lay hands on the sick and call upon Christ and God for healing. As the workers continued to carry out the foundation work of the palace, digging deep trenches, Thomas spent less and less time at the work site and more and more time traveling among the people preaching. Some days, he would leave the area completely and travel around to neighboring villages with his message that the Kingdom of God was at hand.

Thomas' fame and the word of his generosity spread among the people. In addition to giving away the king's money and food, his skill as a miraculous healer became known far and wide. The afflicted would come from the town and from the surrounding region to hear the apostle. Lines of beggars and the diseased would make their way to him, seeking his blessing and miraculous powers. Thomas would lay his hands on the afflicted and the downcast. In some cases, he would even cast demons from the body of the possessed, often to the great alarm of those present.

As the needs of the people grew, Thomas' need for more money and food grew too. And as he used up resources on his mission for God, the work at the palace site slowed. Soon, the work stopped. His religious activities did not go unnoticed by the palace. Initially, the king was preoccupied with matters of state, particularly paying attention to the increasing Persian threat to the west. He failed to notice how little real progress was happening at his palace construction site. Eventually, King Gondophores noted and even became exasperated by his courtiers who constantly reported on the lack of progress. *How was it that they could not seem to manage this Hebrew,* he wondered, frustration marking his face? *Such a small thing.* Out loud, his tone was more direct.

"Can't you see that I am tied up with matters of state?" he would angrily explain to his senior courtier. "Kadphises is a plague coming our way. Build my palace!" he would almost shout.

Thomas' audience also drew a number of bhikkhus—Buddhist priests—who listened attentively to every word that Thomas preached. Each day, they would dutifully report back to the senior bhikkhus on all that they had heard and observed. Initially, the sangha were amused by the teachings. Yet, as the crowds grew, the question of what to do with Apostle Thomas began to slowly grow among the Buddhist community. Thomas' anti-Buddhist teachings began to alarm many. They were tolerant but could only be pushed so far. Eventually, a senior group of bhikkhus approached and raised their concerns with Master Rinpoche directly.

And so it was that Master Rinpoche, the most senior bhikkhu, at the urgings of the royal courtiers as well, finally sought an audience with the king and explained to him fully what Thomas was doing. King Gondophores, now hearing the stories of Thomas' activities from a reliable second source, and from someone more important and influential than his own courtiers, initially still did not want to believe. *There must be some mistake,* he kept thinking. *Was not Abbanes his trusted servant?* Angry and frustrated that he had to interrupt affairs of state for this petty matter, he realized he had to stop what he was doing and go see the situation for himself on the ground.

Clenching his fist reflexively, a longtime bad habit he had developed whenever he felt stressed, he resignedly but tersely called for the royal chariot. Along with several of his close guards, he mounted his vehicle and immediately rode directly to the palace site on the hilltop. The king himself took the reins of his chariot, not content to be driven anywhere by anyone, whipping the horses harder than he intended. It had rained the night before, making the ground wet and muddy, with the chariot sliding in some places along the road. Finally arriving at the hilltop, he fully expected to see some walls raised and perhaps other works. Instead, the monarch found a large muddy hole in the ground.

Gondophores' anger growing, he jumped down from his chariot and paced the grounds on the hill of his future palace. Mud, trenches, gaping holes, and earth! Thomas was nowhere to be found. The workmen's camp was almost empty. A few stray dogs watched wearily from the edge of the camp. Not even the cooking fires for the workmen were warm. Most of the workers had returned home, waiting for when they next might be paid to return to the work site.

Furious, the king called upon his guards to arrest Thomas and Abbanes and bring them to him. Mounting his chariot, he returned to his palace, his anger such that he was of a mind to execute both Hebrews. Finding Thomas was a relatively simple matter. His fame was such that most households knew of Thomas and where he might be from day to day. The king's guards located him at Seri Bahlol, addressing a crowd in front of a great statue of the Buddha, denouncing idolatry. They waited patiently for Thomas to finish his sermon and for the crowd to disperse. As Thomas took to the road to return to Taxila, the guards arrested him. Returning to Taxila with Thomas in a chariot, they stopped at Abbanes' residence and arrested him too. The guards brought the two men before the king.

Walking into the great hall for only the second time since arriving in Taxila, Thomas experienced a much colder reception. The queen and consorts were not present. Instead, several military officers had entered the room and were standing to the side. Master

Rinpoche and two of the senior bhikkhu sat cross-legged on the floor along the opposite wall, watching the proceedings carefully.

The two Hebrews were pushed to their knees facing the king. Abbanes gave the guards a sharp look as they did so. Such behavior was unnecessary. The trader knew the protocol.

The king looked upon Abbanes and spoke. "Where is my palace? What have you done?" His voice and tone were icy and hard. He turned his gaze from Abbanes to Thomas.

Before Abbanes could respond, Thomas, religious fervor still coursing through his veins, and the confidence of Isa rising in his voice, declared, "You cannot see the palace now, O King. But I tell you that when you pass from this life, you will inherent the kingdom and palace of God, the Almighty."

Abbanes turned to look at the apostle as he spoke. Thomas' face was animated, even happy.

King Gondophores was stunned. *What nonsense is this?* he thought. He immediately regarded Thomas as a madman and was sorry that he had entrusted him with so much responsibility. It was a puzzle to him. He had also been blinded by his confidence in Abbanes. This surprised him greatly. Until this moment, Abbanes had been as reliable as the rising of the sun. *How had he not seen this coming?* the king wondered. He shook his head, angry at Abbanes, but also angry with himself for not paying closer attention to this project. *The threat of Kajula Kadphises has been on my mind too much,* he reflected.

The king looked at Abbanes and waited to see if he had anything more to say. He owed him that at least, for his loyalty and hard work in years past. Abbanes hung his head in shame, then looked up upon the king. He spoke slowly and carefully.

"My king, Gondophores," Abbanes began. "I have been exceedingly busy with other matters, and I have failed you. This is all my fault. I should have stayed with my builder to make sure that all the money you sent was spent properly. I should have stayed with him to make sure all the affairs of building a great palace were carried out as you ordered. Please forgive me, my king." Abbanes bowed low at these words, touching his forehead to the carpet and floor in front of him. He continued. "Allow me the opportunity to correct this. If you but release me and this humble servant Thomas, I give you my word that we can restore the construction project."

Thomas turned to look upon Abbanes with compassion. Still looking at his Hebrew friend, he repeated his earlier statement in a loud contrarian voice: "I say again, O King. You cannot see the palace now. But I tell you that when you pass from this life, you will inherit the Kingdom and palace of God, the Almighty."

Abbanes started to speak in response to the apostle's declaration but then stopped, realizing that he lacked the words that would change the situation. It was all in the hands of the king. There was no point in refuting the apostle. Who would believe him?

Gondophores sat there watching these two Hebrews for a moment, shaking his head, incredulous at Thomas' response. He finally laughed quietly to himself, like Abbanes, realizing the futility of further talk. *How on earth had I imagined that this man could build me a great palace?* he thought. The king concluded that no more words were necessary. Not taking his eyes off the two prisoners, he turned to his guards and commanded them in terse words.

"Place these two in prison." He said so with a heavy heart. He still greatly respected the past loyalty of his older servant Abbanes and even felt some love for the man. He knew he could not put Abbanes to death. He would send them both to prison.

Master Rinpoche, in the room and listening to the exchange, found Thomas' reply interesting. He realized that he would like the opportunity to speak to him and learn more about his strange religious beliefs and teachings. Surprisingly, some of what he was saying made sense to him. But, he thought, it also appeared that Thomas misunderstood key tenets of the path that the Buddha himself knew about and corrected. He knew that now was not the moment for that. There would be other opportunities to talk to the apostle about the Middle Path.

Chapter II

But your dead will live, Lord; their bodies will rise.
Let those who dwell in the dust wake up and shout for joy!
Your dew is like the dew of the morning; the earth will give
birth to her dead.

—*Isaiah 26:19*

THAT NIGHT, PRINCE Gad retired to his chambers with his princess, younger sister to the queen herself. Fear and concern were written all over his face. Kujula Kadphises, the rising Kushan prince, was increasingly being talked about at court. Now, this strange Hebrew builder and apostle had appeared in the city and was talking about the Kingdom of God.

What is the meaning of these two omens? He thought worriedly. Surely, there were more challenges that the Kingdom would face now. Problems had a way of constantly cropping up, causing the prince to fret and worry about the future. Gad was superstitious in the extreme. His very weight and size—rolls of fat stuffed into his royal tunic—were markers of his bearing and status for the people. Not pretending to compete with his athletic and stronger older brother for the throne, he made it his duty to offer sage, loyal advice to the crown instead. It was his best strategy for survival. His biggest pleasure was eating and drinking and pursuing the exotic delights his concubines had to offer. He cared little for the active passions of his elder brother the king, such as hunting sher and boar.

As he moved towards the balcony, it happened. He suddenly could not walk, could not speak, and could not move. The prince fell heavily to the ground, the princess crying out as she watched her husband collapse. He hit his head on the tile floor, falling hard, making an audible thump. The princess screamed. Guards at the door shouted and burst into the room, immediately followed by frightened servants who flooded the room with torches and candles. Doctors, healers, and even shamans were called.

Pain. Pain in his chest. Pain in his head. He remembered he had hit his head hard. He had passed out. It was as though he were dead. His eyes were closed, but he could hear and understand what was happening around him. It was as though a supernatural force was preventing him from working his mouth and operating his legs. His vision became black and narrow like he was looking down a tunnel. There was no light, only blackness. He knew he had fainted. There was a small burning sensation in his chest and arms now. His head still hurt though. The pain was intense. God was calling him.

He felt his spirit separate from his body. It was an eerie sensation, like a dream. He suddenly realized he was looking down upon himself. He was at the top of the room looking down. Everything was happening very slowly. He could see his beloved young wife on her knees and weeping hysterically by his side along with his two older children, both crying. At that moment, he knew how much his wife and family loved him. That sense of love gave his spirit courage.

He could see his still body lying on the bed motionless. Somebody needed to do something to save him, he thought. Do something! The sensation was intense. The doctors and healers had come, but they seemed to be unable to do anything. One of the shamans was bent over him, chanting something and sprinkling a colorful fluid on him. How ridiculous, he observed.

King Gondophores arrived. As the king entered the room, everyone cleared from the room, even his wife and children. The king's own physician examined him now. He could see the elderly healer bent over him, shaking his head. Prince Gad's body, his own body, remained almost lifeless on the bed. The prince could still see all of this. Finally, he saw the king, his brother, earnestly take to his knees and pray by his side. Gad saw it all. Yet, the king could see that his younger brother was indeed dead. He hung his head in sorrow and wept. Somehow, the vision of his brother truly sorry at his passing made the prince feel joy. The emotion surprised him.

As Prince Gad, in spirit, watched all this, he could see far and wide, almost like the Third Eye that the Buddha talked about. He heard voices talking to him. And suddenly, he understood the words of Thomas in the court with the king. Our palace is not on this earth, but it will be in heaven. We must repent and join the Kingdom of God. The pathway was through Christ and this new Apostle Thomas, the twin. And then, Gad lost consciousness. He was no longer in the room. He could no longer see himself on the bed. His spirit had reentered his body. He slept as in death.

After a time, the king, sorely aggrieved, left his side, along with the royal physician. The healers and shamans returned to the room and stayed for a while, examining, praying, chanting. After an hour, even these healers left his side, leaving only the servants, a few Buddhist priests, and the princess in the room, grieving for the soul of the Prince of Gandhara. Gad, the Prince of Gandhara, had died.

Finally, the princess and her two sons said goodbye to their husband and father and left the room. The servants whispered that the embalmers had come and were waiting outside the palace doors, ready to come in and prepare for the great state funeral that must be coming. All knew the king was sorely anguished by this terrible loss. While the king expected little of his brother, he nonetheless loved him, realizing that Gad had been one voice that would always seek to defend him. Gad had been loyal.

Several of the servants to the prince had heard Thomas speak. One of them even claimed to have seen Thomas heal and perform miracles. Watching all the healers, physicians, and shamans come and go, several questioned why this strange Hebrew man of God had not been consulted. The princess, who might otherwise be expected to go to death with her young husband, immediately became attentive when the story of Thomas' actions were relayed to her. If her husband were really dead, there was a good chance she would follow him. Despite the love she felt for her husband, she had a strong desire to keep on living. The princess called for her guard to go to the prison that very night and to bring the apostle immediately.

"Bring the foreign shaman, the Hebrew!" Her command was clear and strong. She did not understand what exactly this Hebrew shaman did, but she wanted to find out. He might save her life too. She had nothing to lose and everything to gain.

The princess kept the embalmers out of the room, clinging to this last hope for her husband and for her life. The embalmers were patient men. They knew, that sooner or later, they would be called. No need to rush the princess. Death would take us all.

At the insistence and then order of the princess, two of the prince's guards immediately ran over to the nearby king's palace and then went down into the prison, looking for this strange Hebrew man of God. They soon found Thomas, strangely awake, even cheerful, as though he knew what was transpiring. He greeted the guards warmly and gladly did their bidding.

The officer in charge was initially reluctant to allow the release of Thomas but soon backed down when the guards made it clear that they had been ordered by the princess and were prepared to draw weapons to effect the release. The officer reluctantly relented, worried that later, he would somehow be held accountable for this unusual action. Thomas was escorted back to Prince Gad's room in the palace.

The princess met the apostle at the door of the bedchamber. The young woman explained to Thomas what had happened: how the prince had suddenly fallen and hit his head.

"He stopped breathing," she told Thomas. Sobbing slightly, she finished. "He is dead." She trembled just saying those words as if she were trying them out, as though she needed to convince herself this had really happened.

Regaining her composure, she continued, determination and even courage in her voice. "My servant tells me you have healed the sick. They tell me you have even raised someone from the dead. Is this true, prophet?"

The princess did not fully understand Thomas' teachings and mistakenly thought he was a prophet or perhaps some kind of mystic healer. She was used to seeing shamans and healers of all kinds on the streets of Taxila. *Is this man really any different?* she wondered. She tried her best to look cool and composed. She noted that the man did look surprisingly rested and positive for someone who had just come from the dreadful prison at the palace of the king.

Thomas looked at the young woman with compassion and did his best to reassure her. He smiled upon her and then took her hands in his own for a moment, squeezing them, and then released them. The servants and priests in the room watched the apostle touch the hands of the princess with alarm. Several servants were about to voice their protest at his actions when he released her hands. The princess did not seem to object to Thomas' behavior.

Thomas then stepped away from the princess and towards the still body of the prince. He conveyed a sense of confidence and serenity.

"What is the will of God, the most high, will be," he intoned repeatedly, as he looked upon the motionless body of Gad. At first, he asked the princess to stand back, away from the bed of her husband. Still studying the prince, he changed his mind and asked her to leave the room. He also asked the entire retinue of servants, priests, and bhikkhus to leave the bedchamber. As the assembled men got up to leave, some of the servants and bhikkhus began to voice objections, reluctant to leave a prince of Gandhara with this strange man. They immediately elected to drop the matter when the princess looked at them sternly. She waited in the room until all had left and then, with a nod to the apostle, finally walked out of the room herself.

What do I have to lose? she kept repeating to herself. *What could he possibly do that would make the situation any worse?* She knew that the healing of her husband by this man was improbable, but she just had to try. She was privately grateful that the prince's brother the king was not present. He likely would not have allowed this foreign shaman to touch his younger brother.

With everyone finally out of the room, the apostle looked down upon the young prince lying still. He did not see the chest of the man rising and falling as he would have expected, but his body was not yet cold either. He laid his hands on the temple and silently prayed to the God of Abraham. He took oil from his pouch and anointed the man's brow. Raising his head and looking to the heavens he prayed in a great voice, speaking in Aramaic. He intended to pray, but his words were like a command: "The Kingdom of God has come upon you."

The commanding voice of Thomas the preacher, with his accent spoken in an unintelligible foreign language, could be heard clearly in the hall outside the room and cast a spell over the waiting assembly. The door to the room was not closed and instead, a heavy curtain covered the entrance. The princess stood at the doorway and peered through a slit, able to make out the apostle in the flickering torch light.

Thomas chanted and continued to pray for several minutes, repeating the prayers that he had seen Isa utter in Judea. He placed his hands on the prince and continued to pray silently for the soul of this man. At the end of his prayer, he took a small candle from his pouch and placed it in front of him, on a table just to the side of the prince. He again called upon the God of Abraham for a miracle. He lit the candle.

At the very moment that Thomas lit the candle, the prince stirred and let out a big sigh. He rolled over as one who had been in a deep sleep. Thomas continued to pray over the young prince for several minutes, thanking God for delivering him. The princess continued to watch the apostle from behind the curtain in the doorway. She could only see the apostle clearly but could not clearly see the form of her husband, who lay in an inert mass. Suddenly, to her great astonishment, she made out movement on the bed of her husband!

She thrust aside the curtain just as Thomas was turning to call her into the room. The young woman looked past Thomas and at her husband on the bed. She rushed to his side and touched him. She found her prince looking as though he were asleep. He was breathing! He was even quietly snoring!

Soon, the entire party in the hallway rushed back into the room at the news. A joyous word went out to all. The prince was not dead! Servants roughly told the embalmers to be gone and then literally chased them off the palace grounds. Guards raced to tell the king, only to be told to wait. The exhausted king had gone to bed with strict orders not to be disturbed. The princess considered forcing her way in but decided to wait to tell the king in the morning. Perhaps Gad himself could be the one to share the good news with the king. That would be a wonderful surprise.

To the complete astonishment of the entire Royal Court, Prince Gad slept through the night and was able to slowly regain his feet after he awoke.

Still early morning, clearly on the mend, with the princess by his side for support, he slowly walked the short distance to the palace of his brother the king. Guards and servants at every corner stopped and stared. *Was this not the prince who had perished? What miracle was this?*

Gad continued to walk, a smile on his face, still weakened but determined to show that he had recovered. Being the only man authorized in the entire kingdom, other than a few trusted servants, concubines, and the queen, he walked right into the bedchamber of his brother the king. In a great and joyous voice, Gad announced his return and his good health.

King Gondophores was just waking after a rough late sleep, thinking that his younger brother had perished during the night. He had seen his dead body. To his enormous astonishment, in walked Gad—into his very bedchamber! Still in his bed clothes, the king leaped to his feet.

"Brother," said Gad, momentarily forgetting to address his elder brother as the king. There was a great smile of amusement and joy on his face, as he savored the surprise of his unexpected visit. "I am come to buy the carpenter you call Thomas and indeed will purchase all his debts, including that of the unbuilt palace on the hillock. For I have discovered the real palace. Our kingdom is in heaven and not of this earth."

Gondophores looked at his brother in complete bewilderment. He had seen his own brother dead in his own bed. How could this be anything other than a miracle?

"Brother!" finally exclaimed the king at a loss for words, an expression of joy and great surprise on his face. Breaking protocol, he ran to his younger brother and touched him and embraced him warmly, as though he needed to confirm that he was real, that this was not all some kind of strange dream.

"You can't buy the palace on the hillock, but I freely give it to you," said the king in response, reassuring his younger brother as he embraced him. "I give you that land, and I also give you my indentured servant Thomas, for surely this is some kind of miracle."

Suddenly remembering the terrible mistake he had made in putting both Abbanes and Apostle Thomas in jail, he called for his guard to find them and release them immediately.

In short order, Thomas and Abbanes were both brought before the king and escorted directly to his private chamber. There was no kneeling this time, only a union of great friends. In front of his royal couriers, King Gondophores spoke in a loud and clear voice. "Restore all that is theirs to them," he commanded, gesturing towards the two Hebrew men who had just entered the room. Abbanes turned to Thomas and gazed upon him in wonder. He was only just beginning to understand what had happened, not having been present in the chamber of Prince Gad. He had not seen what had happened there.

Abbanes turned to the king and bowed low, acknowledging the king's generous action. The king's command was particularly important to him. He had stood to lose his house, his wife, and all his holdings in prison. Thomas, in his self-imposed poverty, owned nothing more than the clothes on his back. Now, it was all being restored and more.

He had been worrying that his friend Thomas had been going too far with his preaching and sermons of self-denial. Yet, it was clear that he held some kind of special powers. He had returned Prince Gad to the living!

Chapter 12

Being wholly set upon by the apostle, both King Gondo-
phores and Gad his brother followed him and departed not
from him at all.

—*The Acts of Thomas Chapter 26*

WORD OF THOMAS' miraculous healing of Prince Gad rapidly spread throughout the city. The sangha learned of these strange events and became even more distressed. Some felt that by so openly supporting this imposter, the royal court was questioning the enlightened path of the Buddha and the Noble Eightfold Path.

Thomas and Abbanes found themselves embraced by the royal family and particularly the prince and his immediate family. Thomas was now regularly invited to the prince's palace to share meals with the royals and to preach the word of God. The entire royal household became regular listeners, if not outright followers of the apostle.

"I have healed you in the name of the one true God and through him his son Isa," he told the young, corpulent prince. He took pains to make it clear that it was the Christ and the God of Abraham that had healed the prince. He often had to remind them that he had no special powers except through God.

Thomas, the man of God and no longer just a carpenter and builder, was free to preach. The fact that he did not need to build things anymore delighted him. It was as if a great burden had been removed from him. The apostle now understood the great wisdom of Isa. He had sent him to India to build a palace. But it was not a physical palace. It was to contribute to the building of the Kingdom of God. Thomas could now focus on the divine mission before him and carry out his part of the Great Commission that Isa had laid out for all the apostles.

While preaching to the household and the community, Thomas explained how the path to the one God was really a spiritual and even a physical union with God. "We are his sheep, and he is our shepherd," he would say.

As Thomas continued to preach, his wisdom and understanding of the nature of God and his mission changed too. There was no middle ground when committing to the one God. One had to leave the old life and commit to a new life in union with the one God. There was no other path to follow. The aspect of commitment, of leaving behind possessions and old relationships, took on a new importance.

This new and strengthened understanding of the nature of one's relationship with God convinced him more than ever that all physical unions outside of union with the divine needed to be discouraged. His experience in Andrapolis with Sarida and the cupbearer Natan was always in the back of his mind, a story that he would not tell his audiences but would influence many of his sermons.

He preached that "fornication darkens the eyes of the soul." Thomas' understanding of this deadly sin covered all aspects of human behavior, even the very union between a husband and wife.

The union with God would make the acts of union between husband and wife a sin. This rather extreme theology was tolerated by the king and the royal court, in favor of this man of God who could miraculously raise people from the dead. Still, the extreme view did continue to catch the attention of the Buddhist priests, and even Master Rinpoche himself, the greatest advocate of the Middle Path and the Noble Eightfold Path.

Prince Gad, still taken with his miraculous healing, chose to ignore the details of what Thomas was saying exactly and agreed to conversion and the path of Thomas and Isa. Thomas explained that the way one publicly announced the commitment to the Kingdom of God was to be baptized by full immersion in water. The prince, accustomed to symbolism, gladly acquiesced to this simple matter. He the prince would be baptized. In fact, he asked that Thomas baptize his entire family.

The prince's enthusiasm did not stop there. Wanting to show how much he appreciated the intervention of Apostle Thomas, the prince even asked his brother the king to join him in this foreign baptism ritual. King Gondophores, after thinking over the idea of carrying out a foreign religious ritual, and still amazed at the works and stories of the acts of Apostle Thomas, agreed to do the same. In his mind, religious dualism was possible and even necessary.

I will remain the supreme Buddhist leader of the people and also accept some nominal ownership of this strange religion, he decided. *Am I not the king appointed by all the gods?* He made a mental note to ask Master

Rinpoche to look into this matter and to discuss this with the apostle. *After all*, he mused, *the Lord Buddha did not even claim to be a deity. My actions will not be disloyal to the Buddha.*

Rather than have the entire royal party baptized in the nearby river in public view for all to witness, the king ordered that the public baths be closed for seven days and that no one be allowed to bathe in them. On the eighth day, the baptism of the royal household could occur at the public baths. That way, he could be baptized and yet retain the dignity and distance that his court and position in the world demanded.

And it was done. The public baths were closed. It was announced that no one could enter. On the night before the rite of baptism, unknown to Thomas and even the king, several Buddhist priests quietly slipped into the baths and carried out ablutions to protect the king and his family, if divine protection or even intervention was needed against this foreign influence.

And finally, on the eighth day, at night, to the light of many oil lamps, King Gondophores and his younger brother Prince Gad, and their immediate households, were baptized by Apostle Thomas.

Thomas baptized the king first and then his brother second, before calling in the balance of the household. When Gondophores entered the public baths, he demanded that all leave the bath house except for two close attendants and Apostle Thomas and Prince Gad. He then disrobed and stepped into the pool of water. Thomas, taking his hand, waded into the pool, the light casting an otherworldly glow about the chamber. The two stood in waist-deep water. The apostle anointed the king with oil on his brow and then began to sing and chant in Aramaic, his voice melodious and smooth.

"Come power of the most high," he chanted.

"Come gift of the most high,"

"Come, compassionate mother,"

"Come, communion of the male,"

"Come, she that reveals the hidden mysteries,"

"Come, mother of the seven houses, that thy rest may be in the eighth house."

"Come, elder of the five members, mind, thought, reflection, consideration, reason: communicate with these young men."

"Come, holy spirit, and cleanse their veins and their heart, and give them the added seal, in the name of the Father and Son and Holy Spirit."

Supporting the king's back, Thomas gently immersed the monarch in the water. Raising him up, he continued chanting in Aramaic for a few moments. His melodious voice was soothing. The alien sound of the foreign chanting, along with the flickering lamps, created a mesmerizing, relaxing atmosphere. The king stood up, surprised to feel somehow refreshed and reassured. *This foreign rite was not too bad,* he thought privately. *It was easy.* He stepped out of the pool and put on his robe.

Thomas then motioned for the prince to step into the pool where he repeated the ceremony. The prince afterward felt much the same, refreshed and even relaxed. Like the king, he found the rite simple and straightforward and was slightly relieved that there was no more to it than that.

Both men dressed and left as was their station. Prince Gad, walking out, displayed exuberance, still marveling at what had happened to him. Outside of the baths, several members of the sangha were assembled to greet the monarchs as they passed by, relieved that nothing significant appeared to have happened to them.

Both royal families, the household of Prince Gad and a few members of the king's household, remained in the baths, while Thomas conducted baptisms for each member willing to subject themselves to this new rite. As was his developing practice, the apostle required each member to fully undress while he led them into the water. Concluding the ceremonies, palace youths arrived with torches to guide the royal household back to their chambers.

The next morning, Thomas returned to the palace of Prince Gad and conducted the ceremony of the Eucharist. This rite caused more consternation than the baptism among the bhikkhu. Thomas explained that he would serve them the body and blood of Christ by offering each member a small portion of bread and wine. He explained that the ritual of the taking of the bread and the wine was only symbolic of their faith and that they were entering the Kingdom of God with this act. The bhikkhu advised the king to not participate in such ritual cannibalism. King Gondophores, believing he had done what was needed to acknowledge this healer of his brother, politely declined.

"Thank you, but I decline," he said firmly to the apostle, raising his hands to emphasize that his decision was final on this. *Ritual cannibalism,* he thought. *A ghastly practice.*

Prince Gad, still feeling a sense of obligation to Apostle Thomas, consented to the odd ritual, although he appeared uncomfortable. He asked the apostle to excuse his household from this rite, choosing to not fully explain his decision. He alone would participate in this additional ritual.

After the baptism and the Eucharist rite, Thomas fell into a routine at the palace of the prince. He was given a room for his personal use and where he could come and go. He continued to regularly minister to the royal household as best he could, but as time went by, Thomas began to realize that his palace audience was too small. He had exhausted his sermons on all the staff. Most had converted or at least had publicly accepted Christ in some fashion. Yet, it was increasingly clear to him that he needed to expand his mission beyond the boundaries of the two palaces.

As soon as he felt he could, he took his leave of Prince Gad and expressed thanks for all that he had done for him. "Yet my calling is greater still. I need to return to my mission of evangelization," he explained.

Prince Gad, having heard the message repeatedly, was delighted with Thomas' proposal to expand his mission in the region. The prince even put resources at his disposal. Thomas embraced the opportunity. He continued preaching the word of God in Taxila but also began traveling around the region. He was now preaching in India, just as Isa had envisioned. The Kingdom of God was at hand. He was accomplishing his mission.

Thomas' greatest asset for drawing a crowd was his reputation as a healer. The possibility of being healed brought many to listen to this new man of God. While most were there for healing, the larger audience gave the apostle opportunities to deliver his real message, the path to the Kingdom of God.

"Children of God," he would preach loudly near the end of his sermon. "My brothers and sisters," he would say for emphasis. "Abstain from fornication, covetousness, and the needs of the body.

The greatest sin is fornication. Instead, seek out a new marriage union with the Lord God!"

To some of the Buddhist priests and novices in his audiences, at least part of Thomas' message sounded like a teaching the Lord Buddha might have given. However, as Master Rinpoche had observed, this strange man seemed to have misunderstood some of the basic tenets from the teachings. The Hebrew apostle did not take it to the next level. He did not moderate his message and did not seem to understand the importance of the Middle Path.

All that the apostle said and did was reported regularly to Master Rinpoche, who listened to the reports of Thomas' preaching and activities with great interest. The healings in particular were a great puzzle to the sangha. The foreign preacher was a good storyteller, and his parables were understandable, wise even. But what power did this man have to heal? How did that happen? Where did that power come from?

Chapter 13

Bodhisattva of Tolerance:
In the practice of tolerance, one's enemy is the best teacher.

—Tenzin Gyatso
The 14th Dalai Lama

THOMAS' DEDICATION TO delivering the word of God to the people continued to grow. With the enthusiastic backing of the royal family, he had a ready audience wherever he spoke. He increasingly began to travel further and further in the region, often in the company of his growing number of devout followers. Many but not all of his followers elected to be baptized.

Abbanes increasingly found himself occupied with his many trading and commercial interests and was unable to travel or even stay by Thomas' side as a mentor, translator, and aide. His reduced role with Thomas was something of a relief for the older Hebrew, still not certain his own beliefs were in full alignment with the apostle's extreme teachings.

Filling in the role of chief aide, and gradually becoming Thomas' closest disciple, was a young Buddhist acolyte from the palace named

Xenophon. Youthful, earnest, and hardworking, Xenophon knew the region all around Taxila and was soon invaluable to Thomas as a source of information on where to travel and with whom to meet. Thomas' language skills were expanding, as he was forced to speak for long hours in Gandhari. His initial attempts at the language had been poor, and his strong Aramaic accent made him almost unintelligible at times. Xenophon, understanding Thomas' intent, would step in and clarify what the apostle was saying. Yet, as the months passed, Thomas' linguistic abilities expanded, and he could soon carry an entire sermon in Gandhari with ease.

The sangha, consisting of Buddhist priests from all across Gandhara, were increasingly alarmed by the news that a strange man of God was among them, preaching words that clearly contradicted the great learnings of the Buddha. This man from the west was even reputed to carry out miracles and was said to have caused the dead to rise! He had even raised Prince Gad, the brother of the king from death. Many of the sangha were doubtful about this story and suspected that some kind of fakery was involved. For one thing, had not Thomas asked that all the sangha and doctors leave the room just before Prince Gad was miraculously restored to life? Why did he need to do that? How could that have happened?

Master Rinpoche observed the visceral and angry reactions of his sangha with growing concern. The senior priest was disappointed that his sangha did not display and demonstrate confidence in the Middle Path and Right Thinking. Rather, many of his followers exhibited signs of jealousy and anger towards the Hebrew visitor.

"These behaviors are not what the Lord Buddha taught us or how he lived. This reaction mostly points to the fact that some of the sangha need more time to learn," he explained to other senior priests. Thinking to disarm his own sangha, Master Rinpoche decided to invite Thomas to the monastery adjacent to the great Dharamarajika Stupa to meet and talk with him.

Master Rinpoche reflected that perhaps in debate, the sangha would see there is nothing to fear from this man. Perhaps he could even show him the Middle Path and direct him away from this course of limited asceticism he seemed to be taking. The Hebrew should be directed to the path of Right Thinking and had instead embraced a false path that the Buddha himself once explored and rejected.

The invitation from Master Rinpoche to meet arrived in the form of a small delegation of young Buddhist novices, three young men anxious to see this man of God for themselves. For his part, Apostle Thomas was delighted to accept the invitation and seized the opportunity to proselytize those he considered to be idol worshipers. He looked forward to entering this den of vipers and to openly challenge the hegemony of the priests, as Isa had once done in the temple in Jerusalem years earlier.

Isa. As Thomas prepared for the visit with Master Rinpoche, thoughts of his brother were not far from his mind. The terrible events of his brother's death were easily forgotten. Instead, he would joyfully think of the resurrection. The miracle inspired him.

Where is Isa now? Thomas wondered. He had lost track of his brother in Andrapolis. *Where has he gone? Back to Jerusalem probably.* He never considered that he might never see his brother in person again. Isa always came through for him. Even when he was not with him, Thomas felt the presence of his brother close by.

The walk from the small room that Thomas shared with Xenophon to the monastery next to the great stupa was short. The road was clear, and the enormous stupa was an excellent landmark for the entire town, guiding the apostle to his destination.

As Thomas arrived at the monastery, he was met by the same young earnest novices who had met with him before to extend the invitation. All three novices greeted him warmly, their hands ready in prayer position, bowing to the apostle with smiles on their faces. The young men escorted the apostle to the main hall. Upon entering the great stone and masonry structure, Thomas could see the many beautifully carved stone statues of the Buddha lining the walls and all about the room, most resting on stone pedestals.

Master Rinpoche was seated on a dais at the front of the room and was waiting for him. Seven senior priests sat off to his right, with dozens of other priests and novices scattered in the room all about. A vacant cushion on the floor directly in front of Master Rinpoche indicated to Thomas where he was expected to sit. One of the novices escorted him to this place. Once seated, he nodded to Master Rinpoche, who folded his hands together and bowed his head towards the apostle as a friendly greeting.

Thomas suddenly felt inadequate in front of these learned men. There was a quiet seriousness about them, the air of men who were well read, highly educated, and thoughtful. Servants brought Thomas chai, which he declined. Master Rinpoche took nothing either and remained crossed-legged and comfortable, smiling before his guest.

The priest began the meeting by greeting Thomas warmly, calling him Thomasji. Master Rinpoche added the endearment "ji" as a sign of respect for his guest. He wished to put Thomas at ease. The two exchanged pleasantries, with Master Rinpoche politely asking how Thomas found Gandhara and if it was to his liking. While the tone was polite, there was no hiding the fact that the master was also anxious to discuss other issues with the apostle.

Thomas elected to be polite in return and answered affirmatively, still unsure if this meeting was going to be amicable or not. None of Thomas' disciples attended the meeting with him. He was alone with Master Rinpoche in his hall with his people. His feelings of righteousness, of being the mouthpiece of the one true God, were evaporating as Thomas the doubter arose inside him.

A brief awkward silence ended the initial friendly exchange. Thomas abruptly broke the silence with a simple question. "Who is this God?"

He gestured with his right hand to one of the carved figures of Buddha to his left. It was a simple question. To Thomas, the idea that these stone images were anything but profane deities was obvious. He could see the common people worshipping them. He further considered that the idea that stone idols could be deities was on its face ridiculous. He chided himself for not more strongly condemning these false idols outright, but his confidence was still shaky. His voice sounded almost timid as he asked the question.

Master Rinpoche looked carefully at Thomas for a few moments as he processed Thomas' abrupt question. *The Buddha is certainly not God.* He decided to address the fundamental thinking underpinning all first rather than the simplistic thoughts about a singular concept of one God. *There is no God as such. Only an endless cycle of births and deaths. The representations of the Buddha's life and his* achievement of nirvana would take some time to explain. The Buddha was certainly not a superficial almighty deity.

"Thomasji," he began slowly. "We believe there are four noble truths in the world. I am thinking you will understand them, and you may even agree with me as I explain them, so let us begin there." The Tibetan spoke thoughtfully, carefully. "Do you not agree?"

It was Thomas' turn to hesitate for a moment, but he nodded his head in assent.

The Buddhist priest continued. "The first truth that the Buddha taught us is 'dukkha,' that is, the problem of human suffering. All suffer in this world."

Master Rinpoche went on to elaborate. He recounted the stories of Prince Siddhartha before he attained enlightenment and became a Buddha. He focused on the prince's initial journeys outside of the palace and his discovery of great suffering in the world.

Thomas nodded his head affirmatively to the stories. There was little need to elaborate on this point, he thought. He was not familiar with Prince Siddhartha, but he was in full agreement with the idea. He had walked past terrible suffering just journeying to the monastery, that very day. On his short walk, he had observed an entire young family enduring slavery, hostage to the construction trade, carrying rocks on their heads; young children too, their unformed backs already bent and broken from the extreme labor. They were people without history. They had no rights and made their master wealthy while they did without. These were not the actions of God. These were the actions of men. This was human suffering, and he observed it on a monumental scale all around him.

Rinpoche finished recounting the tale of the Buddha and then waited for a comment from Thomas. Seeing Thomas nodding assent, he continued.

"The cause of this suffering is desire, what we call 'samudaya.' Do you see, Thomasji?" Master Rinpoche's question was a statement. He continued with a story of the Buddha's teaching that if cravings were stopped, then one could end suffering. Thomas listened carefully and again found himself in full agreement, thinking of his own experience and desire for the beautiful flute player Sarida and the disaster that resulted from his desire for her.

Master Rinpoche finished his point and again was looking for some kind of comment from Thomas and found the man only gently nodding his affirmation.

The first sign of Right Thinking is listening, thought Master Rinpoche. *Maybe this youthful man will understand. Some of these ideas can be difficult and hard to understand at first.*

Both of these concepts were very much in line with Thomas' increasingly ascetic thinking and the imperative to deny oneself. Still, Thomas found himself growing slightly impatient. The truths that Rinpoche described were fine, but what about the ultimate being? he thought. Where was the supreme deity? Where was God in all of this?

"Thomasji, the third noble truth is the 'detachment of desire,'" continued the priest. And here Rinpoche described several stories of the Buddha. The first story he told was the Buddha's effort to deny all bodily needs and the terrible mistake that was.

"Denial of all food simply starves the body," he explained.

Rinpoche suddenly stood up and motioned Thomas to follow. Walking towards the entrance of the chamber, he stopped in front of one of the stone carvings sitting on a pedestal to one side of the room.

"This is our Fasting Buddha," he said. "It is a reminder to us that we all must seek the Middle Path. Fasting until death will achieve nothing. We must seek out balance in life."

Thomas wondered if Rinpoche's wording, "our Fasting Buddha," implied that there might be other statues displaying that attribute. He also noted that Rinpoche did not refer to the statue as a deity. Confusing, he thought. He looked at the life-size statue. It was carved in black stone. The figure was emaciated, with ribs and shoulder bones exposed through stony skin.

He had to stop himself from commenting on how a "God" could look like that. He privately considered that the representation almost looked like an evil spirit, dark and foreboding. It was certainly nothing he could worship.

Still, Thomas found himself in general agreement with his host. By removing the distractions of this life, the physical pleasures of women, excessive food, and other needs, he considered, one could find fulfillment by being linked to the living God. Yet, one did not need to carry such denial to the extent that one's body could not function.

Master Rinpoche continued. "The Fasting Buddha teaches us that the Middle Path is the right path. All these great carved Buddhas in the hall symbolize the many different truths that the Lord Buddha taught us. In some cases, the statue represents teaching. In others, it is a representation of the Lord Buddha in meditation and prayer. And some even represent the Lord Buddha in death." Rinpoche said the last sentence with emphasis, intending to return to that concept later.

"The first three noble truths lead all of us to the fourth and in some ways the most important truth. It's not so much a thought as it is a passage for living. No matter what we do on this earth, we will all be subject to the limitations of our bodies. The Lord Buddha understood this and yet, even after his enlightenment, he continued to teach and live among the people for many years. During that time, he was subject to all the sufferings that all humans experience. However, he had achieved the cessation of suffering, called 'nirodha.' This is the fourth noble truth, which we call the Eightfold Path. It is the Middle Path, the balance between austerity and life's needs. It guides the people on the path to Right Thinking and Right Living." Master Rinpoche nodded his head in conclusion as he spoke, inviting Thomas to speak if he wished.

The apostle immediately questioned this odd thinking in his mind. *What Master Rinpoche is saying seems to be a dilution of a more positive path,* he considered. Finally finding his voice, he spoke with conviction. "If you compromise your values and start down the path of needs and desire, you will lose your connection to the pathway to God. My Lord God says we must deny ourselves to achieve everlasting life." Speaking out loud gave him renewed confidence in front of all these learned men. This time, his voice sounded confident.

Master Rinpoche looked back at the man, suddenly no longer sure how much he had really understood. He was aware of the challenges that trapped Thomas' thinking, his knowledge borne in part from his frequent debates with the followers of Ahura Mazda, who seemed to have similar thinking. Rinpoche shifted the conversation to address that. He would need to address the question of the all-powerful God, a fixation in some religions.

"What is a soul, Thomasji? Does a soul matter? Which God controls your soul?" Master Rinpoche asked. He wanted to move the conversation in a more fruitful direction. He would gently demonstrate the futility of that path, anticipating what Thomas would be thinking.

"I follow the one true God and the pathway to God through the Christ, his only son," affirmed Thomas. "My soul will rest in heaven."

The response caused smiles to break out among many of the priests and novices in the room.

"Thomasji," said Master Rinpoche gently, "all life is caught up in an endless stream of birth, death, and birth. The Buddha taught us the pathway to break this cycle and to find nirvana. Nirvana is the ending of the cycle. It is a release."

Thomas realized he was not understanding these priests at all. "Nirvana is heaven, then?" he inquired. "Is that where your soul will live?" he pressed.

Rinpoche realized his friend understood little of what he was saying and was indeed trapped into thinking that the universe had to be controlled by one omnipotent God, as he had suspected earlier.

"There is no heaven, Thomasji," said Rinpoche. "Heaven is a simple idea and vision, the result of undisciplined minds and desires. Why is heaven only ever populated by man's needs and desires," he pointed out, "and not a woman's desires? Heaven seems to be inhabited by what you think you need today: perhaps great food, beautiful virgins, or strong bodies." He smiled and added. "I would not want to be a woman going to your heaven. That thinking is not Right Thinking, an idea that the Lord Buddha taught us. Nirvana is the breaking of that cycle. Nirvana is the true absence of needs and desires. The Noble Eightfold Path leads us to the Right Path and Right Thinking. It can also lead us away from asceticism and wealth. It will lead one to the Middle Path. It is also the path to all deities."

Master Rinpoche explained the Noble Eightfold Path in more detail. The apostle listened attentively.

"I can accept all benevolent gods, even yours," Master Rinpoche finally stated, as he wrapped up his teaching. This concluding statement took the apostle by surprise. Rinpoche noted Thomas' reaction and added, "Remember, the Eightfold Path is the pathway of tolerance for all men and women of the earth. Tolerance!" He emphasized these last words by thrusting his hand forward. "Tolerance," he repeated again.

Thomas was astounded by this strange conversation. He had never heard of thinking like this and was startled by what it represented. *Rinpoche could not really be open to accepting Christ as his Lord and savior,* he thought. Master Rinpoche's declaration did not make any sense.

It was now Thomas' turn to shift the conversation. *"Where is this man's soul?"* he had been constantly thinking. He then said it out loud, "Where is your soul?"

His questions seemed small when compared to this deep thinking and gentle man before him, but to his mind, it was essential. *The soul is the essence of who we are,* Thomas affirmed to himself. *The soul is the starting point.*

Rinpoche was clearly delighted to respond, his face smiling as he explained. "I don't know of a soul in that sense, Thomasji. But I am made up of many parts. My friend Nagasena explains it this way.

You arrived to greet the king on a chariot, yes? Is the wheel of the chariot the chariot? Is the axle the chariot? Is the yoke the chariot? Of course not. All these things make up the chariot. In the same way, I, like Nagasena, am made up of parts, which all together are called Master Rinpoche. But my cloak does not name me. My hands do not name me. My feet do not name me. And all of these parts are constantly changing, just like the chariot. But there is no part quite like the soul you are describing either. Do you understand?"

Thomas was now amused, and it was his turn to push back. "Master Rinpoche," he said, finally addressing Rinpoche in his formal title. He was feeling the need to assert his beliefs to this man, the true beliefs of the Lord God. *These Buddhists do not accept the Lord Buddha as a unitary creator God,* Thomas realized. *This is a core difference in our beliefs.*

Despite the philosophy presented, Thomas saw compelling contrary evidence all around him that Master Rinpoche's followers did worship the Buddha as a deity. Even now, at the far end of the chamber, he could see a man bowed before one of the Buddhist statues in earnest, emotional prayer, eyes closed, crying and shaking. Thomas gestured towards the praying man to reinforce his point. He paused for a moment to be sure that Master Rinpoche understood he was indicating the distraught man. Master Rinpoche nodded ever so slightly, acknowledging the point. *I will have to address the question of our imperfections with this man one day,* he thought.

"You have a soul," said Thomas, continuing and taking on the tone of the preacher that he was. "And God will hold you accountable one day. Your identity is written here in this stone, in this profane temple, and among the incense that you burn to your gods. You say Buddha is not a God, but I see your people praying to him all the time. This man is just one example of many that I see praying to a false god." Thomas unconsciously gestured with his hands for emphasis as he spoke. He was unable to hide the contempt that crept into voice when he said the words "false god."

The apostle, ingrained with the idea of the all-powerful God of the Hebrews, could not conceive that the universe was organized any other way but by a single all-powerful creator God. *The idea of an eternal cycle of birth, death, and rebirth is preposterous!* he thought emphatically. *Still, these Buddhists are brothers in arms in some ways. They understand the importance of denial of oneself as a way to draw closer to the divine.* Thomas struggled to reconcile their beliefs with his own.

Master Rinpoche smiled back at Thomas, electing not to challenge or respond to him on his affirmation of a soul at this time. He was beginning to understand a little bit of what was going through Thomas' head and did not wish to be combative in this first meeting. He truly hoped that Thomas had at least understood his message of tolerance—the most important message. That subject could be explored in greater detail when they next met, along with a discussion of the imperfections of men.

Master Rinpoche also considered Thomas' growing passion. "We are all in different states of learning and development as we journey through this world," he answered slowly. "Our mighty kingdom has found a brief period of peace because of tolerance. King Gondophores has chosen to accept and honor most religions in the region. He wisely chose not to create a true state religion." The king, along with Master Rinpoche, understood that intolerance would drive the country back to disaster and war. Tolerance was an idea that was most often at the forefront of his thinking.

He continued to smile at his guest. "Thomasji," he finally said. "Go back to your palace and sleep on all these words. Perhaps we can have further discussions in the coming days. I do want to talk to you about the actions of some of our devotees and many other matters. We are far from perfect. Let us at least agree that tolerance first must drive all our discussions." The apostle was chagrinned by this statement but elected not to challenge it. *It was their first meeting after all. Perhaps he would be able to convince Master Rinpoche in a future meeting.* Thomas smiled and nodded his affirmation.

With that, the meeting ended, and Thomas stood up and bowed. Master Rinpoche rose with him and escorted him to the door of the chamber, giving him a blessing and a small gift as he left.

Long after Thomas left, many of the priests in the room remained, quietly discussing what they had observed. It was clear to them that this strange Hebrew was failing to understand many of the key points that Master Rinpoche was making so clear. While they loved and honored Master Rinpoche, many thought he did not push back hard enough on the Hebrew, allowing him to infect the royal household with his foreign ways and thinking.

Something needed to be done. And some of the sangha were prepared to take action if necessary.

Chapter 14

A dream that is not interpreted is like a letter that has not been opened.

—Berachot 55, The Talmud

THOMAS, LOST IN thought, slowly walked back to his room from the monastery and the great Dharamarajika Stupa. He walked past the construction site, again seeing the young family enduring slavery. A three-year-old child clung to her enslaved mother, crying. Her nose was running, and her belly distended, indicating worms and misery. The mother was somehow carrying and comforting the child while simultaneously balancing a load of rocks in a small basket on her head.

Thomas looked away. *What can I do for these people?* he thought. Isa had once said, "The poor will always be with you, but you will not always have me." Thomas understood those words now. He wished his brother were with him right now. He wanted to discuss these issues, as he grew in his understanding of the world and its difficulties. He, Thomas, with only the practical training of a carpenter and builder, was now confronted with these real problems.

The apostle continued to ponder what Master Rinpoche had discussed with him. Certainly, this was no simple matter of throwing the money changers and thieves out of the temple, as Isa had once done in Jerusalem. These religious holy men of India were complex. There were no money changers and sellers of cheap goods in their great hall.

He entered the palace courtyard and walked back to his room, greeting Xenophon at the door. The young Buddhist acolyte looked out of breath, as though he had just rushed back from somewhere.

A small fireplace was in the corner of the room with a broad clay flute running up the side of one wall, designed to channel the smoke up and out through the roof. A clay pot bubbled on the small dying fire. On many days, an older woman would bring food for the apostle. Today, Xenophon himself had prepared a meal on the fire to share between them. Thomas gladly accepted the food: a spicy stew with rice. He ate slowly, thanking Xenophon for his contribution.

The small effort caused Thomas to consider how grateful he was for having Xenophon in his life. The young man was there for him, helping him in whatever needed doing, a ready and devout convert. Thomas sometimes thought that if he could have a dozen Xenophons helping him, he could change the course of the world and hugely expand Isa's mission. His mission.

As the day wore on, Thomas realized how tired he was. He suddenly remembered that God had ordained the seventh day as the day of rest. *I am just exhausted from so many travels and labors,* he admitted to himself. *And I have been taking no rest days from my sermons and labors.* Thoughts of Master Rinpoche's description of the "Middle

Path" and the "Eightfold Path" kept coming back to his mind and would not leave him. *On this one matter, I can agree with Master Rinpoche,* he thought wryly. *There is no reason to starve the body or to deny oneself sleep. I need sleep.*

His hunger satiated from the earlier meal, the apostle lay down on his sleeping mat, pulling his cloak over him to rest for a while. He soon drifted off into a deep sleep. He began to dream fitful and frightening dreams. He tossed and turned upon his cloak, calling out the name Isa. "Isa! Isa, where are you?" But his brother was not there.

In his dream, Thomas was walking down a road. He saw a handsome young man lying on the ground ahead of him. He walked towards the man, at first to save him. As he approached the man, his self-awareness grew, thinking that he must do more than just save this man. He suddenly realized he is feeling desire! He knows the man is well-formed and attractive. Thomas was horrified at his reaction. He felt desire that he could not control. But the man's body was still too far away for him to see clearly. As he arrived at the man's side, he saw that the man was dead, and his desire immediately gave way to sorrow. The man was lying on his side on the edge of the highway. *What has happened here?* he wondered.

As he approached the man, he saw a terrible wound on the man's arm. Something had bitten him, and the wound was large, bloody, and jagged. Just as he arrived by the man's side, a great black serpent rose up from behind the man, staring across the body at Thomas. The serpent was huge, with scales and fangs like daggers. His eyes were red and penetrating. He shook the earth as he beat the ground with his mighty tail.

Yet, Thomas the Apostle was not afraid. The Lord of Hosts was with him always and reassured him. Thomas felt confident.

And then the serpent turned his head towards Thomas and spoke.

"I know you. You are the twin of the Christ," said the serpent in a powerful gravelly voice. "You are here to reproach me. For I have killed this man. I saw him with a young girl from the village. I was waiting for the girl, but instead, this man found her. He took her, and he kissed her, and he had foul intercourse with her." The serpent sneered when he spoke these last words.

"Stop!" commanded Thomas harshly, looking at the serpent and raising his right hand at the monster. Gesturing to the man on the ground, Thomas commanded the serpent to suck the venom from him. The serpent seemed fearful of Apostle Thomas. Still hissing with frustration, he nevertheless obediently bowed down and took the wounded arm of the youth into his mouth. Closing his eyes, he sucked the terrible poison from the wound and ingested it into his own body. As the serpent did so, he began to change color from black to a pale white. The horrible beast withered and looked upon the twin of Christ in agony as his body shrank painfully before them. The serpent died quickly.

The youth gently awakened. Thomas looked into the face of the youth and saw that it was Xenophon looking back at him. His Xenophon! Thomas took his hand and raised him up. He explained to Xenophon that God would not reckon against him, nor take account of his past sins, which he might have committed in ignorance. Taking him by the hand, the apostle led the young acolyte towards the "right intentions" and "right views."

Thomas awoke suddenly, the dream ending. As he sat up, he began to look about, slightly disoriented but relieved to have escaped the dream. Sweating, he saw that Xenophon was there in the room with him, watching him, a look of concern on his face. Xenophon smiled reassuringly at him. Thomas sighed and lay back, suddenly remembering the debate with Master Rinpoche. The matter with the Buddhist priest was just too much. *The Buddhist priest's thinking is affecting my own thinking,* he thought, slightly frustrated. *My God is greater than that.* The apostle closed his eyes and slowly fell asleep again. As he slept, night came on with darkness folding into the room all about him.

Thomas began to dream again. A large colt stood before him. The colt could not speak so Thomas commanded it to speak. The colt said, "I know you as the twin of the Christ. You are the highest apostle, companion of Isa, and the one who knows the secret oracles. Your brother has sold you into bondage so that you might bring many into the joy of knowing the true God." The voice was pleasant and friendly.

The colt offered to carry Thomas on his journey, and he readily agreed. Thomas mounted the colt, and the two began their journey discussing "right mindfulness," "right concentration," and "right efforts." As Thomas rode forward, crowds began to form to watch the pair, amazed to see a man speaking with a colt. As the pair neared the city gates, Thomas dismounted and thanked the colt for his efforts. The colt likewise wished Thomas well and turned to leave. As he did so, he immediately fell to the ground and died.

The death of the friendly colt in his dream shocked Thomas, and he violently awakened. He sat up on his sleeping mat. The room was dark and silent. Xenophon was gone.

"What does this dream foretell?" He shivered. "What message is God presenting me with? Why is he presenting these thoughts that I discussed with Master Rinpoche?"

Deeply disquieted, Thomas was afraid to go back to sleep. He tossed and turned and fought the fatigue that was overcoming him, but he couldn't prevent it. The apostle fell asleep again.

A third dream began in which Thomas met a troubled young married woman. A young male lover who was not her husband had come to her at night and had intercourse with her. She was married, but the man gave her pleasure. As Thomas and the woman were speaking, the man appeared and spoke to Thomas.

"I know you are the twin of the Christ," the man said. The voice of the man was just like the serpent's, gravelly and evil. The man, beautiful to look upon, continued, "I know you are here to reproach me. I came for her, and she wanted me. She enjoyed all manner of intercourse with me."

There was mockery and laughter written on his face. The man was clearly enjoying Thomas' discomfort.

Thomas commanded the man to leave, and surprisingly the man departed in peace. The ease with which Thomas commanded and the obedience to his words shocked him. Speaking truth was powerful. He took the woman by the hand and spoke to her. The woman began to sob and repented. The apostle explained the importance of "right livelihood," "right actions," and "right speech." He led her down to the river, where he baptized her. As he was doing so, he heard a distant cock crow. Thomas stirred in his sleep and lost the vision of the woman. The cock crowed again, this time more loudly and even closer.

Thomas opened his eyes, staring at the ceiling of his room in the receding darkness.

The dreams were confusing. He knew he had been given divine power. But he also knew that some of the dream had a message from Buddhist teachings, teachings that Master Rinpoche would have approved. The thought troubled him. He knew he must resist that path.

The world was deeply silent as he continued to awaken and gather his thoughts. He looked towards the door. Through the cracks, he could see. Morning had come.

Chapter 15

*When the apostle heard this he said, "O insane intercourse,
how you lead to shamelessness. O unrestrained lust, how
have you excited this man to do this!*

—The Acts of Thomas: 52

THE COCK WAS still crowing. Thomas sat back up on his mat. He turned his gaze to the door as it was suddenly thrust open. Xenophon stepped in, stopping at the entry, his eyes ablaze with fear. The young man was breathing hard from running. He was sweating, his face flushed, and his clothes disheveled. Thomas saw that Xenophon was wearing the very same tunic he had been wearing in Thomas' dream. His beloved and loyal companion was weeping uncontrollably.

Thomas looked at him with alarm. "Xenophon! Are you all right?" His voice betrayed the fear he felt, as his mind was immediately flooded with concern for his friend. He stood up and went to him and embraced him.

He spoke more gently to the younger man, his voice still cracking and betraying emotion, "What terrible thing has happened?"

His embrace of Xenophon caused the younger man to momentarily stop weeping and to look up at the apostle.

"What has happened, Xenophon?" repeated Thomas, a bit hoarsely, but intending to sound more tender. "Where have you been all night?"

He could discern from Xenophon's face and look of exhaustion that he had not been in the room for most of the night while he had been sleeping.

His young friend broke down and began to sob uncontrollably again. Thomas continued to embrace him until the young man finally found his strength and regained his wits.

"I have been with my lover, tonight," the young man finally stated, his emotions still raw and exposed. "After our union at the inn, we began to talk, and I soon realized that she did not love me and that she loved another. That she was even married to this other man, and before coming tonight, she had already been with her husband. On the same day! Can you imagine such an evil woman!" He spoke these words with emphasis and with a hint of self-justification.

Thomas felt a strange pang of jealousy pass through him. Still, he comforted the man. Xenophon continued in halting words. "I don't know what overcame me, but a great passion, like the devil, entered my being," he said. He shook his head as he spoke these words. "Rage overtook me, and I strangled her." He looked hard at Thomas and added forcefully. "I killed a woman, Thomas. I killed her!" He brought his hands together to mimic the terrible act of strangling. "They will kill me for this," he added softly. His confession seemed to give him a feeling of release, yet the anguish in his face betrayed the torment and pain he still felt inside.

Thomas was stunned by the admission. He had never encountered such evil so close to him before. *Here again, is an example of all that is wrong in the world,* he thought. *Once again, foul intercourse has led this young man down the wrong path. If only he could deny his needs.*

Thomas knew he needed to take charge of the situation quickly. It would not take long for the community to find the woman and then seek retribution against his disciple.

"Come," said Thomas, gently assuring his companion. "Let us go to her and minister to her. Show me her body. Where is she?"

Xenophon took a deep breath. Taking Thomas by the hand, he suppressed a cry. "I took her body from the inn in the middle of the night to the trade road on the far side of town," he said. "There was no one there, and no one saw me. I carried her body on a colt and left her there. I pushed her body into the bushes. Even now, it is possible that wild beasts have taken her. I did not want to be discovered. I did not want anyone to find the body. I do not think anyone saw me."

Thomas, still holding Xenophon by the hand, asked him to lead him to the place. The two men gathered up the colt tied to a post at the palace outside the room. Hand in hand, they walked through the palace gates and on through the slowly awakening town, leading the colt. Seeing two close male friends holding hands was quite normal in Taxila and merely indicated a fraternal bond. Yet, any movement by Apostle Thomas was often exciting and often generated local interest, if not outright enthusiasm. Thomas was a known healer and had developed a steady following among the townspeople. Things, extraordinary things, seemed to happen around him. Soon, a small group of boys was walking with the two companions, curious to see where they were going.

A growing number of adult followers soon joined them, having no idea that they were being led to the scene of a murder. Several beggars and a destitute family joined the crowd along with a few who were seeking healings. By the time they reached the edge of the wood where the body had been deposited by Xenophon, almost fifty people were in attendance, watching the actions of the apostle.

Xenophon walked to the edge of the forest and pointed into the brush along the side of the road, where he had thrown the body of the young woman. He refused to go further than the side of the road and stopped. His raw emotion was again creeping into his being and taking control of him. The proximity to the scene of the crime was just too much for him. He sobbed silently, conscious that many eyes were on him. The apostle nodded understandingly to the young man. He turned to the assembly and with raised arms indicated that all were to stay and not follow him. He then went forth and into the brush. He found the young woman's body a few short meters into the foliage. To his relief, no wild beasts had yet disturbed her.

He saw that the young woman was beautiful and that some violence had been done to her. Great circular red welts marked her delicate and fragile neck, marking the place that Xenophon had tried to strangle the life out of her. Even her face was bruised and discolored. One of her elbows looked broken and displayed a large gash. She had probably fallen on it when Xenophon had flung her into the brush.

Thomas wrapped a spare cloth about the wound and then rewrapped her own cloak about her to cover her nakedness. He gently picked the woman up in his arms, carrying her out to the road and to the assembled townspeople. The woman was slender and light, an easy burden for the powerful carpenter. The crowd murmured as Thomas emerged from the wood carrying the young woman in his arms.

All the people in the growing crowd were now attentive, not understanding exactly what had happened here but beginning to suspect that a foul deed of some kind had been carried out. The crowd's murmuring grew louder. The sun was now fully up and slowly moving across the sky. It would soon grow hot. Thomas decided to carry the woman to the inn for shelter.

Telling Xenophon to walk with him, Thomas carried the woman the short distance back to the building where the events of last night had occurred. Entering the courtyard of the inn, he gently laid the woman in the shade at the far end. The crowd was now beyond curious and pressed into the courtyard to see what was happening. Still others ran off to alert the woman's family and husband that something terrible had happened to their wife and daughter.

Thomas knelt before the body of the young woman. Laying his hands upon her head and speaking in Aramaic, he called out to the Lord of Hosts to heal her. Anointing the woman with oil, he pressed down upon her chest repeatedly and again called out to the Lord of Hosts. Thomas then began to chant, remembering the words of Isa, remembering exactly how Isa had carried out these ceremonies and had raised people from the dead. He remembered the miracle of raising Prince Gad. He called on the God of Israel to heal this woman of sin. Thomas believed.

To the assembly, seeing Thomas, a strong robust, figure chanting in Aramaic, a language they did not understand, all seemed magical. The chanting was other worldly, melodious, and beautiful.

And then a miracle happened. The young woman suddenly breathed. Her chest heaved visibly. And then, to the astonishment of the crowd, she moved her arm.

As the crowd continued to respond in amazement, Thomas continued to pray. He then stood up and motioned for Xenophon to come forward. The young man, relief written on his brow, stepped forward, unsure what was expected of him. Thomas instructed Xenophon to take the hand of the woman and to speak to her and to pray to the God of Hosts.

Xenophon gently took the woman's hand, the hand of the woman not so long ago he had attacked. He prayed to God for forgiveness and asked God for healing. And the young woman awoke and sat up. Seeing Xenophon, her attacker, she immediately recoiled in fear, but Thomas comforted her and knelt down to her and took her by the hand, reassuring her.

He then stood and began to recount the evils of adultery and indeed the evils of all intercourse between men and women.

"Adultery and intercourse are the worst of sins," he cried out to the people. Here was an example of how failure to deny oneself had brought evil and horror. He called on the people to each repent and deny oneself. Many in the crowd watched in amazement, unsure of what exactly had transpired there.

Thomas finished speaking to the assembly and invited all who would be baptized in the name of God to follow him to the river. Thomas led the way with the shaken young woman following.

Thomas baptized her in the name of the one true God and then offered to baptize others.

Present in the crowd, watching all these events, were members of the sangha. They were stunned. They had observed the events with growing suspicion, skeptical that Thomas was a real man of God and increasingly more and more convinced he was some kind of false shaman, a false shaman who had found favor with the king. Their king! Their kingdom! Surely this man had staged this false miracle. He needed to be exposed.

While some of the sangha walked back directly to the Dharamarajika Stupa and the Monastery to report what they had seen to Master Rinpoche, two other priests took a different path and walked to a home of a wealthy patron and devotee of the sangha. There, they met with a dozen other priests to discuss what exactly needed to be done about Apostle Thomas.

Chapter 16

My brother Thomas is a good and honorable servant.
Among his greatest gifts is his unfailing ability to continu-
ously seek the right pathway to the Kingdom of God.

—This is Isa.

THE PALACE OF Prince Gad was bustling as usual, as Abbanes made his way onto the grounds. Abbanes, a wealthy and popular figure, was greeted enthusiastically at the gates as he came in. A full week had gone by since Thomas had healed the young woman who had been murdered by Xenophon, and there was still much talk of those events in the town and indeed in the entire region.

Abbanes had been invited to come to the palace to meet with Captain Siphor, a representative of King Charisius, who ruled an Indian Kingdom far to the south. After the meeting, Abbanes hoped to find Thomas and talk to him about his activities. Abbanes was constantly hearing news about Thomas' preaching and healing. Not all the news was good. He learned from several sources that the sangha were becoming increasingly concerned about Thomas' religious exploits and were considering action against the apostle.

Abbanes knew that Master Rinpoche would never sanction violence against Thomas and indeed was a pacifist concerning matters like this. However, many of the priests around him were not so noble of thought or action. Abbanes knew that some of them regularly broke their vows, often overindulging in lavish meals at devotees' homes or spending large sums of money on expensive prostitutes. While they were discreet in their activities, these indiscretions were still known to occur by many of the sangha. Abbanes also understood enough of the politics of the kingdom to know that many of these priests would not want their monopoly on the largesse of the royal family threatened. In their minds, their very existence, their very livelihood was under attack by Thomas. Hegemony over spiritual matters was one thing, but the apostle might even threaten their food bowls.

"Thomas' popularity is really becoming notable," Abbanes mused, as he walked the palace grounds thinking the situation over. While he often heard of the good things like healings, he also increasingly heard that he was preaching unnatural things like sexual abstinence, not just for priests but for all. He was even advocating sexual abstinence between husbands and wives. *This is too much,* he thought. *I will just have to talk to Thomas about all of this. I am quite certain that what Thomas is preaching clashes with the Middle Path doctrine of Master Rinpoche and his loyal adherents. How did Thomas' thinking evolve to this? How did he come to believe in this restrictive doctrine?* The thought would not leave his mind. He remembered Thomas' amusing reaction to the beautiful flute player, Sarida. Yet he did not know the whole story, including the attack on Natan and how he was devoured by a lion. He shook his head as he continued to puzzle through these developments.

Abbanes understood Thomas was a man of many contradictions. He had learned to admire and even believe in some of what the younger man said and did. He had even allowed himself to be baptized. However, he finally concluded that the extremes that Thomas went to made him uncomfortable. He was a devout Hebrew of the Buddhist Middle Path, he thought in amusement.

An idea occurred to him. His meeting with South Indian Captain Siphor might be fortuitous. Siphor had come from the city of Muziris, in the land of Tamilakam on the southwestern coast of India. Abbanes had had long-standing trading relations with Muziris through the small Hebrew community there. If things were getting too dangerous for Thomas here in Taxila, he could send him there. In fact, he realized that he himself might be able to go with him. He had been planning a trip down that way for some time. It had been a long time since he had visited his family there. He would need to take the road to the south and then hire an ocean-going boat that would take him down to the great port city.

As expected, the meeting with Captain Siphor went well. In fact, the South Indian seemed extremely enthusiastic when Abbanes suggested that he wished to accompany him if he could. The road was long and dangerous. It was always better to travel in greater numbers. Siphor thought too that Abbanes would be most welcome in the Jewish community, telling him how excited that community in Muziris would be to see him after such a long absence.

Siphor gave little thought as to who exactly would be Abbanes' traveling companion. Abbanes explained that he had a young carpenter with him from Judea.

"Bring him with you, of course!" exclaimed the captain. "Your friend and guest is my friend and guest."

As Abbanes was walking off the palace grounds, a young acolyte no more than ten years old walked up to him. Bowing low before the Hebrew trader, he motioned to Abbanes to follow him. Abbanes was amused by the formality of the young boy and his bow and smiled. Unsure of what this was about exactly, he elected to follow his young guide, recognizing it as a polite, but discreet summons of some kind. The acolyte entered a stone building that served as quarters for some of the sangha. Entering the structure, the boy led Abbanes into a dimly lit hallway, and then he was shown to a small room. As he entered the room, two young monks stood and greeted him, smiling but clearly nervous too. The open doorway and a small square window cast light throughout in what otherwise would have been a darkened chamber.

Abbanes, his curiosity now peaked, immediately endeavored to put the young monks at ease. He clasped his hands together in the prayer pose, pressing them to his forehead and bowing to them.

"Good day, my friends," said Abbanes with a warm smile. The monks had his full attention. This meeting was unusual.

The two priests, slightly relieved by Abbanes' attitude, returned the greeting. They had been unsure how receptive Abbanes was going to be to their secretive approach. After a slight pause, the more confident of the two priests spoke up. Both monks were dressed in red cloaks, indicating to Abbanes that they were likely aligned with Master Rinpoche and his theology.

"Good day, my Lord Abbanes," said the young man, promoting Abbanes to a rank he did not technically have. His voice sounded small but grew stronger as he spoke. "Thank you for meeting us like this. I know this must seem unusual. However, I have an urgent message for you, and I could not figure out another way to pass it on to you. You are well known, and your travels are followed closely by many. Most of the other priests and monks are not here right now. They are in the main hall at the palace of the king."

The monk continued, "We are all followers of the Middle Path, and we honor and respect other views as the Buddha himself taught us to do. He taught us to be tolerant and to challenge what we hear, not to blindly believe. We are students of Master Rinpoche." The young man could not help teaching, his very being bursting and ready to take up the duties of a teacher. He also wanted to clearly convey to Abbanes that what he was about to say was approved by Master Rinpoche himself.

"We know and respect the works of your servant Thomas," he continued. "We have heard of the great things he has accomplished, even healing the sick, saving the life of our Prince Gad, and, in the recent case, the raising of a woman from the dead. We do not know the truth of these things, but many are following him." The man paused for a moment, and Abbanes motioned to him to continue. "We also know that Thomas is respected in the palace by our king and his brother." The young monk again paused, again looking for affirmation from Abbanes.

This is interesting, thought Abbanes, equally on guard for what might be coming. "Please continue," he said out loud, nodding and wishing the man would just explain what was on his mind. He was choosing his words carefully.

"We are all loyal to our chosen path and to Master Rinpoche especially," continued the monk, again reaffirming the connection to the senior Buddhist priest. "Yet, there are some who do not take their vows so seriously. Some even renounce their vows for a time and say they will return to Right Thinking and Right Actions later. Others do not even do that, but simply violate the holy vows they have taken." The young man explained all this as though his audience might find his revelations as a surprise.

Abbanes nodded his head in agreement. He knew.

The priest continued, "Some of these unholy monks are not in favor with Master Rinpoche. They do not like your servant Thomas either. In fact, today, I am talking to you because I want to warn you that some of these priests who do not favor their vows are considering harm to your servant Thomas."

Abbanes had already begun to realize that this was exactly where the man was going with his story. Still, it was shocking to Abbanes to hear these words spoken out loud from the mouth of a Buddhist priest. He knew about the overindulgence of many monks and priests. Yet, clearly, priests considering harm to another human being were miscreants on a different scale. Adherents not following the tenets of the Middle Path and prepared to dramatically violate their vows represented a grave danger.

"I am surprised by your words, venerable ones," said Abbanes. He used a respectful address and his tone was solemn. "Can you tell me more of this matter? What do you mean that they will harm my servant? Don't they know that Thomas enjoys the support of King Gondophores?" A pang of fear was creeping into his mind. He did not want to see Thomas harmed under any circumstances. He must protect him. Thomas was his responsibility, even if he did not fully agree with all of his teachings.

The young man politely smiled at Abbanes, "The king's loyalty changes each day. But yes, and especially with Prince Gad, Thomas does have much protection. Yet, I fear such protection will not be enough."

"You still have not told me what you mean by 'harm' to my servant," said Abbanes again.

"I cannot fully explain what I do not truly know," said the man. "Those in authority have become confident that several of the priests intend to kill your servant. Of that I am sure. I have been directed here to warn you." The words of the priest were clear and defined. He was on a mission to leave no doubt in Abbanes' mind of the danger.

Abbanes opened his mouth ready to inquire further and then realized he had heard all that he could expect from these two monks. His admission of a warning was clear and clearly came from Master Rinpoche himself. Undoubtedly, Master Rinpoche was aware of these dissenting views in his ranks but was not fully empowered to stop them. The elder Hebrew trader thanked them for the information, not revealing the rising concern he felt in his heart for his friend. Now more than ever, he needed to speak to Thomas.

The two monks, seeing that Abbanes fully understood the warning, made haste to leave, wanting to return to the great hall before anyone noted their unusually long absence.

Abbanes was no longer in great haste to leave the grounds of the Palace of Prince Gad. He immediately walked over to the guard and inquired as to the whereabouts of Thomas. Directed to a small yard behind the quarters, Abbanes, at last, found Thomas with Xenophon by his side. The men were outside their room, loading the colt and preparing for yet another journey into the countryside.

Greeting the apostle warmly, Abbanes asked Thomas to sit down with him. Thomas readily accepted, seeing his friend was troubled about something. Speaking in Aramaic to prevent anyone from overhearing their conversation, Abbanes recounted to Thomas his conversation with the two young monks. Xenophon could not understand the conversation, but he could see the great distress that it gave Thomas, who had surprise and perhaps even a bit of anger written on his face.

Thomas was righteous at first. "I am the messenger of the one true God," he said. "My God will not forsake me. He will protect me. Isa has sent me to this land, to India, to bring tidings of truth and the pathway to eternity. The Kingdom of God is at hand. I cannot leave my commission. I cannot have evil drive me away from my mission and charter, a commission that Isa himself gave me."

Abbanes put his hand up, palm facing Thomas, indicating that he should stop with such talk.

"I understand how you feel my friend," soothed Abbanes. "However, there is little good that would come from your death. I am certain too that even King Gondophores will not be able to stop his own priests from attacking you. There are so many ways they could do this. They could even poison your food, Thomas," noted Abbanes somewhat morosely. "They likely would not even take credit for the act. Many would be left wondering what exactly happened. How would that serve the purpose of Isa?"

Abbanes was emphatic on this point. Xenophon continued to watch the two in conversation in the foreign tongue.

Thomas did not respond and sat there pondering what his friend was telling him.

Abbanes continued, "I have been thinking about another trade trip for a long time. Here in India. Even before I had heard this terrible news and warning. There is a captain named Siphor, who is here right now, visiting from the south. He is from a land that is still in India, another kingdom, and very much a part of the place that Isa wanted you to go to." Abbanes felt it was important to keep reminding Thomas that his proposed trip was still in "India." "Rather than become a martyr here so quickly, why don't we send you to Muziris?" pleaded the trader.

There was an earnest, confident gaze in his eyes, but a look of his concern was writ large on his face. In spite of his famous confidence and ability to move forward against all odds, Abbanes, the seasoned traveler and survivor of many dangers, could not suppress the pang of fear he felt in his heart for his friend.

The prospect of once again traveling with the amazing and formidable Abbanes was appealing to Thomas, and he continued to mull over the idea. Thomas excused himself for a while and went into his room alone to pray, seeking guidance from the only source he knew, Isa. He needed Isa's divine guidance now more than ever, even when he was not physically present.

The early evening descended upon them as Thomas left his room and rejoined his friend Abbanes, now seated on a cushion by a fire. Servants brought chai and refreshments, and the two Hebrews continued their conversation for several more hours. Night came on with a clear sky, starlight so bright that it was easy to see about the compound.

The logic of what Abbanes said was becoming clear to Thomas as he gazed upon the heavens. In his heart, he began to realize that this change was his destiny, something ordained by Isa too. He should not avoid this challenge. He felt at peace. He now knew that he must go. His work was just getting started. *There are loyal followers here who can continue my mission here,* he told himself, as he considered his choices. *My commission is bigger still.*

And so, at last, it was finally decided. Thomas would go to Muziris with Captain Siphor. *Perhaps I will return to Gandhara at some later day after I have preached the word of God to the people of Muziris,* he reasoned. In truth, Thomas had no idea how far away Muziris was and how likely or unlikely it would be that he would be able to return one day.

Chapter 17

*"If you do not change direction, you may end up where you
are heading."*

*—Lao Tzu and attributed to others as well.
6th Century BC, China*

THE NEXT DAY brought new hope. After the dark news of yesterday, Thomas awoke to a bright and sunny sky. The idea increasingly appealed to him that he would move on and continue his ordained mission to preach the word of God in a new place. Abbanes was making arrangements that morning for Thomas to meet Captain Siphor.

At midday, Captain Siphor came to the palace of Prince Gad and asked for Thomas. He was shown in and soon found the apostle sitting outside his room. Xenophon was in the room and came out to observe the two men in conversation. Thomas and Siphor sat down in the courtyard in the shade of the tree and began to converse. Captain Siphor had been hearing about Thomas for some days. He had learned of some of the wondrous things attributed to this man of God. Now, sitting down with Thomas, he saw a vigorous young man before him, who had charisma and a warm smile. He saw that perhaps there was some truth to the talk about this man. Thomas looked upon the captain with gentle concern and a welcoming smile. After greeting each other, and before the captain discussed the journey, he asked Thomas if he could tell him a story.

"Please," said Thomas wanting to put his guest at ease. The captain thanked him and began to tell his tale.

"Three years ago, while I was off traveling with my king, Misdaeus, and his kinsman, Charisius," began Siphor, "my wife and our daughter traveled to celebrate the wedding of our cousin. The wedding was held in a village not even a day's walk from Muziris. Normally, the road is safe, and I was not worried for their safety. I have heard that the wedding itself was a great and wonderful event."

Siphor's voice took on a more sober tone. Emotion seemed to be percolating just under the surface. He swallowed and continued. "On the return from the wedding, my wife and daughter were delayed. They attempted to walk some of the way at night, with servants to guide them, of course, but they nevertheless became lost. They soon found themselves in a forest, and they were confronted by a coarse man and his son. The men chased off the servants and then raped and violated my wife and my daughter." Siphor's voice cracked, and his eyes were closed as he said these words, vainly attempting to contain the emotion that he still felt.

Siphor deeply loved his wife and his daughter. He could not cast them out as many might after a spouse or a girl child has been violated. For a few moments Siphor could not speak further.

After a time, he regained his composure. "My two beloveds were sorely injured and could not heal. Their physical wounds healed over time, but they remained silent and hurt inside," the South Indian continued, suppressing the need to weep, uncertain how to fully describe the emotional horror and shock that had so terribly harmed his family.

Thomas immediately felt great compassion for the man. *Here is a man who is not lost to human deviancy but still has suffered the terrible consequences,* thought Thomas. *This is precisely the situation that Isa had anticipated. Isa had known that I could help these people by showing them the right path to the Kingdom of God.* The arrival of this man from South India reaffirmed to Thomas that he was making the right decision to travel with him.

He asked, "Do you believe that God can heal them?" Siphor nodded affirmatively. "Do not believe in this idol worship," stated Thomas, sweeping his arm broadly, to indicate the entire region. To Thomas, the Buddhists were all idol worshippers, refusing to make the distinction that Master Rinpoche made in which all these stone carvings were really just representations of ideas and teachings. "Instead, believe and accept the Christ and that he will heal and succor them."

"Yet, even now, they are so far away," Siphor responded. "How can that be possible?"

"Yet, even now, so far away, the God of Hosts will heal them." Thomas had great confidence in the power of healing by his God. "The Christ is building his Kingdom for the whole world," he added, "not just here in Gandhara." He continued to describe the Kingdom of God and the pathway of Christ.

As the two men talked, the captain felt more and more confident that Thomas might actually be able to help his family. The apostle's words were inspiring and gave him great hope. He had heard the stories of this man. Here was a chance to heal. He had to take the opportunity this man of God presented to him.

"Come with me, Thomas," implored Siphor, not certain that Abbanes had already convinced the apostle to travel with him. "I believe you would be well thought of in Muziris, especially with your great powers. The people in Muziris and especially of Cranganore have need of you."

Thomas smiled back. "It is not my power, my friend," he said softly. "It is the power of God. The Christ will heal your family if you but believe." Nodding reassuringly to Siphor, he simply ended by saying, "I will come."

The discussion settled, there was still much packing to do for such a long journey. Captain Siphor continued to prepare his large trading caravan for the long return journey to Muziris. He was in a great hurry now and announced he would leave in three days' time. He was anxious to see what miracle may have transpired upon his wife and daughter in his absence. *Have they been healed?* The thought entered his mind over and over again. The very possibility of their healing dominated his thinking each day. He needed to know. He needed to get to Muziris quickly. A sense of urgency in all that he did dominated his planning.

Abbanes gave Captain Siphor still another reason to make haste. "They are plotting to kill him," Abbanes said gravely, as he recounted the monk's warning to the captain in a private conversation. "It will not be an open assassination. But they will find a way to kill him if they want to. If it's unclear what actually caused the death of Thomas, the sangha will be able to claim they had had no part of it. I am afraid that even now, they might poison his food. They do not know that he is leaving. Haste is our friend."

The captain listened attentively. "Thank you for telling me this grim tale, Abbanes. I am no stranger to the dark machinations of courtesans and men of God. I believe Thomas will find a much more welcoming situation in Muziris and especially in Cranganore. Given this danger, I believe I can make better time if I cut straight south to the port instead of taking the longer Indus route. I have a very large caravan with plenty of good horses and other beasts. If I take the inland trail and cut across the Kutch, any assassins will not be looking for me on that road."

Abbanes considered the proposal for a moment. He hesitated. The Kutch was a hot dry place. He knew there were trails that way, but he had also heard of hardships and danger on that road too. He had personally never traveled that way to Bharuch. Yet, Siphor raised a good point. Assassins would not be looking for Thomas on that road. Thomas might just quietly slip away.

Pursing his lips, he finally said, "I agree, captain. Take the Kutch road, but go with care."

As he said, this, he already knew that he would need to take a different path. He was still preparing his own caravan for his trip to Muziris, part of which would have to be on the Indus. There were river ports he needed to stop at to barter for goods. He also needed to purchase supplies and other goods right here in Taxila. And he had to brief King Gondophores on his plans.

"I will meet you at the port, then," Abbanes finished thoughtfully. "I will see you in Bharuch."

Siphor nodded. "There is our community of Hebrews in Muziris too," added Siphor. "They will welcome Thomas with open arms. As you know better than I, they are close by Muziris, in the community of Cranganore, where I live. I am sure they will be so pleased to meet your apostle. Many of them seem to be wise teachers like your Thomas."

Abbanes shook his head affirmatively, while privately thinking that he was not so sure about the welcome that Thomas might receive from his fellow Hebrews. The Hebrews were not of one mind on Thomas. Abbanes knew the Hebrew community in Muziris well. Captain Siphor had forgotten that he had already been there many times. He did not know the captain well, but he knew he already had a few allies there. He even had a small family there. Yet, Thomas' preaching was different and might be a surprise to the Hebrews of South India.

Xenophon had been present during Thomas' conversation with Captain Siphor. The young man, at last, understood that his master was really going to leave him. Tears had come to his eyes as he listened to Thomas and the southern Indian captain plan their journey.

"I need you to stay here," Thomas told his friend gently. "You are my deacon, the light of Isa, and must remain here to shepherd the people of Gandhara. Come, let us see Prince Gad and say goodbye. I will tell the prince that you are my deacon, my representative here in Taxila. You will speak to the people and show them the path to the Kingdom of God. Keep your faith in the Christ."

On the day of departure, after Thomas and Xenophon had visited Prince Gad, Abbanes sought out the apostle one last time. Finding him at the front of the assembled caravan outside of the palace, he embraced Thomas and wished him a safe journey.

"I would follow you to Kutch if I could, but I have other duties. I will meet you at the port," he told him reassuringly. "On the coast, we can join up and together take ship together to Muziris, to South India." Just uttering the words "South India" gave Abbanes a feeling of comfort that Thomas would be safe.

Farewells complete, Thomas boarded a chariot with Captain Siphor and took to the road, two powerful black horses pulling their vehicle slowly and leading the way for the rest of the caravan. Captain Siphor was anxious to move south quickly and soon picked up the pace of the entire caravan.

Later in the evening of that same day, eight hours after Thomas and Siphor had ridden off in their chariot, black crows gathered in the trees about the great Stupa Dharamarajika and all about the monastery, producing a great chorus of cawing as they delighted in the cool of the day. The crows were a fixture all about Taxila, and their evening chorus was a marker of time for the townspeople: evening was approaching. And, as on each evening, the monks returned from their daily labors. Some had been out begging, as was expected of followers of the Lord Buddha. Some had been out working in the fields. Still others had been out teaching the sangha and the people or just praying and meditating. And so too did Xenophon sadly make his way back to the monastery and his brethren.

As the priests entered the great hall, Master Rinpoche was on the dais. As the monks, acolytes, novices, and priests began to chant, Master Rinpoche noted the presence of the acolyte Xenophon. Xenophon's eyes were searching the dais, fearful and lost. As he did so, his eyes met the eyes of Master Rinpoche. Their eyes locked.

Master Rinpoche smiled reassuringly at the young man, holding his gaze for a moment. The gesture was powerful and meaningful to the young man. Xenophon suddenly felt the release of his burdens. Xenophon, deacon of Christ no more. Xenophon, follower of the Lord Buddha.

Chapter 18

⚬

*And he said to them: Judas Thomas the Apostle of the
new God commands you: Let four of you come, of whom
I have need. And when the wild asses heard it, they ran
with one accord and came to him, and when they came, they
did him reverence.*

—The Acts of Thomas: Chapter 70

RAM STAYED STILL in the brush. Frozen, but with every muscle
tense, as he studied the near horizon. The young man was covered
in dung and mud, bending under the brush of an acacia bush for
cover. Three of his young companions just behind him watched
silently. Before him was a great herd of wild asses. The People of the
Wild Asses protected these herds and in return were rewarded with
meat, skins, fuel, and sometimes, even draft animals, although that
was controversial among the people. Not all shamans agreed that
trapping the spirit of the wild ass was the right thing to do. They
believed that all things should run free.

The most important task of the people was to protect the herds.
The well-being of the people relied on the well-being of the herds.

Sometimes, this was an easy matter. If the people alerted the herd to the presence of a predator, that was all it took. The animals would save themselves and either fight or flee from the danger. Seeing the animals flee was exactly what was on Ram's mind today, fleeing, and the problem of predatory lions.

Just upwind from him, he could see three lionesses moving in close to the herd. The lionesses were amazingly strategic and intelligent. They would attempt to drive the herd towards others of their kind and ambush one or more of the hoofed animals. Each of the lions hugged the ground with their bodies, slowly crawling forward within the grass, inch by inch. Their muscles were tensed and ready to explosively charge upon their prey.

The plains of Kutch were hot and arid in the summer. The grass was dry and brown, providing excellent cover for the lionesses. Ram could see that the attack by the lionesses was imminent, and after waiting patiently, he suddenly decided to take bold action. Turning and signaling his companions with a nod of his head, spears in one hand, bow and arrows in the other, the men, all four of them nearly bleached white from the concoction they had smeared on their bodies to disguise their smell, suddenly stood up to be seen. Every adult ass within a two-hundred-meter radius abruptly raised its head and looked about towards these strange humans with whom they had a symbiotic relationship. Their presence alone would not cause them to run, but the abruptness of their actions was alarming.

Ram and his companions then ran hard in the direction of the lionesses, yelling and shouting, waving their weapons as they ran. The asses, now on high alert, were tensed, ready for flight. The lionesses, knowing their cover was blown, suddenly stood up in the grass. As they did so, all five hundred and fifty-two wild asses, young and old, turned and ran off in one direction, in unison, not unlike a school of fish avoiding a predator. The sudden movement kicked up a huge dust cloud, as the animals charged off, generating a thunderous sound for all to hear. As soon as the herd moved, Ram and his companions stopped running at the lions. Ram looked at his companions, smiling and laughing with delight at their success.

The lionesses, now numbering five, spread out over a quarter kilometer, fully revealed themselves. They stood up, two of them half-heartedly still trotting forward in the general direction of the fleeing prey. They quickly stopped and turned, knowing their efforts were in vain. Looking in the direction of the humans who had so strangely popped up in their midst, all five snarled their frustration at these human spoilers. For the lionesses, there was nothing to do but regroup and try again. By nightfall, they would be ready.

Not far away, Captain Siphor called a halt to the march. His caravan was increasingly facing dangerous circumstances. Water was in short supply. The great lake he had heard about had nearly dried up, and what water remained was brackish and salty to the taste. The heat was overbearing. In his haste to move quickly to the south and make the port on the gulf, he had gone through almost all his horses and other livestock. The summer heat was just too much, and he had been running his stock too hard. He had heard that this route could be done, and indeed there were guides in his caravan who had done so. However, not at this speed, which was becoming a disaster. It was killing the draft animals. Captain Siphor spit into the dirt and threw his staff hard to the ground in frustration, cursing. He had not accounted for all these factors.

"I just want to get home, God," he implored quietly. *"I just want to see my family. Bring me a miracle. I want to see them healed."*

A halt was called, welcome news for most of the caravan. The captain regained his composure and began organizing a more permanent camp to reestablish order. He also sent out scouts to identify local tribal people who might be willing to sell them all manner of livestock, including horses and camels. He even considered attempting to capture some of the wild asses he had seen in large numbers in the area. He had people with him who could break them and then put them to work pulling the loads. Such an endeavor would take time, and Siphor unhappily realized he might have to take that time. He cursed himself again for being so foolish and trying to run so hard.

As Siphor went about his business, several of the scouts, some very familiar with the region, came and briefed him on the local population, pointing out in the distance various thorny corrals that until now Siphor had not realized were actually inhabited by people. At a distance, most of these corrals looked like natural thickets of impenetrable thorns. He now realized that these corrals had been deliberately planted and constructed to keep out wild animals. Within their enclosures, some held what amounted to groups of extended families. The larger corrals held what were essentially small villages. One scout had run into Ram and his companions and invited them into the camp to meet Siphor as well as Apostle Thomas.

While most caravans passed around Kutch, occasionally they did try to march through the area. When they did move through, Ram was always cautious when contacting them at first, because some were less friendly than others. However, Siphor's scouts proved to be friendly enough, and it was clear to Ram that his presence was welcomed. For the tribal people, living in harsh desert conditions, a friendly caravan loaded with trade goods was very welcome.

The appearance and way of living of these people was startling to Thomas. Although he had encountered tribal people on his journey before, these people were unique. They had wattle and daub huts covered in dung, mostly recovered from the wild asses and the cattle they owned. Even the floor of the huts was covered in dung that had been specially prepared and dried, creating a soft, carpet-like surface. They kept their livestock, including cattle, goats, and asses, in high, thorny corrals they constructed around their huts. They called themselves the "People and Brothers of the Wild Asses" and seemed to take pride in that.

The tribal people of Kutch lived between the great civilizations to the east and those to the west. The great lakebed of the region filled up during the rainy season and then dried out in hot summers. Most of the small bands of tribal people were related, and most were pastoralists like the People of the Wild Asses. Great herds of animals lived on the margins of this desert, often following the track of water as it receded after the great rains and then migrating to wetter zones. Many of the nomadic bands followed the herds, protecting them but also living off them.

As it became clearer and clearer that the travelers wanted to speak to the people and desired help, Ram notified the elders. Captain Siphor was clearly in charge, but Ram saw that great deference was given to Apostle Thomas too. Speaking through one of the scouts, Ram invited Thomas and Captain Siphor to the largest of the corrals. Siphor was delighted, hoping to purchase additional animals and perhaps talk these strange men into helping him reach the coast. The huts of the "people" were dark affairs, surprisingly cool, but nonetheless impractical as a meeting place.

Captain Siphor elected to wait to meet these men after sundown. It was just too hot to do it any other way. Establishing his camp not far from this largest of corrals, he was able to walk easily over to the corral with the aid of torches and his guides, escorted by their new friend Ram. Upon entering the corral, Ram directed the two honored guests to sit in front of one of the structures on woven reed mats placed on the ground for just that purpose. Fires and torches all around lit the night sky. Moments later, three older tribals appeared, nodding to these exotic visitors as they sat down in front of them. Smiling, they said little, unsure how to greet these foreigners who did not speak their common tongue.

Each man wore nothing more than a narrow loin cloth with colorful bands around their arms and legs. Equally, each had broken teeth, and one of the elders sported a large, swollen stomach. None spoke Gandhari or even a dialect of Persian, but the tribal people did speak a form of Kaatchi, the common trade language everyone locally used for commerce. Several of the scouts could speak the language, and one acted as an interpreter for Siphor.

As Siphor consulted with his scout before speaking, one of the elders suddenly stood up. This man, long white hair flowing, pointed at Thomas and began chanting. Soon, the entire village was looking at Thomas and clapping and singing happily.

Both Thomas and Siphor looked at the interpreter for help. What were these people saying? Their manner was festive, so they did not feel threatened.

"They are speaking a tribal dialect and not the Kaatchi I know," the interpreter responded. "But I think they are saying that Thomas is the messenger of one of the Gods." Surprise and even concern were written on his face. He turned and queried Ram, who responded immediately. "Yes," the scout affirmed more confidently. "I do not know how they know this, but they know our holy man Thomas." The scout's demeanor changed, and he smiled and laughed lightly. "They know Thomas is the healer of the king's brother as well as many other things about him. I know about the works of Thomas from my own travels, but somehow news of Thomas has already arrived here. They know him," he stated firmly, looking puzzled. "Another caravan must have traveled through here and shared some of the news of Gandhara with them."

Thomas smiled back at the man and bowed his head in his direction. The old man, delighted that he had identified Thomas and had even received an acknowledgment, sat down grinning broadly. News of Thomas' fame and the healing of the Prince of Gandhara had traveled far and wide. Even in distant Kutch, the story was still being told.

"It seems your presence here is indeed fortuitous, Thomas," remarked Siphor. "Remarkable." He shook his head. "Hopefully, these tribals will be disposed to help us. They live in a very primitive state, but I also see they have many animals. Better yet, they know how to handle them," he added, matter-of-factly. Turning to the scout, Siphor asked, "Ask them for guides and help with our journey. We have a long way to go, and we barely know where we are. These men know this desert and the region well. They can help us cross the desert safely and find the port on the other side. We need to find good water too. We will pay them."

While none spoke Gandhari, some knew enough words to understand his last sentence about paying them. Siphor noted that his comment produced smiles from many Kutchis who heard him. He immediately resolved not to speak so openly about payment in any language in the future.

The scout, taking the liberty to explain the situation to the people, did more than translate the captain's words. He laid out the problems the caravan was facing and explained how the people could help. When it was again reaffirmed and clearly understood that Siphor was prepared to pay for the assistance, cooperation was immediately forthcoming.

The chief offered up Ram's services, plus three other young men as guides, the very same young men who along with Ram had earlier protected the herd and spoiled the hunt by the lions that morning. The chief also agreed to sell them dozens of asses and cattle to use, although he explained that the asses were his children. Once the asses had taken the caravan to the coast, the asses would have to be returned to Ram, who would see they made the return journey back to Kutch.

The fortunes of the caravan changed dramatically with the new alliance with the desert dwellers. The caravan was embraced by dozens of corrals in the area. Soon, caravan trading goods were packed and repacked on fresh animals, water and watering holes were visited, and a more comfortable journey finally seemed possible.

In addition to assistance with the livestock, the tribal people helped the caravan replenish food supplies. Siphor was amazed at all the produce they were able to pull from the desert.

More than a few young tribal maidens visited the caravan camps and reciprocally welcomed caravan drivers, horsemen, and scouts to their own corrals, night fires, and sleeping mats. In most cases, these liaisons happened under the watchful and delighted eyes of elders and parents, who had turned their own hut over to the respected visitors. And many of these liaisons resulted in young women carrying a valued child as a parting gift from these rare and important travelers.

Interlude

The IndiGo Jet landed at Cochin International Airport mid-morning. Lieutenant Orna Kiretz and her boyfriend Isaac had already passed through immigration and customs in Mumbai. The young couple was looking forward to a week of sun and sand on the exotic beaches of South India. Orna could feel the difference the minute she walked off the plane. The air was lush and tropical. She absolutely needed this break: the beach, houseboats, exotic food, a spa, and relaxation!

"My name is George," the small, distinguished-looking man was saying, reaching out to shake their hands. George had a twinkle in his eye and almost a mischievous grin hiding in his face. He had the air of an unemployed college professor. Orna and Isaac had just walked out of the baggage hall and into a large covered open-air plaza and packed shopping mall that doubled as the arrivals and departures area for all passengers traveling in and out of Cochin. As only India can be, the place was organized, noisy, smelly, and bustling, but still welcoming.

"Nice to meet you, George," responded Orna. "This is Isaac. So where are you parked?"

The conversation was brief until they had loaded the baggage into the minivan.

"This is your driver, Aruna," said George, motioning to the young man behind the wheel of the van. "I'm not your driver, I'm your guide," he added.

Orna smiled, nodding to both. George seemed nice enough and began to chat earnestly about all the things they could see and do in the great state of Kerala in India. A distinguished, elderly man, he had been in the tourist trade for many years, welcoming foreigners to his corner of the world. Orna soon learned that George was indeed originally trained as a college professor. He had become unemployed and shifted gears to become a tour guide.

"Better money," he explained to the Israelis.

Curious, Orna asked, "So George, how did you come by a Christian English name? I would have expected you to have an Indian name like Raja or something." As usual, Orna did most of the talking, while Isaac listened in and only offered supporting comments.

George was accustomed to odd and sometimes inappropriate questions from tourists but was delighted to answer, anyway.

"I'm a Thomas Christian," he said proudly. "If we have time, I'll take you to see some of the important tourist sights, both Christian and Jewish. You're Israelis, correct?" George omitted pointing out that George was not actually a Christian name either.

"Kerala is the only state in India with a very large Christian population," he continued, momentarily forgetting the State of Goa and other locations. "The only," he repeated for emphasis, wobbling his head back and forth proudly in customary South Indian fashion. "And that is why we're also one of the richest," he announced firmly with no explanation.

"Thomas Christians?" Orna responded back. "Never heard of them. Is there a big difference between Thomas Christians and Catholics? Yes, we're Israelis and not up on all that."

George laughed. "Thomas Christians! We are the descendants of the first converts of Apostle Thomas. We number in the millions, we are so many. My Apostle Thomas came here after the crucifixion of Christ. Our history goes back two thousand years." His voice was bursting with pride as he described his people. "There are so many things you can see here."

"I didn't know," answered Orna thoughtfully, noting George's use of "my" when referring to Apostle Thomas. "Interesting. I'm looking forward to visiting the synagogue and maybe other sites, but yes, tell us all about these Thomas Christians too."

"Yes, madam. Later today, I will take you to the Paradesi Synagogue and Museum. Most interesting place! And if we have time, I will take you to the Mar Thoma Pontifical Shrine too. It's even sanctioned by the Pope and the Catholic Church! There is a holy relic there. The right hand of Apostle Thomas is kept there. We have it." George beamed proudly.

Isaac perked up at the thought of visiting these historic places. Orna smiled wanly at the macabre thought of visiting the right hand, a body part, of a long-dead Hebrew in India. She had seen lots of shrines in her day. Jerusalem was filled with shrines. *Still,* she thought, *how on earth did one of her ancient countrymen find his way to this beautiful but distant place?* She found herself wondering why people couldn't all just get along. If Christians and Hindus could find peace, maybe there was hope for Arabs and Jews too?

Chapter 19

"All we are is what we have thought."

—*The Lord Buddha, as quoted from the opening lines of
the Dhammapada*

THE REMAINDER OF the journey to the port of Bharuch on the Indian
Sea was long and hard, but with the help provided by the Kutchi tribal people, the situation was much improved. Ram and his brothers
proved to be good guides, and there was little additional drama on the
remainder of the journey to the coast. Thomas' days were dominated
by long, hot, dusty periods riding in chariots, bullock carts, and occasionally walking on foot, a method of transportation that the Apostle
of the "One God" always preferred. Ram knew all the watering holes
and grazing sites for the animals between the interior and the coast. If
he didn't know, he had such an affinity to the land that he could sense
where water or a passage ought to be. The young Kutchi proved to be
a jovial, positive traveling partner and was regularly sought out by the
herdsmen, particularly for advice on the care and feeding of livestock.

Two weeks later, the caravan finally arrived in Bharuch, only to
find that Abbanes was already there, making preparations for their

continuing journey to the south. Abbanes had taken the more sensible and established trade route, which mostly tracked with the Indus River. When Thomas and Captain Siphor had hastily left Taxila, Abbanes took his time. He was much more interested in being sure that all his affairs were in order and that his journey was well organized. His organization created speed.

The Hebrew was privately amused at the delay of the earlier caravan and was sorely tempted to point out to Captain Siphor how rushing about often makes waste, one of the great wisdoms of King Solomon. He soon dismissed the idea as too paternalistic. *Undoubtedly, Siphor now fully understands his mistake,* he mused, chuckling to himself. His delight was also generated by his sense of relief that Thomas was safely out of Taxila and no longer in real danger from assassins.

Captain Siphor's caravan set up a temporary camp near the port, while Abbanes and Siphor set about arranging for the transfer of all the trade goods to the ships that would take them on to Muziris. Thomas had become accustomed to the rhythms of caravan life and found himself in the familiar position of being shouldered aside, as master loaders, sailors, and laborers took over the process of transferring cargo from bullock carts, camels, asses, and other beasts of burden to the ships.

Left on his own, he wandered about the port city, discovering that, unlike Taxila, Lord Buddha was far from being the primary religion in this city. In Taxila, Buddhism was the dominant religion, even though there were many gods and religions observed there. The very architecture style of Taxila reflected this, with most buildings displaying dominant Buddhist structures and a distinct skyline. Here in Bharuch, the Nazarene discovered there were many deities but only a handful of Buddhist temples. Many of the shrines and temples were dedicated to gods he was unfamiliar with, carved into stone or formed by clay images. Many shrines appeared to be linked to a goddess named Lakshmi. Thomas also found temples dedicated to Ahura Mazda, Ganesha the elephant-headed god, and Shiva. These were gods he knew little about and considered their images an abomination. He had come to realize that with every kilometer he traveled to the east and south, more and more people appeared to be pagan in his eyes and worshipped elaborate idols and other strange gods. As the apostle walked about the city, he realized he was unable to clearly distinguish or define the Hindus he was encountering. He failed to understand the complex world he was entering and tended to place them all into one category—that of idol worshippers.

The biggest shrine in the city was dedicated to the goddess named Lakshmi. Thomas visited the temple and quietly observed the religious practices. He found the symbolic puja offerings repugnant and unintelligible, with lots of chanting and bell ringing. Devotees lit lamps in front of her image, prayed, and made offerings of flowers, food, money, and other goods.

Observing the rather alien approach to the worship of God, Thomas suddenly felt tired. He knew his calling was to go to Muziris and Cranganore in the south, but he also knew that the calling was not going to be easy. Once again, Thomas felt like a stranger in a strange land, as doubts crept into his mind. All the activity was too much for him. He walked to the edge of the town and found a quiet place to pray. Great stone boulders lay jumbled along a hillside. He found a shaded area under one such rock and knelt down to talk to his God. After praying for an hour, he felt his mind becoming clearer and his energy returning.

The quiet time presented him with the chance to reflect on the journey he had taken from Jerusalem. He missed his brother and hoped he was in the region somewhere. *Where is Isa? Has Isa finally abandoned me and returned to Judea?* he wondered. He knew he could do nothing to find his brother. He committed himself to using his time in Bharuch to pray and regain his strength and courage. He would not preach here. The decision to minister to his own needs gave him a sense of relief.

Thomas' decision not to preach in Bharuch also brought a big sigh of relief to Abbanes. The people in Bharuch were generally tolerant, but he knew that both he and Thomas would not have the same royal cover and protection that they had in Taxila. There were citizens of all the world here in Bharuch, representing many religions, ideologies, and forms of worship. And he knew the Hindu priests themselves were generally tolerant, but he also knew they could not always control the people. Religious poaching among the various beliefs would likely break the peace. And they might interpret Thomas' sermons and healings as an attempt to steal their followers and bring them into a false religion, he contemplated. *Many would not likely take kindly to some of the practices of my fellow Hebrew.* They might take particular offense to his obsessive views on male and female relations. He shook his head slightly, as he thought about this and smiled wryly. *How can Thomas really think such a belief is even feasible? It seems so unnatural. Something terrible had happened on his journey that had driven him to this view. What? Still, despite his imperfect views, he understands how to tap into the divine, evidenced by his inexplicable power to heal.*

The Hebrew trader was also increasingly worried about how the Jewish community in Muziris would receive a man like Thomas, whose views of God deviated significantly from the established view of Yahweh, the one who was so holy that his very name could not be uttered. Thomas was advocating something more than an updated Hebrew doctrine. He was advocating and preaching an entirely new religion—one associated with the Hebrews but that still had no name.

Abbanes continued to think of both himself and the apostle as representatives of the Hebrews, as they traveled the world. He also knew that people would always look to categorize strangers and travelers, partially to consider whether or not the visitor represented a threat of some kind. Hebrews were a known people. Thus, Abbanes and Thomas would always be "Hebrews" or "Jews," whether accurate or not, to most people they encountered.

While Abbanes had come to accept that his friend Thomas preached a new religion, he also knew it was a new dogma that his fellow Hebrews would not likely accept. *Fortunately, my good Apostle Thomas seems to recognize that he does not need to preach here in Bharuch,* Abbanes considered with some relief. The thought stayed in the front of his mind and all that he did. *I am hopeful that we will find more tolerant and open minds in the south,* was his constant wish and silent prayer.

Thomas remained melancholy and withdrawn for a few days, learning about and adapting to the new land around him. After visiting the city and observing the many different forms of worship, the apostle returned to the margins of the temporary camp of Captain Siphor and waited there for the final sailing to the port of Muziris in the south.

The ships were ready in a matter of days, all heavily loaded. Abbanes was once again in his element, his robes flapping in the breeze as he, along with Captain Siphor, shouted orders from the deck of their command ship.

And once again, Apostle Thomas sailed to a new city. As he boarded the craft and found his accustomed resting place out of the way of sailors, he remembered the first day of his great journey to India. He had boarded a craft at Alexandria on the mighty Nile River. Isa had been with him then. *Not this time,* he thought almost sadly. *He was traveling far on his own.* As the craft maneuvered out of the port of Muziris and to sea for the journey south, Thomas studied each boat, half expecting to see the figure of Isa sitting serenely on the deck of one of the ships, his hair gently waving in the breeze.

It was a good image, thought Thomas. *But Isa is not here.*

Chapter 20

"Primal Shakti, I bow to You!
All-Encompassing Shakti, I bow to You!
That through which Divine Creates, I bow to You!
Creative Power of the Kundalini, Mother of all Mother
Power, To You I Bow!"

—*Mantra of Adi Parashakti*

DRESSED IN A fine white dhoti, Pandit Natarajan sat on the floor, his legs firmly crossed. It was still early, and he was taking his morning chai. He had completed all his ablutions and meditations and was preparing for the day ahead. His knees seemed to unnaturally bend out from his body, the result of a lifetime of sitting comfortably cross-legged for extended periods of time.

Natarajan used his time each morning to meditate, some days selecting a complex subject, other days meditating with a clear mind. This morning, he had considered aspects of the story of Lord Ganesha and the absolute proof of the power of the feminine embedded in it: the power of the Goddess Parvati, mother of Ganesha. The story was that Lord Shiva, Ganesha's father, was away from his wife

Parvati for a long period of time and did not know he had a new son, Ganesha. Upon discovering him and thinking he was an imposter, Shiva promptly cut off his head. Parvati rushed to her son's aid, but she was too late. The all-powerful deity Shiva, in his grief and upon learning the truth, elected to replace the head of Ganesha with the head of the first creature he saw. The first creature he encountered was an elephant.

"But the real power of the story is the feminine," Natarajan reflected. "Parvati made Lord Ganesha from the earth and then saved him from certain death.

His young niece, a teen dressed in a simple sari, dutifully brought him his morning meal wrapped in a banana leaf. Spreading the leaf on the floor in front of him, she unfolded the bread she had moments earlier pulled from the flat pan. She then ladled out a portion of yellow dhal onto the broad green leaf, making sure to cover parts of the flat bread too. She then placed a ripe banana on the top of the leaf. She walked back out of the room. Natarajan, using only his fingers, slowly began to eat his meal.

He considered the day before him. Muziris had become an international port for many people, and his diverse community was growing ever more complex. Pandit Natarajan was a devotee of Lord Shiva and especially that of his consort, the Goddess Parvati. His calm understanding of the world taught him the truth of universal tolerance and Right Thinking. He knew that the essence of most religions could be accepted as true. Ultimately, there was only one holy power in the universe, and all true religions led there. The power of women was also fundamental to his understanding. Men became lost in egos, war, and domination. Those were all paths to destruction. The feminine aspect of Shiva was far more tolerant and powerful and brought peace to the world.

The growing and diverse religious community of Muziris would regularly meet in different forums. It was always up to Pandit Natarajan, the senior religious leader of the community, to keep the peace during those times. Many were caught up in the dogma and bigotry of their own narrow religious beliefs. The small Jewish community generally kept to themselves and said little, not engaging in any dialogue. Yet, there were fierce debates between some of his priests and those of the Lord Buddha. *They are both wrong,* he would often think. Some of his own followers forgot that what the pujas carried out was actually just symbolic of the divine. Likewise, many of the Buddhist adherents often forgot that the Buddha himself was tolerant and commanded his followers to be open-minded and to question dogma and beliefs.

Natarajan knew the Buddha was a divine incarnation of Vishnu. He also knew the teachings of the Buddha better than the Buddha's own devotees, and he would often remind them of their own teachings. Natarajan always prayed to Parvati for her divine power and wisdom in these matters. He was a firm believer that there was room for all worshippers and all religions – in one word, tolerance. Tolerance was fundamental to peace and prosperity for all humankind.

As Natarajan finished his morning meal and looked out upon the sea, Thomas unknowingly looked right back at him from the distant gunwales of his ship, still far off shore. The apostle carefully studied the shoreline as it came into view, forming his first impressions of what he assumed would be his new home. He could see the great river, called the Periyar, along with settlements all around. A large herd of mud-blackened, domesticated water buffalo lounged by the riverbank. In the distance, on the far side of the herd, Thomas could see two tiny figures on the banks, likely boys no more than six years old he guessed. The boys were armed with sticks and used them to swat at the great bovines. Despite their size, the relatively massive animals obediently and tolerantly allowed their small handlers to direct them about. Further down, he could see two elephants carefully walking down the shallow embankment. Each elephant sported a young mahout, riding their mounts as the animals joyously entered the cooling waters of the river. To Thomas, all this activity was a stunning and exotic sight.

This land looked different from anything he had seen earlier. He found the humidity from the sea and the accompanying heat stifling. It was hard for him to imagine that this land could ever feel cold. Much of the land was covered in tall palm trees with dense shrubs and green forest. Near the mouth of the river, the craft was able to enter a large lagoon with clear calm waters. As they approached the shore, like so many other times in other ports, half a dozen smaller boats immediately took to the water to greet them. Thomas had become accustomed to this routine. Soon, these small boats were alongside them, offering the travelers fruit and other goods for sale.

Abbanes, one foot on the gunwale, arms folded, greeted the vendors with a broad smile. He good-naturedly bartered with one and soon had a small woven palm basket of fruit in his arms. He tossed individual mangoes to the crew and then one to Thomas. Thomas, unfamiliar with this fruit, watched as the men tore into the ripe fruit with their bare teeth, a real treat.

"Mango season," said Abbanes simply, beaming as he looked over at Thomas.

In short order, the craft were in the port, and the entire operation turned into an unloading and logistics enterprise. Captain Siphor was clearly in charge and back in his home element, but also anxious to be off to see his wife and daughter.

After only half an hour, he handed off responsibility to several port officials and then, grabbing Thomas by the arm, pulled him into an ornate bullock cart. He commanded the driver to take him to his home. It was clear that Captain Siphor's arrival at the port had not gone unnoticed. His family and indeed his entire household were out waiting for him, smiles on their faces. There, standing at the gate, were his beautiful wife and daughter, dressed in saris. Seeing both women healthy before his eyes, he embraced them, weeping with happiness. To his complete astonishment, they were healed! The terrible marks and scars on his wife and daughter seemed to be gone. More importantly, he realized that their spirit of well-being and safety had returned. When he looked into their eyes, he saw joy, something that had been missing for a long time.

His two women, the center of his life, had been brutalized and harmed. Now, they were whole again. His women were strong again. The two women gave thanks to the power of the divine feminine and explained they had been worshipping in the temple of Parvati when the miracle happened.

Thomas, not fully understanding the language spoken, heard the women say "Parvati" and then apparently describe the idol and worship of that god. While not completely understanding the conversation, he understood enough to realize that Siphor's wife was crediting a foreign god for their healing. Shaking his head, but still smiling, the apostle interjected quickly, "Give thanks to the one true God." He was still struggling with the concept of religion in India. Hearing the words of this woman underscored to Thomas how important his mission was.

Siphor embraced his wife in an extremely rare show of public affection. Some of the staff looked on in wonderment at this breach in social etiquette. The captain glanced at Thomas before turning to his wife, speaking in Tamil. He explained what had happened in Taxila and more, that their healing must have come from the new great God, "the Christ," and his apostle, Thomas. Before he could explain further, the entire happy party was ushered into the home for a celebratory meal, Siphor's now happy daughter taking his hand and leading the way.

Siphor's home was the home of an adherent to the Goddess. There were also images of Shiva and of Ganesha with his elephant head as he rode upon his mount, a mouse. Siphor insisted that Thomas stay with him that night and longer if he wished.

"I accept your hospitality, Captain," answered Thomas graciously. Then he added, "Tomorrow, let us all go the river so that I may baptize you and your family into the Kingdom of God."

This request continued a discussion the two men had been having during the voyage. Now that Siphor could see that his beloved wife and daughter were truly healed, he could do nothing else but be baptized under the banner of this new God.

"Yes, Thomas, let us all go together to the river tomorrow," answered Siphor. "Today, let us rest from our long journey."

That was a suggestion that Thomas readily agreed to. Captain Siphor was exhausted from all his labors.

After the meal, Thomas was escorted to a central guest room in the captain's large house. The open yard of the house was alive with activity. Peacocks and other fowl had the run of the grounds and were constantly creating a din. Small children and servants rushed back and forth. Women could be seen arriving with clay pots of water, bundles of produce, and stacks of firewood.

Still at the port, Abbanes secured his trade goods and set about meeting with his Jewish community contacts in the city. They were expecting him and were overjoyed that they would again have an opportunity to conduct business with the famous trader from distant Gandhara. Abbanes always brought wealth, opportunity, prestige, and news from the outside world. He had even been to Jerusalem, the holy city! How much he could tell them.

Seth appeared at the port and embraced Abbanes. "We are so overjoyed to see you again, my friend," he said.

The two men continued to talk for a while, sharing news and stories from both worlds. News from Jerusalem was especially prized. Abbanes recounted his visit to the holy city in great detail, realizing he would need to repeat the tale many times in the coming days. Abbanes also told him of the man of God he had brought with him, Thomas the Nazarene. Seth looked sideways at Abbanes at the mention of the apostle and shook his head.

"We need to talk about that, Abbanes." His voice was guarded and flat after his keen excitement about the news from Jerusalem. "You are most welcome here, and you even worship in our synagogue with us. In many ways, you are one of us. Your family is here. Yet, now you bring this heretic to us. We have heard of this twin brother of Isa, this Nasrani. We do not like what we hear about this man. He even says the name of God. How can a Hebrew use the name of God like that, the one so holy his very name cannot be spoken? Some say he even is to be worshipped as God. You know that is not the truth and not what we believe. How can a man be God?"

Abbanes listened attentively to his friend but said nothing. Seth continued more soberly. "As a practical matter, his preaching and shaman practices might make things difficult for all of us with these Brahmins." Seth pronounced the word "Brahmin" with a trace of scorn in his tone. Seth referred to all Hindus, Jains, and sometimes even followers of Buddha as Brahmins. He considered all beliefs other than the one true belief in the God of the Hebrews to be abominations. While thinking as such, the Hebrew community survived by being discreet and not announcing their views. Their strategy was to remain apart and distant. They made no attempt to proselytize the local population—a strategy appreciated by all.

Abbanes continued to listen to his friend but said little. He now realized how difficult it was going to be to reconcile his own people with the outspoken preaching and personality of Thomas. He had expected some resistance from the local Hebrew population, but he had not expected it to be this fervent or this quick. Abbanes also did not want to do anything that would jeopardize his good relations with these people. He came often enough that he even had a young wife and children in the town too. He could not afford to make it difficult for them, because he was gone most of the time. They were always looked after by the community in his absence, in part because the Hebrew fathers valued and respected Abbanes.

Chapter 21

"Let there be one scripture only, one common scripture for the whole world. —Bhagavad Gita. Let there be one God for the whole world. —Sri Krishna."

—Lord Krishna in the Bhagavad Gita

THE NEXT DAY, Thomas, along with Siphor and his entire household, walked down to the river. The path was well traveled and neatly maintained. A steady stream of people made their way back and forth to this vital source of fresh water. In Cranganore and throughout Muziris, it was the custom for the men to go to one place on the river upstream and for the women to go to another place downstream, one that was better suited for them to wash clothes, lay them out on the rocks to dry, bathe children, and when time allowed, bathe themselves. As the party began to separate by gender, Thomas stopped and motioned that the entire household was to follow him to the women's area. The entrance to the river was shallower there, and one could easily walk to deeper water.

With the entire household standing on the banks of the river watching, Thomas took each member by the hand one at a time, and praying over them, led them into the slightly murky, waist-deep water. He placed his hands upon their head and supported their back while he briefly submerged them, baptizing each in the name of Christ and the Lord of Hosts. He chanted in Aramaic, using the words he had heard Isa say in prayer so many times. This strange foreign ritual attracted the attention of many of the local people, who gathered to watch along the banks, impressed by the exotic and new religious ritual. Captain Siphor's presence added still more legitimacy to the proceedings, in case some might be offended by Thomas conducting the ceremony where the women normally bathed. The act of baptizing Captain Siphor's household was anti-climactic, yet it began a Christian tradition that would endure through the ages.

Abbanes was up early too, arriving at Siphor's home just as the party returned from the baptism. As was his custom when entering a new port, Abbanes' first priority was to visit with the local authorities. In this case, it was Prince Charisius, younger brother of King Misdaeus. He thought it would be important to bring Thomas with him and help him meet as many influential people in the community as possible. Abbanes had already decided that he would try to avoid or at least delay a meeting between Thomas and Seth, fearing any meeting with the resident Hebrew community would not go well. He was hoping the Brahmins would prove to be more tolerant. Siphor excused himself from the meeting with Prince Charisius, saying he had other responsibilities and was expected to meet with King Misdaeus himself later in the afternoon. Thomas readily agreed to all the arrangements. He was still considering how best he could begin his great ministry. The healing of Captain Siphor's women and the baptism of his household greatly raised his spirits.

Thomas walked by the side of Abbanes to the meeting, indicating to all who saw them that Thomas was an equal. Thomas realized that while the title of the prince was impressive; he also had the distinct impression this kingdom was more modest than the kingdom he had encountered in Gandhara. The buildings were not as impressive.

Prince Charisius turned out to be an enormous man, fatter than anyone Thomas had seen in all his travels. The prince's girth was such that his form appeared to be completely round. Adding to the effect, he was short in stature and consequently struggled to even walk. He constantly required two attendants to stay with him whose primary job was to balance him when he moved about. He could no longer sit on a horse easily or stand steadily on his chariot. A journey to the temple was painful, and so most often, he asked the pandits and priests to come to him.

His great and obsessive impulse was to eat. His traders brought him exotic foods from all over the earth, even from China. While he labeled himself as a "prince," and his brother as "King Raja Misdaeus," they both acknowledged the sovereignty of the more powerful Tamilakam kings to the east. As long as the brothers kept the coastal trade open and the ports functioning, all prospered. If they failed in that one job, Charisius knew that he would be "prince" no more.

As fat and grotesque as he was, he was generally thought of as kind and tolerant by the people. He rarely interfered in religious matters and preferred to leave governing to others. He was surrounded by wise and tolerant religious leaders who helped him keep the peace. However, his supporters did not include members of his own household, who were subject to all his private horrors. Charisius' appetite for perverted sexual pleasure matched his grotesque appetite for food. And to satisfy that terrible urge, he forced all his wives and concubines, including the princess, to carry out whatever deviant impulse seemed to please him.

For the wives, especially Princess Mygdonia, the prince's behavior was nothing less than horrifying. Every week, there was some new terror that often involved the obese prince finding some kind of sexual gratification at their expense. The princess was still young, having been taken by the prince in marriage when she was still a teen. Having borne two sons for the prince, her most important function in life was now complete. She earnestly looked forward to the day when the prince was in such terrible health that he would not be able to function sexually, a condition she expected to occur soon because of his terrible diet.

Thomas and Abbanes were ushered into a small holding room as they waited to meet with the prince. Their meeting was nothing more than a courtesy. Abbanes knew that a gift was expected, and he had prepared a gold medallion, claiming it was from King Gondophores, as a special personal gift for the prince, as well as several exotic food items. Of course, King Gondophores knew of no such gift for this minor regent in distant Muziris. Abbanes, always thinking ahead, thought it best to show this prince his good standing with other powerful men and to play to his ego as well.

After a short wait, the men were further directed into the principal chamber of the palace. Here, the Hebrew visitors found Prince Charisius laid out on a divan with stuffed cushions to support his immense form. He was dressed in a finely embroidered gold and blue cloak, the royal robes so broad they could have doubled as bed-sheets for most men. On close inspection, one could see the robes were slightly soiled with food stains. Unable to sit up properly, the prince propped up his head with his arm and rested the back of his head on a large pillow. Speaking in a soft, high-pitched voice, he welcomed the visitors and invited them to come forward.

Princess Mygdonia was unable to sit with her husband on the divan since his body was so large, so she sat on a separate especially prepared divan just for her and several other ladies in attendance. She watched the proceedings with care, studying Thomas in particular, seeing a handsome man in his prime. The princess knew nothing of Thomas but had seen Abbanes come and go on his many voyages. She loved to hear of Abbanes' travels and would sometimes dream of an impossible time when she would wake up as Abbanes' personal consort or perhaps even travel the world like a man.

Opposite the princess and across the room, sitting on a series of colorful mats, were the prince's advisors, including the Pandit Natarajan, sage and sometimes guru. Natarajan was nothing less than the unseen power at the court, the wise man and moderating mature voice all sought out in the absence of strong leadership. Natarajan watched the proceedings with interest, particularly noting Thomas, the foreigner.

Thomas in turn was shocked at the presentation of the unsavory-looking prince. *How is this miserable-looking man a prince?* he wondered. There had been no official announcement of the arrival of visitors. The palace was grand but nothing like the palaces he had seen in Gandhara, or even the one in Andrapolis for a satrap. Seeing the obese man before him, the truth was clear to him: *Here is a man who must deny himself and take up the path of the Christ. He must give up all he has and seek poverty. He must give up his physical needs and seek union with God alone.*

Abbanes greeted the prince in halting and limited Tamil, a language that Thomas did not speak but was keen to learn. The two exchanged pleasantries for a few minutes. Abbanes had been meeting with the prince for years, coming to see him on each of his trips. He had not fully mastered Tamil, but he could speak well enough to be understood. He knew his fluency was cyclic. The longer he stayed with his Tamil wife and family, the better his Tamil became. He would then leave for a year or two and soon forget some of the language until he returned.

Abbanes described his journey to the prince and discussed some of the trade items he brought with him. After an hour, and after the presentation of gifts, Prince Charisius turned his gaze to Thomas, indicating that it was an opportunity for Abbanes to introduce his companion. Abbanes, delighted to avoid talking further about trade with the prince, explained that Thomas did not speak Tamil and that he would do his best to translate for him. He explained that Thomas was a man of God, like a prophet. As soon as Abbanes said that, Charisius' eyes turned to Natarajan. He motioned him forward.

Natarajan was a well-read man and spoke many languages. He had traveled to northern India as a younger man. The pandit could manage to speak some Gandhari, although he was limited in his vocabulary. He was delighted to have the chance to use these skills again.

Thomas explained that he was an emissary of Christ, the one true God. Christ asked everyone to deny themselves and surrender their human needs and desires and seek union with him. "I have come to baptize you and guide you into the Kingdom of God," explained Thomas through his slightly puzzled interpreter. Natarajan did his best to suppress a smile and remain friendly and polite to this strange man.

Abbanes watched his friend closely as he explained his message. Having repeatedly heard the message of the apostle, Abbanes could anticipate almost exactly what Thomas was going to say. As time went on, Abbanes was increasingly unsure what he believed about Thomas. Isa had certainly been amazing. Thomas seemed to be getting caught up in some unnatural issues and was struggling to move past them. Thomas' insistence that one needed to form a union with God, even at the expense of the relationship between a husband and wife, did not sit well with him. Abbanes struggled to interpret and was assisted by Natarajan.

Natarajan was immediately struck by the fervent and impassioned words of this unusual apostle and decided to slightly temper the message, as he translated what Thomas was saying to the prince. The prince yawned as the conversation continued, making it clear that he was not interested in this discussion.

As the conversation continued, Abbanes and Natarajan looked at each other and nodded slightly. Further realizing that the prince would not appreciate elements of Thomas' unnatural dogma, the pandit strategically suggested that the prince allow him to continue discussions with Thomas in the adjoining room; the kinds of things that Thomas might raise would be of no interest to the prince. The prince readily agreed to this plan, stating he wished to retire to his chambers. He thanked the pandit for his suggestion and dismissed the visitors.

As he did so, Princess Mygdonia, more than a little intrigued by this interesting and handsome foreign man, immediately interjected that she too would like to attend this meeting with Pandit Natarajan. The prince nodded a gracious assent to her request.

Thomas, Abbanes, and the Pandit Natarajan were ushered into an adjoining chamber. This room was about half the size of the chamber was often used for private royal audiences and was less ornate. As the three men sat down, they were instructed to wait a few minutes before continuing the conversation. After a time, Princess Mygdonia herself entered the room. Seating herself near Natarajan, she nodded her assent to the pandit to begin.

"You said something very interesting, Thomas," began Natarajan, continuing the earlier conversation, as several junior priests and acolytes entered the room and seated themselves on mats in the back of the room. Natarajan had invited them, wanting to expose his community to new ideas and new ways of thinking. He spoke in Gandhari and translated generally for the princess.

"You said that we are to deny ourselves and enter the Kingdom of God through Christ. Are you not a Hebrew of the faith that says that no one may speak the very name of your God? We have a small community of Hebrews here, and I have spoken to them many times. If this is true, then your views are not those of my Hebrew neighbors. I am quite surprised by the different approach you take. You are naming your God?"

He said this last using a quizzical tone but more for emphasis. As the discussion continued, the pandit displayed only limited knowledge of the Hebrew beliefs, evidenced by his questions. He did not share the fact that most of his attempts to engage the

Hebrew community in religious discussion never got far. He was often politely but firmly rebuffed.

It was finally Thomas' turn to respond. Seeing the apparent wickedness of the prince, Thomas felt inspired. Isa had guided him here for this very purpose so that he could save these people. Now he understood his mission.

"The Lord God is named," he said with authority and finally addressing Natarajan's question. "He is the Christ. If any man is to deny his needs and follow him, he shall find the glory of God in heaven."

"What does that mean exactly?" asked the Brahmin gently. "Here, we understand the concept of self-denial. We Brahmins are particularly good at denying oneself." Natarajan said this somewhat wryly. "Our land is filled with sages and sadhus doing just that. We also have the followers of the Lord Buddha here who also believe in a form of self-denial. And then the followers of Lord Mahavira are here too. You will come to know them as the Jains. They are small in number, but some of them take such extreme vows of poverty, they don't even wear clothing and only eat a few types of vegetables!" Natarajan elected to not even raise the question of what "heaven" was, a complex question that perhaps this man of God had not fully considered.

Thomas explained, "A man must deny all his physical needs." Anticipating a response from the Brahmin and remembering his discussions with Buddhists, and the "Middle Path," he continued. "There is no Middle Path as in Buddhism. A vow of poverty is necessary. It is true, as my brother Isa once said, it is easier for a camel to pass through the eye of a needle than for a rich man to find the

Kingdom of God. And the commitment is greater still. One must choose union with Christ and be as married to him. Devotion to the one true God is essential in all things. Thus, if a man has desire for a woman, then he must deny that desire. Even if the man and the woman are married."

Thomas went on to explain how the greatest sin was fornication itself. He was tempted to explain how he had discovered this and his experiences with desiring Sarida and the resulting death and sin that had occurred, but he elected to remain silent on that issue. *Perhaps I can explain that story to the pandit some other day,* he thought.

Natarajan did not respond to Thomas immediately. He knew that the dogma and Thomas' comment about fornication between husband and wife being a sin were preposterous. *I will have to work on this man,* the Brahmin thought, knowing the apostle's views would be seen as unnatural and even heresy by most of the community. Yet, he chose to smile politely, not wishing to challenge this man on their first meeting.

Natarajan slightly raised his hand, indicating to Thomas that he should stop for a moment while he attempted to translate for Princess Mygdonia. When the princess heard that Thomas was saying that the denial of a physical union between a husband and wife was a pathway to the Kingdom of Heaven, her face lit up. She listened attentively as Thomas and Natarajan continued their conversation, with Natarajan stopping every few minutes to give a rough translation of the conversation. Neither man was a native speaker of Gandhari, and so the language skills of both men were being stretched.

Yet, for most of the discussion, the main point was clear: the importance of self-denial. Fornication was the greatest sin. For the princess, the prospect of not needing to satiate her husband's deviant sexual cravings animated her. She had originally looked at Thomas as a young woman looked at a handsome man, a young woman unhappy with her marriage partner. She now looked at him for religious succor.

"Natarajan," she finally said. "I need to return to the prince. However, I find this man interesting. Please accommodate him and ensure that we give him any assistance he needs."

Pandit Natarajan smiled back at his princess and assured her that he fully intended to do just that. After she left, the two men continued their conversation for another hour. Natarajan wanted to fully understand this man's beliefs, but during the course of the conversation, he realized that Apostle Thomas was not open to learning about Natarajan's own belief system. Perhaps that will come later. The pandit sighed.

Chapter 22

*The disciples said to Jesus, "Tell us what the Kingdom of
Heaven is like." He said to them, "It is like a mustard
seed. It is the smallest of seeds. But when it falls, on tilled
soil, it produces a great plant and becomes a shelter for the
birds of the sky."*

—*The Coptic Gospel of Thomas, Verse 20*

THOMAS THREW HIMSELF into the study of Tamil with the aid of
Captain Siphor, and before long, he was preaching the word of God
to assemblies all around Muziris. Several of Captain Siphor's servants were learned men themselves and welcomed the chance to
assist Thomas with his language studies and thereby escape from
the menial duties they were forced to perform in the captain's
household.

As Thomas preached about the Kingdom of Heaven, he began
to tap into disgruntled members of the community, especially the
various castes that felt disenfranchised. He also connected with
some Iyer Brahmins and even Buddhists who felt left out of the
power structure that was dominated by others and where they did

not have a voice. Although many were doubtful of Thomas' strange philosophy about denying oneself, many noted that some of these ideas sounded similar to what some of the sadhus and gurus said when they greeted them at their temples each day. Still others were attracted to Thomas when they heard of the miracles he performed, healing the sick and even raising people from the dead. They were all delighted that he was not asking them for money—a factor that gave him great credibility.

Pandit Natarajan spent the next few days mulling over what to do about the strange foreign sadhu. The princess had even asked for another private audience with Thomas and had asked Natarajan to arrange it and join them. Natarajan did not know with certainty what was on the mind of the young princess, but considering the condition of the corpulent prince, he could guess what her motivation might be. By becoming an adherent, a follower of Thomas, and especially if it were sanctioned by Natarajan, the princess might be able to excuse herself from her wifely duties.

Natarajan had tried to involve the Jewish community with Thomas but was repeatedly rebuffed. He quickly learned that this Hebrew had no friends there. The Isa cult was known to some of them, and none in the Hebrew community supported Thomas and his blasphemous beliefs. He might be a Hebrew, they said, but he was not one of them. He was a Nasrani. The word meant "one from Nazareth," and it had become a pejorative for some. Many did not have a good understanding of what the term meant or even that it referred to the town of Nazareth.

What to do? Natarajan meditated and pondering on the situation. Considering the circumstances, he finally settled on a new strategy. He would embrace the apostle. He would offer Thomas a place of worship, a temple the Hebrew could call his own. There were many fine temples all around Muziris and specifically in Cranganore. He would find an older, poorly utilized temple and give it to this man from Nazareth. Most of the temples had carvings and dedicated followers. Natarajan calculated that most of the followers of a temple would likely stay connected to it, especially if sanctioned by Natarajan himself. They would naturally be inclined to become his followers.

By showing him support and by physically incorporating him into the community of Hindus, Natarajan speculated, perhaps Thomas would be inclined to moderate some of his beliefs. Exposure and daily interaction with the common people as they lived their lives might cause Thomas to realize that he needed to allow for a Middle Path. He could not see why Thomas might not one day even embrace the worship of the Goddess too. *Why not try?* he thought with enthusiasm. The more he thought about the idea, the more he liked it. Generously offering him a place of worship might co-opt him and change him. This approach would also be consistent with the charge that the princess had given him—that he should take care of this man. Giving him a temple with some devotees even would certainly reinforce her instruction. His actions also fit nicely into his own philosophy of tolerance. There is room for all.

The next meeting with Princess Mygdonia and Thomas was nothing short of a surprise to Natarajan. The three met in the same chamber at the palace where they had held their first meeting. The meeting began with the princess asking for Thomas to repeat his message of God and the meaning behind it. The conversation was conducted in a mixture of Gandhari and now even some Tamil, as Thomas attempted to show that he was learning the language. Between both languages and having learned some of the vocabulary from his earlier conversation with Natarajan, Thomas was able to be more specific.

Natarajan watched the princess appear to be almost enraptured by the Hebrew and his enthusiasm for his mission. She hung on his every word, asking questions particularly about aspects of denial of self. She stared deeply into his eyes and watched his every move. The Brahmin grew more and more uneasy as he observed the princess. *The princess seems quite captivated,* he thought. *Where is this going?*

The pandit, wishing to break the connection between her and Thomas without offending her, looked for a chance to make his offer to the apostle. Seizing a momentary pause in the conversation, he asked permission to speak. The princess readily granted it to him with a smile, suddenly aware that she may have appeared too enthusiastic in her questioning of the visitor. Natarajan smiled back and thanked the princess with a respectful nod of his head.

"Thomas, I have considered carefully your mission here for some time." He spoke in a gentle tone. "The number of followers interested in your message is growing. Yet, you are still working from the house of our captain Siphor. Don't you need a temple of your own? If you agree, I would like to give you a temple, a building for your very own use. It would be a special place to hold your meetings. You could even live on the grounds there if you chose to."

Both Thomas and the princess were surprised by this unexpected development. They looked at each other with delight.

Thomas thanked Natarajan, unable to mask the broad smile on his face.

While thanking Natarajan out loud, the Nazarene's mind was suddenly racing ahead with possibilities. *I will take such a building and tear down the idols and make it truly a place of worship for the one true God,* he thought excitedly. *Here, I will build my church. Here again, is proof that Isa was right to send me to India.* Thoughts flooded his mind.

"Thank you, Pandit," said Thomas, still learning what the appropriate form of address was for this man. "I would be so pleased to accept your generous offer."

Already developing the customs of a South Indian, he clasped his hands together and then bowed slightly to accent his thanks. Still speaking politely, Thomas changed to a more businesslike tone. "I can accept such an offer, but it would have to be understood that I would likely need to modify some of the structure."

This was Thomas' soft way of warning the pandit that the idols he found in the structure would have to be removed, and perhaps other things as well. He elected not to say too much on that account, excited by the actual offer and the opportunities it presented.

"Of course," responded Natarajan. "I am sure the devotees of the temple will be willing to help you in due time. I will talk to them."

The two men continued to speak, with Natarajan telling him a few more details of the Shaivite temple he had selected, soon forgetting they were in the presence of the princess.

"The devotees of the temple will be delighted to help rebuild and repair the structure," repeated Natarajan, wanting to allay Thomas' concerns. "They will become your devoted followers."

Natarajan did not fully understand Thomas' potential objection to objects or idols in the temple but was gambling that he would be able to overcome any objections the devotees might have.

Both men turned to the princess, who had quietly raised her hand, indicating that she wanted both men to stop talking. She had listened to the two men with interest, struggling to follow the conversation as it moved between poorly spoken Tamil and Gandhari. But now, she needed to change the direction of the conversation. It was time to address her own concerns.

Hesitating for a moment, she was suddenly unable to contain her emotion and began to weep quietly as she put her head down. Thomas asked tenderly, "What is wrong, my princess?"

As he did so, he looked at Natarajan, hoping for some guidance or an explanation for this unexpected outburst. Natarajan was surprised that Thomas had addressed Princess Mygdonia as "my princess" and equally by the fact that she had suddenly shown emotion. *Clearly, the offer of the temple is a reinforcement to Thomas that he belongs here,* he mused, *and that this may become his permanent home.*

Regaining her composure, Mygdonia looked up at the two men and then into Thomas' eyes.

"I cannot bear the king, anymore," she cried softly. "He is awful." She wrinkled her face as she spoke. "When he is on top of me, he smothers me. He smells. He makes me and the other wives engage in all kinds of deviant pleasures. He laughs greedily and seems to never be satisfied."

She mimicked the high-pitched gurgle of delight that the prince would utter.

"Lately, he seems to like to hurt one of us and then watch as it happens. You cannot even imagine what I have seen him do. You cannot imagine what I have had to do. And the other girls. It is just a horror!" The princess continued to weep quietly.

Thomas looked at the princess with compassion in his eyes.

"Come with me today and be baptized." He spoke these words softly and solemnly, intending to be comforting. "As a child of Christ, you can throw off the sin that follows you. You can tell your husband that he must abstain from touching you. Intercourse with your husband is polluted and evil. Deny the world and come into the Kingdom of Heaven, says the Christ. Follow me."

Thomas reached his hand towards the princess as a welcoming gesture. Natarajan did not intervene, yet he was concerned. *How might I stop this?* he puzzled. *The prince is a problem.*

Princess Mygdonia hesitated, trying to regain her composure. Thomas was offering her a way out of her nightmare. She could become a follower of Isa of the Hebrews, still not fully understanding what that might entail.

She nodded her head slowly and smiled at the apostle through her tears. Not wanting to wait any longer for change, she asked Thomas, "What must I do to be baptized?"

She had come to understand that baptism was the strange ritual that signaled you were now a follower of this sadhu. Thomas stood and, breaking all protocol, reached down to her. This time, he took her hand in his own.

"Follow me," he said. "Follow me to the Kingdom of Heaven." Thomas felt exultation in his heart. Clearly, this was his mission.

The princess stood up, still holding Thomas' hand. He led her back through the doorway and out into the large open courtyard. In the center of the courtyard, there was a fountain that supplied water to three large, tiled, decorative pools of water. Thomas had noted the pools when he had entered the palace. Like many palaces and homes of the wealthy, the courtyard was the center of all activity. All about the courtyard, servants and attendants were busy going about their assigned tasks.

Open to the sky, a large mango tree and several smaller tamarind trees populated one side of the yard. At the far end was the entrance to another hall. Nearer, and to one side, was an open doorway that led to the kitchens and to the outside. A few black crows inhabited the mango tree, their regular cawing punctuating the silence.

Each tiled pool was circular, a short three meters in diameter, and less than one meter deep. Decorative koi and other fish were kept in one of the pools along with lily pads. During festive times, the servants would float candles on the surface of the water, creating a wondrous holiday effect at night. One of the pools was clearer than the others and did not contain koi. It was to this pool that Thomas walked. Stopping in front of the pool, Thomas had the princess stand for a moment, explaining that they would enter the water. He asked her to undress. The princess, now beyond all caring, hesitated at first and then accepted the request. She unwrapped her sari with some help from the apostle. The apostle explained that she was removing the past and all sin and past evil from her life. The water would purify her.

Servants all around the courtyard stopped what they were doing and gasped. Natarajan watched this performance with concern but knowing the determination of the princess, elected to not interfere. *Even if I stop her now,* he reasoned, *she will find an opportunity to do it another time.*

A slender gold chain encircling her hips was the only article visible on the princess' slender form. Holding her by the elbow, Thomas helped her step over the side of the shallow pool and into the water. Thomas then stepped into the pool with her. Placing his hand on her head and supporting her back, he baptized her in the name of Christ and lowered her into the pool.

Mygdonia felt the water rush over her. It was cool and refreshing. Rising up out of the water, she felt like a newborn, as though her life would have new joy and meaning. A great burden was being removed from her. The burden of the marital bed with the prince was being vanquished. Thomas' voice echoed in a magical way to her as he spoke the words of baptism in Aramaic. As she stepped out of the pool, servants scrambled to meet her and to cover her nakedness.

And several attendants ran, not walked, to the chambers of the prince.

Chapter 23

The disciples said to Him, "Not everyone can accept this word, but only those to whom it has been given. For there are eunuchs who were born that way, and there are eunuchs who have been made eunuchs by others - there are those who choose to live like eunuchs for the sake of the kingdom of heaven. The one who can accept this should accept it."

—Matthew 19 Verse 10–12

As THE MONTHS passed, Abbanes came to realize that it was time for him to return to Gandhara. He had done all he could as a trader in Muziris and was ready to return to his family and his home. Never a full believer in Apostle Thomas' message, but always a loyal follower when needed, he said goodbye to the brother of Isa.

"You will need the protection of God to journey so far," said the apostle. Thomas blessed him and prayed over him, quoting from Psalms:

This I pray for you, that the Lord will rescue you from every trap and protect you from deadly disease. He will cover you with his feathers. He will shelter you with his wings. His faithful promises are your armor and protection.

Thomas placed his hand on Abbanes' brow and was about to say more when Abbanes, impressed that Thomas could quote the Psalms so effortlessly, embraced him warmly. Smiling while considering the image of a protecting bird as a blessing for his journey, Abbanes spoke.

"Thank you, Thomas," he said, his voice slightly tinged with emotion. "Thank you for being the best traveling companion a true friend could have. We have seen some of the world, haven't we? You too go with God's grace, protection, and *wisdom*."

He emphasized the last word. He still worried about Thomas' safety and continued to have doubts about some of the apostle's teachings. He cared about his friend and felt responsible for him, but he also recognized there was nothing more he could do for him. Thomas was on a mission chosen by God.

Thomas was increasingly confident as a minister of God. Since leaving Judea, he had learned to speak to larger and larger audiences, and he knew how to hold their attention. He understood that part of the success of a good sermon was to tell a relatable story. He would then put on a performance like a healing or a laying on hands to drive out demons with skill and legitimacy that evoked confidence among his followers and observers. His renown as a strange sadhu among the Brahmins was steadily growing. Abbanes sensed this growth from his friend. The elder Hebrew knew he had fulfilled his pact with Isa.

Where is Isa? The question ran through the minds of both Hebrews with less regularity now. Isa had followed them on the early part of their journey and then stopped. Abbanes kept thinking Isa might reappear miraculously among them again. And yet, Isa did not reappear. He also knew Thomas had grown without the presence of Isa. *Perhaps that was what Isa had intended,* thought Abbanes.

The elder Hebrew did not think long on the matter and was soon on his saddled horse and off to the port. His ships were already prepared, laden with spices, gemstones, and other exotic goods he knew King Gondophores would greatly desire upon his return.

Thomas was sad at his friend's departure but also recognized that it was time for a change in their relationship too. As a practical matter, he no longer needed Abbanes to look out for him. His ministry continued to expand greatly. The Jewish community remained hostile to him, but many in the Brahmin community began to follow him. Pandit Natarajan was a tolerant leader and continued to speak favorably of Thomas. Influenced by Natarajan, many of the Brahmin faithful associated with Thomas' Shaivite temple were good-natured and tolerant, though not particularly dedicated to Thomas' way of thinking. Some of his nominal followers continued to view themselves as Hindus, certainly followers of the Goddess above all, but appreciated some of the religious elements of being a follower of Isa too.

Thomas had noticed some of his followers, even those who had been duly baptized, often visited Brahmin temples too. This strange duality in beliefs worried the apostle but did not stop him. Thomas had seven communities that now claimed to be "Followers of the Christ." These seven churches represented a foundation on which to build his church in India. This foundation would grow into millions of followers one day. The apostle expected these dual believers would eventually repent of their ways.

Thomas' greatest Muziris patron and disciple was Princess Mygdonia. Mygdonia had publicly announced her conversion to the new God of the Hebrew Thomas. The importance of this announcement soon became clear, as more and more followers felt comfortable attending Thomas' sermons.

When Princess Mygdonia first announced to her husband that she was a follower of Apostle Thomas, Charisius paid it no mind, as though his wife announced that she had changed the color of her hair. She eventually worked up her courage and told her prince she could no longer have intercourse with him, that it was a sin before her new god. Charisius laughed when Mygdonia first brought this up, thinking it was a passing fancy. He spent much of the first day after this announcement laughing to himself. He had other wives and concubines who kept him satisfied. However, as time went on, and days stretched into weeks, he began to miss his wife. Mygdonia was the most beautiful woman in his life. Yet, she had become a forbidden fruit that tormented him. He longed to feel her under him, to be inside her. He had to have her. His feelings on the subject went from amusement and laughter to growing hostility and frustration.

Princess Mygdonia gained more and more confidence every day and completely refused to enter the prince's bedchamber. The prince's conversations with her had become more and more difficult. Most meetings were fraught with underlining tension.

"I cannot have foul intercourse with you," insisted the princess firmly. "I am a bride of the Christ and a follower of the one true God."

The Prince would argue with his wife but to no avail. She would not change her mind. Growing frustrated with the situation, Charisius began to seek out counsel.

"Could he not order the death of his wife if she refused him?" he asked. "Could he not cast her aside? Divorce her?"

Ordering the death of his wife or divorcing her was not what he desired. He wanted her.

As the situation continued and seemed unresolvable, Charisius finally confided in his older brother, King Raja Misdaeus. The raja, in the presence of his court, laughed heartily when he first told him that his wife would no longer sleep with him. Soon, the entire palace staff, guards, servants, cooks, servers, gardeners, and courtiers had all heard the story. A prince who could not command his wife? The secret was out and rapidly spread around and beyond the community. The princess was commanding the prince, not the other way around! Laughter rang out in palace hallways, market stalls, and teashops.

"Brother, you have to seize her," the raja responded one day, unable to contain his mirth, as he considered his portly younger brother's misfortune. "There is no other way to do this. You have to show her that you are the prince. My wives fear me. Your wives should fear you too," admonished the king, still chortling at his brother's uncomfortable and embarrassing situation. He continued forcefully, "It is your right as her husband to take her. She is your wife! Take her!"

Later that day, Misdaeus pondered on what Charisius had told him. Several of Princess Mygdonia's sisters and cousins were counted among his wives and concubines. But Mygdonia was the most beautiful of all the sisters. He could feel his loins burn at the thought of taking her. It was often in the back of his mind, even now, despite the misfortune of his younger brother. He considered how he might profit from this situation but dismissed the idea quickly.

I should have taken her when I had the chance years ago, he thought sadly. Mygdonia was a strong woman, and this made his desire even more acute.

Armed with advice from his older brother, Charisius returned to his palace, determined to change his circumstances. Over the next week, he considered what he might do. After two weeks, and now unable to even find his wife in the palace, he ordered his guards to find the princess and bring her to his chambers, by force if necessary. It was not long before they returned, the princess walking voluntarily with them. Yet, the woman who came before him and entered his room was barely recognizable as his lovely wife. He was shocked by her appearance. *This is my beauty?* he thought. *What has happened to her?* Charisius was stunned.

As a devoted follower of Apostle Thomas, Princess Mygdonia no longer kept herself well and had not bathed in days. Her hair was slightly matted and uncombed. She wore a simple sari and not the robes of her station. The apostle had advised her that by doing this, dressing plainly, she would not be a sinful temptation for all men she encountered, including her own husband.

Studying her somberly for a moment, Charisius inquired with alarm, "Where have you been? Have you become ill?"

"I have been with the physician," she responded coldly.

"What physician have you been with? So, you have been ill? Is this Hebrew stranger whom you see all the time a physician?" asked the prince skeptically.

"Yes," responded Mygdonia. "He is a physician of souls. He has the power to heal the body and also to heal the soul. He has healed my soul. I cannot lie with you, anymore, O Prince. I am wed to the Christ."

Charisius was furious with this answer. But seeing her unkempt state, he no longer desired to take her by force either.

He dismissed the princess and fumed about what to do. Determined to take decisive action, he called his guard back and instructed them to go find Apostle Thomas and bring him before him. The guard quickly discovered that Thomas was not in Muziris at the moment and returned to report that a search was on. They eventually located him with the help of the Pandit Natarajan. Prince Charisius instructed the pandit to come to the palace with Thomas immediately upon his return. He wished to speak to both of them.

Natarajan had become a friend to Thomas. The two would often debate on the pathway to God. Natarajan continued to attempt to moderate some of Thomas' extreme views and tried to get him to see a more moderate pathway to God. He was rarely successful. Yet, their relationship was that of a senior pastor and mentor and a less informed but charismatic junior. The two men regularly remained in touch. Natarajan also remained the spiritual advisor to many of the older adherents of the Shaivite temple that Thomas now inhabited. He counseled all on the value of tolerance and duality, to accept the views of Thomas but also to see that the truth remained in the ancient path. For many, the duality did not represent a difficult problem, generally accepting the idea that it was better to be on the good side of all deities.

Sending a messenger to Thomas, Natarajan knew immediately that he must accompany Thomas to the meeting with Charisius. Knowing that Mygdonia had become a devout follower of Isa, he knew that put her in direct conflict with her husband. *The other wives and concubines have been unable to fulfill whatever needs the prince has,* he thought. He had hoped otherwise.

Thomas returned to Muziris two days later, unclear as to what the prince desired. He sought out the Pandit Natarajan first, and the two men arrived at the palace together. The mood of the courtiers was sullen, and Thomas realized this was no social call. Charisius sat up upon his divan, this time his portly frame propped up by a dozen pillows. His saggy face looked pained, even angry. None of his wives were present. In their place, a dozen armed young men lined the walls, standing at attention. The pandit knew this was not going to be an easy conversation and was on guard. He would do his best to moderate the words of his friend and find a middle ground, if possible.

"Greetings, Sadhu," said Charisius, sounding cold, almost hollow, as he looked at Thomas, momentarily ignoring Natarajan. Charisius, not a leader of men, was unsure how to appropriately greet this holy man. He decided to be reasonable at first, although inside, he felt impatient and furious.

"Captain Siphor tells me of the wondrous things you have done in Muziris and in the whole area," he began diplomatically. "You have healed the sick and reached many with your words of wisdom. Natarajan tells me you now have seven temples with many followers and that the number of your followers is growing daily."

He managed to keep his tone polite, although all in the court could tell that his voice was strained. Thomas bowed his head slightly towards the prince, acknowledging the compliment. The prince then continued.

"While I understand many words of wisdom, please know that I myself cannot follow you. I, along with my brother, must represent all the people, all religions, all gods. You can understand that I think?" Charisius looked at Natarajan for confirmation. The pandit wanly smiled back, nodding his head.

Pausing for a moment, he continued. "Sometimes, the acts by one in our kingdom affect the many. In this case, your acts are now affecting me personally. And I myself am the kingdom, and with my brother, all of the kingdom." The prince was straining to keep his voice civil. "So, why have I called you here, you must be wondering?"

Thomas looked at Natarajan. He was struggling to keep up with the prince's speech in this formalized Tamil. *"What is the prince planning to say here?"* he reflected. Almost as if Charisius could read Thomas' mind, he answered the question for him.

"My wife is refusing to sleep with me. She is not bathing anymore and goes about with unkept hair and dirty clothing. She tells me she is a follower of your God. She says that she was baptized by you. My servants say she disrobed herself in front of all to be baptized by you in water!" No longer able to contain the emotion he felt, his voice cracked.

Charisius raised his voice. "What kind of God does these things to a princess?" His tone was accusatory. "My wife the princess now tells me she is a follower of Isa, even married to him! She calls our union in the marriage bed polluted!" His tone was no longer friendly. Any pretext was gone. "Can you explain this to me, Nasrani?"

Charisius anger was rising. Like many others, he was only a slight understanding of what the term Nasrani even meant, having vaguely understood there was some sort of town way off in the west called Nazareth. Yet, he had learned that the local Hebrew population referred to Thomas derisively that way.

Thomas was taken aback by the prince's growing hostility. He knew it could be dangerous to speak the truth, but he was still the Apostle of the one true God. He had to speak the truth to this man and to all who were present. He must trust in Isa and have faith in the truth.

"My prince," he began, "the greatest sin of all is fornication. That is what your wife is telling you. You cannot enter the Kingdom of Heaven unless you purify yourself. You must deny all physical pleasure."

As soon as Thomas uttered these words, Natarajan was finally struck by the total impossibility of Thomas' teachings. The apostle did not even try to mitigate or explain this strange message. He had been in error to even entertain the idea that he could moderate this man's thinking.

Hoping to somehow soften the message before the prince, Natarajan quickly interjected before the apostle could continue. "Thomas, surely you cannot mean that all men and all women cannot procreate? How can any people live like that?"

He was hoping Thomas would give a more thoughtful response to the prince.

Yet, Thomas did not hesitate to indict himself and did not consider for a moment that he must moderate his message. He was speaking for Isa. He was not defending his faith; he was promoting it. More forcefully, he repeated, "I am saying that the greatest sin of all is fornication. We must deny ourselves if we are to arrive at the Kingdom of Heaven. The prince must get rid of all his wives."

Natarajan was incredulous. He was trying to save the apostle, but he was not getting help from him. He had been extremely tolerant and open to Thomas from the beginning, yet he had not fully allowed himself to believe that Thomas was this inflexible in his thinking.

Soberly, Natarajan asked Thomas several more questions in a vain attempt to get Thomas to show some leniency in his views. No tolerant view was forthcoming. Just the opposite, Thomas argued more forcefully that he was following the path that God had set out for all men. Finally, Natarajan bowed his head and stopped asking questions. He knew what was coming.

Charisius had been closely watching these two holy men continue their exchange. He now understood that Thomas was not even pretending to act under the religious supervision of the pandit. Natarajan did not sanction or control this man. He listened to Natarajan attempt and fail to moderate Thomas' views. Shaking his head, he could not believe that anyone would follow this crazy foreign sadhu. He broke the silence.

"This is madness!" His voice rang out clear and strong.

Thomas and Natarajan turned towards the prince. Charisius looked hard at Natarajan and held out his palm at the pandit, a clear message that he should no longer speak. He then motioned to the guards to come forward. With great effort, assisted by the two young attendants by his side, he stood up, his corpulent body almost shaking with the effort. Charisius liked to be standing and forceful when pronouncing judgment. He thought he looked more princely and commanding when he did so.

Pointing at Thomas, he ordered the senior guard. "Place this man in chains and take him to prison. His words and actions are an abomination before all the people. His own words seal his fate. There is nothing more to judge here."

The prince's words were a judgment for all the people to clearly hear and understand.

Natarajan's face went cold. He knew this was the only possible outcome, yet he still felt sadness for his friend. There was no battle to fight, here. What Thomas was preaching was unnatural before any God. He would have to be held accountable. It could not continue.

Prince Charisius turned directly to Thomas, pronouncing his personal judgment on the apostle. "Thomas, I will keep you in prison until you instruct my wife to come to my chambers. She must return to my chambers today and that will be the end of it." Charisius was firm and clear. He did not wait for Thomas to respond. His judgment was law and a command.

Natarajan relaxed a bit, relieved that the pronouncement by the prince was not more severe. Natarajan had worried that Thomas might receive a much harsher sentence, even death. Perhaps Princess Mygdonia could be reasoned with, and she would return to the prince.

The guards came forward and seized Thomas, who readily surrendered to them. The prison was underneath the palace of King Misdaeus, a short distance away. They escorted him outside and placed him on a chariot. Two guards jumped onto the chariot with Thomas, handling him roughly, and rode the distance to the king's palace. They were met at the entrance by the prison blacksmith who fit the Nazarene with a chain about his leg.

The apostle, still trusting that God would provide, began to softly pray in Aramaic as he was placed inside the prison, chained to a wall. He had once assumed that the conversion of Princess Mygdonia would offer him and even some of his followers some protection from the vagaries of this foreign court. Now he understood the perils too.

Chapter 24

For it was I who had obeyed his commands
And it was I who also kept the promise,
And I mingled at the doors of his ancient royal building.
He took delight in me and received me in his palace.
All his subjects were singing hymns with harmonious voices.
He allowed me also to be admitted to the door of the king
himself,
So that with my gifts and the pearl I might appear before
the king himself.

—The Hymn of the Pearl; Verses 100-105

THE PRISON WAS a single large chamber. It was nearly black inside, except for a few spluttering torches on the walls and an equally modest watch fire lit by the guards near the entrance. The fire cast flickering shadows on the far wall. Several prisoners sat lined up along one side, each chained at the ankle, as was Thomas, with one prisoner chained at the neck to one of the pillars. The floor was sandy and smelled of urine. Rats could be heard scurrying about in the dark, skillfully avoiding being seen in the shadows and recesses that were occasionally illuminated ever so faintly by the watch fire and torches.

The apostle began the night in prayer. At times, he imagined that Isa was there to comfort him. He could sense the presence of his twin in the prison chamber with him. He would turn ever so slightly and look for him, expecting to see him even, but Isa never appeared. But he knew that Isa was close somewhere. He understood that a union with his brother was coming. At times, he could joyfully think of nothing else. Halfway through the night, he finally fell into a deep sleep, dreaming of the Kingdom of God.

By the next morning, Muziris and, indeed the entire region, had learned of Thomas' imprisonment. Most were soon telling ribald jokes about the reasons why. Prince Charisius' predicament and the loss of his wife to the teachings of this strange foreign sadhu had become common knowledge. While Charisius was not unpopular, the thought that a princess could refuse to enter the chambers of her prince to carry out her sexual responsibilities was just too funny. The story was soon told throughout the port and beyond, often in greatly embellished detail.

The story of Charisius' situation and the extent to which the people were ridiculing the prince reached the ears of King Misdaeus. While the king initially found Charisius' problems amusing, he was now concerned with the dignity of the royal family and the importance of respect for his crown. His subjects were mocking his brother too much. This situation caused the king to think more carefully about the negative impacts the foreign Hebrew sadhu was having on his subjects and their relationship to their divine ruler. Misdaeus found Thomas' teachings unnatural, ridiculous, even an abomination. The king approved of Thomas' incarceration and was prepared to do more if necessary.

The morning light cast a few slivers of sunlight down into the prison chamber. Thomas awoke feeling refreshed and renewed. His mind was on fire. He remembered his dream and thought it a clear revelation from God. It was a story, a hymn even. He struggled to find the right words in Tamil, but they would not come. His mind had received this great message from the one true God in Aramaic only. How to express it?

As he looked about, he saw that several of his fellow prisoners were awake. He called out to them and asked as to their circumstances. The prisoners on the wall, four in all, said they were in prison for petty crimes and were hopeful they would be released soon. One man who said he was called Velu had been imprisoned several times and was accustomed to the prison routine. One young man was chained by his neck to a pillar and could not speak. He lay there quietly moaning. As more and more light came in, it was apparent that the man had been badly beaten.

Thomas led the prisoners in prayer, and soon several of the guards joined them. They had heard of this Sadhu Thomas and knew it was said he had miraculous healing powers. There was certainly no reason to offend him. Before long, Thomas was preaching to them all and proposing baptism for those who would enter the Kingdom of God and acknowledge Christ.

Princess Mygdonia, initially believing Thomas was away for a few days, did not learn of Thomas' imprisonment until that morning. As soon as she heard what had happened the night before, she carefully bathed herself and dressed according to her station in a fine sari that only a princess of her rank could wear. Her servants applied oils to her dry skin and perfumed her body. In denying herself, she had also been neglecting herself. Now fully restored to her previous glory, the effect was stunning. Mygdonia was again the beautiful woman who could command the attention of every man she encountered. Mygdonia walked to Charisius' chambers to demand an audience. None was given. Charisius had suspected that his wife might come looking for him, demanding an explanation for the incarceration of Thomas. Expecting just such a reaction from his wife, he refused to see her.

"I am Princess Mygdonia!" exclaimed the princess. The senior attendant was called, who explained that Charisius wanted to first hear that his wife was giving up on this foreign sorcerer and that she was now willing to return to the prince's chambers to fulfill her duty as a wife. The attendant, an elderly and skilled diplomat, knew he had to be careful explaining the denial to such a powerful person. He smiled gently at the princess, hoping she understood that the decision to deny access to the prince was not his decision. He was simply carrying out his instructions.

Mygdonia threw up her hands in frustration. Unable to speak to her husband, she decided to change her strategy. She boldly walked directly to the prison, located on the palace grounds of her brother-in-law, the king. Mygdonia was well aware of the lustful stares Misdaeus would shower upon her. At times during court events, the king would show her excessive deferential treatment, or even preferential treatment, to her slight embarrassment. She knew that if the right discreet moment presented itself, the king would have taken her. She was not above allowing the king to think of such things, now. He would be a far more pleasant partner than her husband, even if forced to perform against her will.

The royal guards at the king's palace were surprised by the arrival of the princess and accommodated her request to visit the prison, but also immediately alerted King Misdaeus to her presence. One of the guards led her to the prison chamber, but not before discouraging her.

"It is not a place for the princess," he kept repeating, all the while continuing to escort her to her destination. But Mygdonia was determined to find Thomas and set him free, insisting the guard show her the prison.

The prison chamber did not have a functioning door. An ancient metal gate, rusted and forgotten, was pressed against the side, broken and unused. The jailors had discovered long ago that they had no need of a locked door to keep the prisoners in. There was simply nowhere to go. All prisoners were expected to be chained to the walls inside the prison with armed guards at the ready. The guards controlled the only passageway into and out of the prison chamber.

As Mygdonia, guard escort in tow, neared the prison chamber, she realized she could hear the voice of Thomas faintly in the distance.

Am I imagining this? she wondered as they moved along the corridor. *He is speaking. No, he is singing!* The voice became clearer as she approached. Mygdonia could not understand the words. The apostle was chanting in Aramaic:

> *When I was a little child, in my father's palace,*
> *And enjoyed the wealth and luxury of those who nurtured me,*

*My parents equipped me with provisions and sent me out from the
  East, our homeland.
From the wealth of our treasury, they gave me a great burden,
Which was light so that I could carry it by myself:
Gold from the land above, silver from great treasuries,
And stones, chalcedonies of India, and agates from Kushan.*

*And they girded me with steel,
And they took away from me the garment set with gems and spangled
  with gold
Which they had made out of love for me
And the yellow robe which was made for my size,
And they made a covenant with me
And wrote it in my mind that I might not forget:
"If you go down to Egypt and bring the one pearl
Which is in the land of the devouring serpent,
You shall put on again that garment set with stones and the robe which
  lies over it.
And with your brother our next unto us, you shall be an heir of our
  Kingdom.*

Thomas sang these last words just as Mygdonia entered the chamber. Smiling and overcome with religious ecstasy, he continued with the Hymn of the Pearl, enchanting all those who listened. The words were not understood, but Thomas' melodic voice was captivating and peaceful. The hymn itself was a word from God, a dream that explained Thomas' mission and purpose. The pearl was his message.

Thomas wished Isa could be there with him in person at that moment, yet he felt his presence. The hymn was part of the answer to the riddle for the apostle. The hymn was a message from Isa and the one God. It carried words of comfort and empowerment as he conducted his work in India. The hymn inspired Thomas and reassured him that he could carry on no matter what adversity was to come.

Princess Mygdonia looked about the prison. She cringed at the horrific smell emanating from the room, so strong it induced an involuntary retching reflex on those not accustomed to such foul odors. She listened to Thomas, as he continued to sing, despite the overwhelming stench. Still gagging from the powerful odor of the prison, Mygdonia managed to regain her senses. Shuddering involuntarily, she turned to the guards in the hall just outside the room. She looked straight at the slightly better-dressed guard in the group, unsure who exactly was in charge.

"Release the apostle," she demanded brusquely.

The young guard looked about desperately for higher authority but dared not contradict her. Realizing he had no option but to obey, he stepped outside for a moment. He quietly spoke to the prison blacksmith to come quickly.

In short order, a large, barrel-chested man arrived. His arms were scarred from a lifetime of handling, hammering, and cutting metal, and the thumb on his left hand was missing. His teeth were red from constantly chewing areca nut, and he carried a hammer and other tools. Seizing Thomas' ankle gruffly, he raised up his leg and quickly knocked free the pin that held his ankle chain. The chain fell off with a clang.

"Hurry," implored Mygdonia, looking at Thomas. Her voice betrayed a sense of relief that she had found Thomas alive, but her tone was also urgent. "You must leave the prison immediately. You are free, but you should also leave Muziris now."

Thomas, smiling blissfully, shook his head and continued to rejoice in the presence and power of God. Still looking at the princess, he kept singing the hymn and did not show any interest in departing.

At that very moment, King Misdaeus himself arrived in the prison. Several well-dressed and powerful-looking guards were at his side. They pushed aside the prison guards, making room for the monarch. The king did not flinch from the prison smell. His visage was stern and strong. It was not the first time he had been to his prison.

"Princess Mygdonia!" said Misdaeus forcefully, but not before running his eyes over her form. "What are you doing here in my prison? This is no place for you," he added more softly.

Before she could respond, Thomas interjected. "I am the disciple of Isa, the Christ, the minister, and the vessel who will show you the pathway to the Kingdom of God."

Thomas' tone was sober. The magic of the singing of the Hymn of the Pearl had rapidly dissipated with the arrival of the monarch. The moment was gone.

"I am sure you are," Misdaeus answered sarcastically.

The apostle continued with words on his lips, but King Misdaeus, still looking at the princess, raised his hand, indicating that he wanted the Hebrew to stop talking.

"Princess, why are you allowing yourself to fall within the power of this charlatan, this supposed sorcerer?" Misdaeus asked.

"What has become of you? Return to my brother the prince," he ordered. More gently, he continued with a tender voice, "Mygdonia, forsake this man and return to your husband. If you do that, I will let your sadhu, this man Thomas, out of prison. He will be free to go."

The princess was silent, uncertain what to do. She knew she did not want to return to the terror that was her husband, yet she knew she had no choice.

Thomas stood up. He felt compassion for the princess but also realized that there likely would not be another choice. With resignation in his voice, he supported Misdaeus.

"Princess Mygdonia, obey your king and return to your husband," he uttered solemnly. Thomas felt like he was betraying the young princess when he spoke these words. They cut into him deeply, giving him a sense of failure.

Mygdonia wept at Thomas' words. "After all that you have told me, you will now compel me to act against the will of our God?" she sobbed. Her tone was accusatory. "You have taught me that wealth is transitory and will not last, that if I renounce this life, I will receive life eternal. All pleasures of this life pass away, but we seek the pleasure that abides in us forever. I am married to Christ and cannot be married to my husband. I have forsaken that bond."

The young woman ran from the prison weeping, overcome with emotion, before Thomas could respond or explain why he had instructed her to return to her husband. Feelings of guilt enveloped him.

Misdaeus watched the princess leave and then turned and looked hard at Thomas, shaking his head. He needed to contain his anger at this man, recognizing how important he was to Mygdonia. He would spare this man's life, but he would do no more than that. If anything else came up with this man, he might indeed order his death.

"You are a sorcerer and a man who does not speak plainly," he said harshly to Thomas. "Further, you are destroying the life of my younger brother, Prince Charisius." The king hesitated for a moment, allowing the substance and tone of his message to sink in, as though he were passing judgment and a verdict.

"Leave us," he commanded Thomas. "Go from this place and come back no more to Muziris. There are many towns and cities you can visit. You do not need to be here, anymore. Leave us," he repeated forcefully.

He then turned towards the passage in search of the princess. *She will need some comforting,* he thought somewhat amusedly to himself. *Maybe now would be a good time to explore that option.*

Thomas watched the king leave. Saying little to the guards, he walked out of the prison to encounter the new day.

Chapter 25

So we shall write a poem, with songs, illustrating the three truths that

1.   *Dharma will become the God of Death to kings who swerve from the path of righteousness.*
2.   *That it is natural for great men to adore a chaste lady of great fame.*
3.   *And that destiny will manifest itself and be fulfilled.*

—The Silappathikaram
An Epic Poem in Tamil from antiquity.

THE RAINS HAD finally stopped, and Thomas was glad for it. The monsoons were proving to be a terror on his journeys. Days would go by with nothing but hard rain all day. Roads, streets, and trails would turn into impassible temporary rivers of mud. Fortunately, they would often dry out quickly. There was nothing to do sometimes but find a dry place and wait it out. The land beyond Muziris was diverse. Hot, dry plains were punctuated by high ghats: blue-colored mountains that proved to be surprisingly cold when crossed. The countryside teemed with life and activity. He encountered many villages, filled with cattle, water buffaloes, goats, and verdant rice paddies. In the foothills each morning, he often would wake to the sound of a male peacock strutting about and calling for a mate. Bright green parakeets regularly filled the skies, some with a beautiful red ring about their neck. Aggressive black crows were a constant companion too.

The apostle had steadily learned to live the life of a sadhu since leaving Muziris. At times, true to his commitment to deny himself, he had to beg for food, living a life of extreme poverty. On the whole, villagers were generous and seemed to be accustomed to helping a sadhu. Most were quick to offer a modest meal, usually of rice and lentils, despite the fact they were impoverished themselves.

Thomas gained a small number of followers as the months passed. He attributed his success to his improving fluency in the Tamil language. He would typically arrive at a village in the late afternoon and find a ready group of humble farmers returning from their labors in the fields, happy to listen to the foreign sadhu preach to them and tell them stories. His new and unusual stories were an enjoyable distraction from what was otherwise a backbreaking difficult existence. To Thomas' delight, some of the villagers would even agree to be baptized, often looking for guidance from their village headman or Hindu priest, who often would often grant permission, comfortable in the ambiguity that life presented.

Despite these small successes, Thomas struggled to establish a strong community of believers in the way that he had succeeded in Muziris. It was proving to be impossible unless he had the support of the local Brahmin priests. Many of the Hindus he converted seemed to accept almost everything he said but chose not to believe it exclusively. They would also cling to their Hindu belief systems.

Recognizing this difficulty, Thomas decided to go to the large town of Madurai, where he knew there was a large temple and many priests. Perhaps he could gain a ready audience there, as in Muziris. He might even debate some of the Hindu priests on the nature of God and thereby draw an audience.

The apostle arrived at the bank of the Vaigai River in the early afternoon, just as a light rain began to fall. Looking across the river, he could see a colorful but modest temple in the middle of the town.

"You are coming to worship the Goddess Meenakshi?" asked a cheerful voice. Thomas turned to see a young man walking up behind him, closely followed by a few others. He was dressed in a white shirt and a simple dhoti which was wrapped up past his knees.

Thomas elected to not respond directly to the man's question. "I am going to Madurai, but I will need to find passage across the river," he answered, smiling back.

The young man was clearly interested in Thomas, a rare, foreign-looking traveler who did not seem to belong there. *Perhaps this will be an interesting man to talk to,* the young Tamil thought. He nodded his head and with his arm motioned Thomas to follow him.

During the dry season, it was possible to navigate across the river by walking from one exposed granite slab to another. Yet, during the monsoons, the water level was too high. When that happened, young boys would take travelers across the river by boat for a small fee.

The young man who had called out to Thomas bargained with a young boy, barely in his teens. Fixing the price, and hoping to generate some good karma, he waved Thomas and two other priests who had just come up on the river into the watercraft. They all stepped gingerly into the venerable but sturdy bamboo craft, long poles lashed together with tapered ends.

Two young boys with oars and poles skillfully handled the longboat, with one standing in the front and the larger boy in the back. Despite the high level of the water, granite surfaces were still visible, sharply jutting out from the water's surface. The young men skillfully maneuvered around the obstacles and towards the other shore, allowing the boat to be gently pushed further downstream with the current. Both used paddles, at times dropping them to pick up the long poles that they used as leverage with rocks and even the shallow bottom.

As the boat was crossing the river, the monsoon rain was firmly setting in, and it began to rain harder. Clouds rolled in, reducing visibility to a short one hundred meters. As the boat arrived on the opposite shore, there was no time to speak, only to run for shelter from the downpour. Thomas had no idea where to go and so ran with his young friend, the one who paid his fare. Most ran for the temple.

The apostle quickly learned why the temple was the destination of choice. Immediately in front of the temple was a large red-tiled roof and open platform that served as an entry point and celebratory place for the temple community. It also doubled as a place to keep devotees out of the hot sun or, in this case, the hard monsoon rains. Thomas and the rest of the party raced into the shelter, soaked to the skin by the time they arrived.

As Thomas entered the shelter, he discovered that there were dozens of others who had already run to the same shelter. Each was sitting or squatting on the earthen floor, dry for the moment. The rains continued as the afternoon ended and nightfall came on. The wealthier patrons who had been caught out in the rain left as soon as they could. In some cases, servants came to fetch them with large umbrellas made from palm leaves. The rain continued, but the numbers in the shelter steadily dwindled, as all the women left the shelter for their homes. Only a few dozen men remained for the night.

As darkness crept over the land, a temple official appeared and lit a fire under the platform for warmth and light. He left and returned a short while later with a large basket. The official, along with another, distributed packets of food wrapped in leaves to all who stayed under the platform.

Thomas remained in front of the fire and did his best to dry out from the rain. The man who had helped Thomas across the river stayed by his side, chatting with him. Thomas seized the opportunity and began to speak to all those around the fire. He told them he came from lands far to the west, on a mission ordained by God, who had sent him to India to bring the good news that the Christ was crucified so that all mankind might live. He explained that in order to enter the Kingdom of God, all must deny themselves, giving up a life of wealth for poverty.

At the mention of poverty, several around the fire began to laugh. "Well," said the young man, "we all meet that requirement. We are all poor already!"

He looked about the fire as he spoke, seeking amused confirmation. Thomas continued with his message, choosing not to further elaborate on poverty.

"Denial is in all things physical, including any union between a man and a woman. Fornication is the greatest sin," said the apostle.

It was a theme that he could not resist raising, always mindful of the pain and suffering he had seen in his own life.

Several of the men around the fire looked around at each other, some still smiling from his earlier comment and now laughing at these new words. Still others looked uncomfortable, including Thomas' new friend, wanting to befriend this stranger but unsure exactly what he was about. Several of the priests heard these words too and turned to study Thomas carefully.

"There are no more women under our shelter tonight," Thomas commented. "Not having women here will remove temptation and help all of us clear our minds for union with God," he concluded. This far-reaching comment shocked all the assembly for a moment and then produced a loud nervous laughter from everyone.

Thomas was startled by this reaction and puzzled. He looked around at the men who shared the fire with him. He had never received such a response when presenting the word of God. He was not sure if they were laughing at him or at his witticism for noting the absence of the women.

"Sadhu," said one of the priests, finally, "your host tonight is the Goddess Meenakshi. This is her temple; this is her place. We are her children. We all miss the women and wish they were here with us. Perhaps you did not realize that she is with us, here. That is why so many of us laughed." The man's tone was friendly. He smiled encouragingly at Thomas, expecting that he would now understand their reaction.

Before Thomas could respond, the priest continued. "But let me tell you a story of the importance of women to our people. Let me tell you the story of the Silappathikaram."

As the priest said these words, all the people in the shelter gathered around closely. They all knew the great tale of Silappathikaram well but eagerly waited for the retelling of it, anyway.

Thomas nodded his head, unsure of what he was agreeing to.

"Many years ago, not far from right here in Madurai," the priest began, "a young couple, a man named Kovalan and a woman named Kannagi, met and fell in love. It was a great love, arranged by their families but also a love match. They lived in great harmony."

After pausing for a moment, he continued, "But as you may know, Sadhu, sometimes, over time, things change. The young husband met a beautiful young dancer and courtesan serving in the king's court. Her name was Maadhavi. Maadhavi was very enchanting and beautiful—so beautiful!" Many in the audience nodded their affirmation. "Soon, the husband, the man named Kovalan, could not resist, and he left his devoted wife for this beautiful courtesan. The two were very happy for a time, and they lived together. Kovalan spent lots of money on Maadhavi. He was so infatuated with her that he took care of her every whim!"

The priest made a fist and struck it against the palm of his hand for emphasis.

"Now, the young wife, Kannagi, was heartbroken that she had lost her husband. Yet, she was a dedicated and good wife, and even though her husband was unfaithful to her, she decided to stay loyal to him. She waited for him!"

There were several "ahh"s in the audience, as some voiced their approval of this behavior.

Thomas looked about the firelight and could see eager faces listening carefully to every word the priest uttered. The apostle himself was captivated by this tale. The priest continued.

"During the festival of our God Indra, there was a singing competition. Both the wayward husband Kovalan and the courtesan Maadhavi joined the competition. Each separately sang a song about how they had been injured by a past lover. As Kovalan listened to the words sung by the courtesan Maadhavi, he began to understand that her song was about how she had been unfaithful to him. Maadhavi heard the song that Kovalan sang and thought the same of him - that he must have been unfaithful to her. Kovalan finally understood the error of his ways and decided to return to his loving and loyal wife Kannagi. Can you imagine!" the priest exclaimed for good effect all around.

Again, several in the audience nodded approvingly at this behavior.

"And Kannagi was a good and loyal wife, Thomas," emphasized the priest. "Despite all the terrible things that had happened, Kannagi still loved her husband. Kannagi agreed to take her husband back, and soon they began their life together again. In fact," said the priest, pausing momentarily for effect, "Kannagi loved her husband so much she even gave him one of her jeweled anklets to sell so that he could raise funds to start his new business and their shared life.

"When he went to the merchant in the market to sell the jeweled anklet, the merchant thought the anklet must belong to the queen, it was so beautiful. It looked just like one of the queen's anklets!" The priest raised his arms for grand emphasis. "The merchant called the guard and had Kovalan arrested! He accused the poor man of theft! Can you imagine!"

The priest repeated, an obvious habitual refrain when telling a story. Concerned that Thomas was not following the complex plot closely enough, the priest repeated his statement.

"The merchant had him, Kovalan, arrested even though it was an anklet from his wife," he explained again. "And the king, without first checking to see if the anklet really belonged to Kannagi, had the husband executed! Just so quickly, so quickly," the priest repeated for effect. "Can you imagine this?"

Of course, all the Tamils sitting in the shelter could, and most knew this favorite story by heart.

The priest enjoyed telling his story and continued with more flair, as he realized he had the close attention of every man under the shelter. The rain was coming down softly now, and everyone could hear his voice ringing in the night.

"When her husband did not return, Kannagi went looking for him and discovered that he had been executed by the king. What to do?" The priest wobbled his head and twisted his hands to emphasize his point.

"She was distraught. She went to the king's court and dramatically threw her other, matching jeweled anklet into the court, proving the anklet was hers and not the queen's." The priest pantomimed the motion of throwing something into the middle of a courtyard. "The king saw the matching anklet and immediately acknowledged his mistake. He repented, but it was not enough. The king immediately dropped dead." The priest made the tone of his voice sound mournful. "Immediately," he repeated.

"But the situation was now changed," the priest continued. "Kannagi had loved her husband. She was loyal to him. But now, he was dead. Even the death of the king was not enough. She was angry, now. Kannagi ripped off her breast from her chest and cursed the town of Madurai. That is this very town, my friend. Kannagi cursed the town. She created a very powerful curse."

The priest dramatically clutched at his breast and then threw an imagery object away from him as he spoke. His face showed fear as he imagined the curse cast upon the town.

"This happened in this very town that you are in now, Sadhu," said the priest, again repeating himself for emphasis. He paused for dramatic effect, wanting to be sure that Thomas understood. "Then sadly," the priest continued, "Our town was burned to the ground because of her curse and the consequence of her suffering." The priest's voice faltered as he said these words. He was wrapping up his story, but his audience wanted more. The dramatic flourish returned to the priest's voice.

"The gods watched the terrible injustice being played out in Madurai. With the blessing of Indra, they decided to bring Kannagi to the heavens where she could meet with Indra! The god Indra, Thomas." The priest paused to ensure the apostle understood this weighty development. "And it happened that she, Konnagi, went to see Indra and repented her anger and the curse she laid upon Madurai. So, in return for her gracious gesture, Indra made her a goddess. Kannagi became a goddess, Sadhu!"

The priest turned towards Thomas. "This is all true, my friend. I can take you to the shrine of Kannagi right here in Madurai. You can see for your own eyes! The point of this great story, Thomas, is that we must honor women. Women are our equal partners in this life."

There was a glint in the eye of the priest when he finished his story. Some of the men in the shelter were quietly still laughing at the idea that Thomas had presented earlier, that all relationships between a man and a woman were somehow wrong.

Another priest spoke up. Looking at Thomas he said, "There are many lessons from this story, Sadhu. Yes, we respect our mothers and the women in our lives, but the biggest point of this story is karma. In this case, the couple was also affected by their past lives."

This comment produced a general discussion about the meaning of the story, some adding further elements to the story, such as the fact that the courtesan and the young couple had all known each other in past lives. There was also some friendly dispute and banter between some of the priests over which god had actually agreed to see Kannagi and what had become of her.

The apostle listened to the conversation, unsure how to break into the discussion. Experiencing first-hand the deep-rooted beliefs that many of the people had, he realized it was going to be very difficult to convert these Hindus to the true path of the one God. As the conversations under the shelter began to wane, most of the men slowly began to settle down for the night, wrapping themselves in cloaks and anything they could find to keep them warm. Thomas found a comfortable dry corner to stretch out in too.

The apostle slept soundly all night in the shelter of the Goddess Meenakshi's temple.

Chapter 26

Om Nama Shiva. I bow to Shiva. Shiva is the supreme reality, the inner self. It is the name given to the consciousness that dwells in all.

—Mantra of Lord Shiva

SADHU VANARAJ, A devotee of Lord Shiva, squatted on the tile floor under the stone roof of the monastery as the afternoon monsoon hit the village. These powerful rains came every year in a predictable fashion. To his mind, the rains were part of the repetitive cycle of life, a mere reflection of the repetitive and cyclical nature of all things, including birth, death, and rebirth, called samsara. It was only through extreme self-denial that one was able to stop the eternal cycle and achieve moksha, the liberation from samsara. Sadhu Vanaraj understood all these things. The monsoon came down so hard, and it cascaded off the roof with so much force, it formed a wall of water that looked impenetrable to those sheltering beneath.

The small village near the monastery, a cluster of huts separated by muddy passages, endured the rains each year. The sadhu was still furious with the monks at Kanchi Matha he had been speaking to.

Wrapped in a simple cloak to hide his nakedness, he summoned his consciousness, a technique he used to quell his anger, but it was also an effort to keep the sensation of cold from passing into his core and body, thus disturbing his thoughts. A Master of Yoga, such concentration was a simple matter. His body was still smeared with ash, and on his forehead, three clear lines announced to the world his devotion to Lord Shiva.

Vanaraj had met with many of the monks over the course of the last few days to better understand their new teachings. It did not take him long to alienate them. They did not appreciate his beliefs and clearly did not want him to be there. There had also been some discussion about this strange Sadhu Thomas who had come to Tamilakam from the sea. He did not speak the language of the people very well, but it was understood that he was advocating unnatural behavior, that an individual should be married to "God." The students, teachers, and sages all found this proposition to be preposterous and felt that it represented a complete lack of understanding of the divine. Even if this Sadhu Thomas had been speaking metaphorically, it still would make no sense. On this matter, Vanaraj could agree with them.

While most of the devotees were adherents of the Goddess, there was one impressive and knowledgeable priest who had singled him out. He took Vanaraj aside and explained that the Raja Mahadeva wished to speak to him. Could he come to Mylapore? The priest took pains to remind him of the important role Lord Murugan, God and son of Shiva, played as a protector of the people. He also emphasized the raja's devotion to Lord Shiva. That the raja was a devout Shaivite pleased Vanaraj, and the invitation to meet with him was a good sign. Still, the request from the raja was unusual. *Why me?* Vanaraj thought carefully. *I, Vanaraj, am not important to such high counsel. Why ask to see me?* The sadhu knew there was probably much more that the king wanted, more than a discussion of the divine.

Vanaraj nodded his head slowly as he considered the discussion. The role of protector was consistent with the qualities of Shiva. The sadhu, trident in hand, was not afraid to take up that role. The villagers all knew Vanaraj as one of the sadhus who would drink from the skull of a human, proof that he did not fear death and could dismiss it. He was fearless. Why would he be called upon to be a protector in this case?

The rains finally stopped and Vanaraj stepped out into the muddy lane, beginning his long journey to Mylapore.

Just a few kilometers away, Thomas was also slowly making his way back towards Mylapore too. Several months had passed since he had visited Madurai and heard the story of the Silappathikaram. After that visit, he had continued to travel around the region preaching the Word of God. He called on the people to repent and to deny themselves and enter the Kingdom of God.

In and around Muziris, he had developed a strong church and foundation for his ministry. The seven churches continued to grow without him, baptizing new ministers, laying on hands, and healing the sick. The Brahmin Natarajan continued to speak of tolerance and peace for all, and it seemed to work. Muziris continued to prosper.

The success Thomas had in Muziris gave him a certain amount of pride. He knew he had left seeds of growth in that church and that community. It would endure through the ages. That church was strong.

But the apostle could not find such strength in any other community in the area. As Thomas traveled about the interior, he found it much more difficult to gather followers. Many people viewed him as just another sadhu, a holy man with extremist views conducting false miracles and living in self-imposed poverty. Thomas' message about self-denial, including his proscription that fornication was the greatest of all sins, did not sit well with many, particularly the wealthy and the higher castes.

When he had visited Mylapore, he had found many interested priests who were tolerant of his message and some who even encouraged him. Yet, he also found that while some appeared to accept his message, most did not stop conducting pujas or acting like Hindus either. Even some that Thomas baptized kept up these practices, some discreetly, but not all.

"What to do?" he sighed thoughtfully. *"Has God brought me all this way to do only this?"*

The thoughts of his success in Muziris and Cranganore initially gave him encouragement and strength to keep trying, despite the lack of success elsewhere. Perhaps God had just wanted him to plant the seeds of the church with the seven communities around Cranganore and over time, it would grow.

The apostle was eventually successful in establishing a small following just outside Mylapore, although this tiny church was still not housed properly. There was no temple or structure from the community given for this purpose. In Muziris, he had had a friendly ally in the Pandit Natarajan. Thomas had been given a temple to use as his own. The temple even included devotees, many of whom quickly accepted his teachings about God too. There he had felt free to move about and to speak and preach as he wanted to. Mylapore was different; he sensed that the people there were not going to give themselves up as freely to the pathway of God. He continued to make contacts with the local religious community, friendly Hindu priests mostly, but none of them offered much assistance. The Mylapore church met in the shade under a large mango tree, in the field below the surrounding hills.

Still, there was no patron like Pandit Natarajan in this new place, he wistfully considered. He had no temple and no wealthy patrons. He had no place to live but managed to find a small cave on the hillside that suited his needs. Many of his followers were from the lowest castes, the downtrodden and diseased. Many of them saw in Thomas a way to improve their lot in a wretched and difficult life. Often baptized, many secretly continued with other worship too, thinking it was probably in their interest to worship all the gods.

Initially, Thomas' past experience with princes and kings led him to believe that it would be better for him to avoid new entanglements with royalty. While his church prospered in Muziris, King Misdaeus had made it clear that he was no longer welcome there. In truth, Misdaeus was tolerant and had decided to ignore Thomas as long as he stayed away from his business, and especially as long as he did not attempt to convert any more wives to his preposterous creed.

Thomas sensed the tolerant views of the king and made a few discreet return visits to Muziris and the area but generally found that he had worn out his welcome. He even risked losing the progress he had made with the seven churches. The princess was no longer available to meet with him and could not be found.

Isa's statement that it is too difficult for a rich man to enter the kingdom of God is so true, thought Thomas. Nevertheless, his lack of standing around Mylapore led him to reach out to Raja Mahadeva, the great king of the region, and propose an audience despite his misgivings. He did not understand the relationship between this king and the titled king and prince of Muziris, but he could see that at least outwardly, Raja Mahadeva was the greater. Mighty cities, temples, and towns sprung up all about Mylapore. He would regularly see chariots and warriors on the road, all showcasing the power of the raja.

Thomas attempted to reach out to the king through a friendly Hindu priest he frequently encountered on the road. The priest had explained that he often attended audiences with the raja. The priest's friendliness and confidence initially caused Thomas to believe that he might expect a positive response from the king.

It was not to be. The response from the raja was clear and unequivocal: Mahadeva was not interested in speaking to a strange sadhu who preached unnatural behavior. Mahadeva had firmly declined the request. The priest, no longer so friendly, made it clear that there was no reason to expect that the raja would ever change his mind.

The response left Thomas severely depressed. There seemed to be no path forward for the apostle. He retreated to his cave on the hill. *How can I reach these people and do thy bidding Lord?* were words that would not leave him. *Where was Isa?* He needed guidance.

The request from the Hindu priest for an audience was too much. Raja Mahadeva had already heard enough. It was time to act. This strange foreign sadhu was preaching unnatural behaviors that were an affront to the gods. Before he had even been approached about a meeting, the raja had received reports coming from his friend and subordinate Misdaeus that even the wife of one of the brother princes had been talked into undressing in front of this man and then had subjected herself to some kind of primitive ceremony involving being dunked in water. *Sacrilege! An outrage!* The raja was not going to let that happen here.

His councilors had initially advised him not to get directly involved. His response to the priest who raised the subject of meeting with the apostle had been crystal clear: no. The priest was further commanded to distance himself from this crazy foreigner and to not associate with him anymore.

"This is a matter for the religious community," his religious advisors had helpfully offered to him. "Let the religious community solve it." The raja acknowledged the wisdom and simplicity of such sage advice. There were other ways to advance a solution and the religious community's advice held the seeds of an answer. Yet Mahadeva elected to be the catalyst to help his often divided and indecisive religious subordinates bring the matter forward. *These priests were good talkers,* he knew. *But taking real action? Not at all.*

Vanaraj entered the royal compound of Raja Mahadeva with caution. He still did not know what the raja wanted from him. The priest at the monastery had not been clear. The sadhu did not view this as a summons so much as an opportunity to answer questions of the divine for the king. At least that was his hope. *I will not answer an actual summons,* he thought stubbornly.

The sadhu was getting on in years and knew that he was approaching the final stages of his life. He had lived a good and divine life. Achieving moksha was even possible in this life. Vanaraj was confident of that. All other things were a distraction, even a visit with the raja. Still, he came; he was here to carry out his duty.

Vanaraj entered the palace grounds humbly, but with his head held high, the appropriate posture for a man of God meeting with royalty. He was met by a young male courtesan who motioned him to follow. He was guided through the palace doors and down a hall to a small chamber, one usually reserved for private meetings with the raja's councilors and senior officials. One end of the chamber held a modest dais and a large chair. Vanaraj was shown where to sit on the stone floor, declining to accept any luxury, including a carpet or even a pillow. He sat against the wall and waited. A servant entered several times, noting his presence, and finally brought him a tumbler of water, which he gladly accepted. The servant explained that the raja was delayed but would arrive soon.

Vanaraj, finding the floor cold, elected to stand after a while. Still waiting after more than an hour, he began to grow impatient. Finally, after two hours, Raja Mahadeva briskly entered the chamber, stopping briefly to place his hands together and nod to the sadhu before him. He gave the impression of a man in a hurry. Raja Mahadeva was not a man of protocol. He was a man of action. He stopped and studied the holy man standing expectantly in his chamber. Vanaraj turned to the raja as he entered the room, placing his hands together and bowing his head slowly.

As the raja sat down on the dais, he thought to himself, *Yes, this is the kind of man I expected.* He smiled faintly. He noted that the sadhu had a rough, unkempt look about him.

"Greetings, Sadhu Vanaraj," the raja finally spoke. "My apologies for my late arrival. Affairs of State." He smiled and shrugged.

"Greetings, mighty raja," responded the sadhu in reply. His voice was coarse, almost harsh from a lifetime inhaling smoke and ash and from living outdoors. He had waited a long time and was not happy. He wanted to get right to the point.

"I have come because you sent a priest to tell me that you were seeking me. I met him at Kanchi Matha," Vanaraj continued. "How can I, a simple sadhu, help a mighty raja?"

"Blessings to you, Sadhu," said the raja, sounding almost repentant. "I am sincerely grateful for your visit and presence. I know you have come a long way, and again I am deeply sorry for keeping you waiting so long." Several courtesans struggled to suppress smiles. The raja was most definitely not sorry nor humble and normally would never apologize to anyone for anything unless there was a purpose. Catering to the sadhu's ego, the raja continued, "But I need the help of the divine. Who else can help me but one such as Sadhu Vanaraj?"

The sadhu did not appreciate the raja's weak attempt at flattery. He was impatient. Again, moving the conversation directly to the point, he asked simply, "How can I help you, mighty Raja?" The sadhu's tone was flat.

From the response, the raja sensed the intelligence of this man and also his impatience. He decided to speak directly to the point.

"When you visited Kanchi Matha and perhaps in other places, you have heard of this new sadhu named Thomas?" queried the Raja.

"I have heard of him yes, Raja," affirmed the sadhu. "I have not met him, but I hear of the unnatural things that he preaches."

"The problem this sadhu presents to us is a matter for Shiva, I think," continued the monarch. "This foreign sadhu has caused many problems for our allies in Muziris. Do you know that he even had one of the princesses undress and take part in some kind of unclean and primitive water ritual? I cannot accept that here." The raja's voice was firm on this point.

"I have heard of that too," answered Vanaraj. "This sadhu also preaches that one is to eat bread and drink wine as though it is of the body and blood of another. Of a god, I believe. This is ritual cannibalism. A very primitive sort of religion."

The raja shivered and shook his head with contempt upon hearing these words. "You see," he said, "our people cannot accept such dangerous thinking and actions happening in our midst." More thoughtfully, the raja asked, "So how do we solve this problem, Sadhu? Can you help us? We need the intervention of the divine to solve this problem. We need the divine intervention of Shiva and maybe Lord Murugan to save us. Do you understand what I am asking? Can you help us?" The tone of the raja now sounded almost like he was begging.

Sadhu Vanaraj regarded the raja thoughtfully. After a pause, he said, "Mighty raja, Shiva is the protector of the people. You are right to call on him to help in this matter. I will seek the guidance of the divine. I will seek the help of Lord Murugan.

The raja smiled at the Hindu man of God who clearly understood. He was happy with these words.

Chapter 27

*Om Tarakasurasanhartre Namah I: Praise be to the
slayer of the Demon Tarakasuran.*

*—Mantra of Lord Murugan, the son of Shiva, the
brother of Ganesha*

THOMAS WAS LOST in prayer. The apostle was back on the hillside of
the small mount. Just below the summit was an opening to a small
cave he used as a temporary shelter and chapel. Large boulders,
worn by erosion, were scattered across the hillside. Thomas knelt
before one such stone, a natural granite block carved by the elements to form an altar. He continued to pray as the sun slowly rose
in the east.

The apostle's great success was in Muziris. *That church would
endure among the seven communities. But my time in Mylapore was almost
finished.* The new church he had established here was not on firm
footing, but he had at least connected them to the stronger church
in Muziris. *Maybe some of the faithful will travel there and find fellowship and
sanctuary.*

He continued to dwell on his predicament. In Mylapore, he had
not found the committed followers he needed upon which to build

a stronger foundation in the region. At first, he was frustrated by this development. He would seem to make inroads with the people in the villages, but it was never for long. They would not fully repent from their Hindu ways. They seemed to willingly accept duality and multiple paths to the divine. They would not accept the one true path to God. *They seem to accept all gods,* he thought resignedly.

Over time, he began to accept that preaching in Mylapore was still the path that God had selected for him, but there was more. God was unfolding a new revelation and establishing a permanent church in Mylapore was not one of his tasks. God had other plans for him here on the mount. He tried to clear his mind from all these thoughts.

He needed to seek out the divine again. In prayer and meditation, a new revelation would come. Isa had always guided him to the right path, no matter how difficult. He had traveled to India. He had endured incredible dangers. He has succeeded in planting the seeds of the Kingdom of God in India. What more was there to accomplish? The Christian Church in India would endure because of his sacrifice. He again cleared his mind of all these thoughts.

Thomas remained in a prayer pose as he considered all these issues; prayer pose but not praying. In truth, he was often meditating like his Hindu friends. Pandit Natarajan had imparted that skill to him. His mind was not disciplined at first, but over the last few months, he had learned to control his thinking and his breathing, which were surprisingly related. At times, he was not sure when he was praying and when he was meditating.

Forcing all stray thoughts from his mind, he knew that he needed guidance. He needed to hear from the divine. What was next in his ministry? Finally, he began to pray again. He prayed to the God of Abraham, to Christ, and to the one true God.

"I am not Isa," he prayed to the divine. "I am but your servant. I am a minister, my God. I accomplish your will, my God. I am your instrument, my Lord." The apostle chanted the prayer over and over in Aramaic. The sound of his voice in his native tongue comforted him. Speaking the Tamil language took supreme effort.

And then, new words came to him. He felt inspired, not unlike the moment that he had sung the Hymn of the Pearl in prison. *"And that which is not a death but is merely that which sets the soul free from the body."*

Thomas said these last words carefully and then repeated them. The words were startlingly clear. It was as though God gave him those words to speak. He did not think them up on his own.

At first, he said the words almost aimlessly, but his voice grew louder as he continued, and with each chant, his understanding expanded. Thomas understood the meaning of the words. This was God's new revelation to him.

This new wisdom of death invaded his thinking: "that which is not death, but merely setting the soul free from the body," was the chant. How had these words of wisdom entered his mind? The next stage in his mission was coming. This new understanding offered him release and peace. The knowledge was soothing.

The new words offered a sense of finality and conclusion that suddenly filled Thomas with joy. He cast his fear aside. His frustration was no more. This sudden awakening renewed his spirit. He stopped praying and stood up, thanking God for his new gift and revelation. Thomas felt newly courageous. God had armed him. God had prepared him. Isa had faced this same problem at the crucifixion. Isa had shown courage, knowing his death would save people and bring them back into union with God the Father. The apostle was prepared for what was to come.

⊷▮ ▮⊶

Sadhu Vanaraj, protector of the people, prepared himself. He conducted his morning puja and meditation with practiced discipline. He was staying near Mylapore, not far from where the foreign sadhu abomination was said to be living. He had been in the area for a few weeks, scouting out the area, talking to other sadhus and priests. Sadhu Vanaraj had thought long and hard about this day. The divine was directing him to this point. He had had several conversations with villagers who had explained their interactions with Sadhu Thomas. His teachings were an abomination. There was a danger to the people.

He resolutely picked up his trident. He had meditated much of the night and early that morning on the task at hand. This problem required absolute clarity and certainty. *If I kill this foreign sadhu, will that action affect moksha?* The thought would not leave him. He had spent his entire life in devotion and purpose. He did not want to see all his sacrifice lost. And then, as only the divine can do, the answer appeared before him. Three other sadhus, Shaivites like himself, suddenly appeared early that morning as he was conducting his ablutions. They were carrying their sacred tridents too. Vanaraj did not know them; they seemed to have come from afar. Yet, nothing more than a few words in passing needed to be said after that. The path of the divine was clear to all. Their very presence was a clear message from the divine of what action needed to be taken.

The actions of today are the actions of the universe, Sadhu Vanaraj thought. *My actions and those of the other three sadhus are not ours alone.* The new truth gave him relief and freedom. He suddenly understood that for a time, he would truly have the divine power of the Lord Murugan to protect the people and slay this foreign demon. The thought energized him.

This man who perverts the divine. This man who suborns the natural order of things. Even the Buddhists and the Jains see the inherent heresy and demonic tendencies in this man, Vanaraj thought, somewhat self-righteously. *There is no Middle Path, no Right Thinking, with this devil.*

Sadhu Vanaraj walked towards the small hillock where he knew Sadhu Thomas was said to be living. Vanaraj had used his time wisely in the last few weeks and knew the area well. The road was clear and unobstructed. There was little traffic to impede his path. Cattle and other livestock seemed to understand his mission and stepped aside as Vanaraj and the three companion sadhus walked briskly past them single file.

He had decided not to approach the demon stealthily. He did not need to hide. Lord Murugan had empowered him! Vanaraj walked openly, boldly, his three Shaivite sadhu companions following quietly but equally resolutely just behind him.

At last, Vanaraj saw the demon itself! It was further up on the hillside, almost directly in front of the cave that many of the Shaivites used. *Undoubtedly, this demon has defiled that holy place too,* Vanaraj thought. He then pushed all thoughts from his mind and concentrated on the task at hand.

The three companions of Vanaraj saw the demon too. As they closed in on their quarry, they silently broke away from the small group, each finding a cardinal direction from which they could approach it.

This is easy to do. All four sadhus had the same thought at the same time, another signal from the divine. *The quarry. The demon will not run.*

Sadhu Vanaraj approached the demon first.

Apostle Thomas, armed with the new and divine truth, a message from God, could see the Brahman sadhus approaching, coming up the hill, demons too, but instruments of the one God.

He was not afraid. The sight of the Hindu holy men and their appearance was not unusual to him: nearly pale white from the ash smeared all over their bodies, wearing scant saffron robes and carrying tridents. Thomas had seen many such holy men on his mount. Yet, Thomas now knew these holy men were coming for him with divine purpose.

Seeing Sadhu Vanaraj approach closely, Thomas raised his hands to God in praise. "Come deny yourself and follow the path to the Kingdom of God!" he cried out. In Thomas' religious euphoria, he was unable to speak Tamil, and his words did not carry to all the men approaching. He spoke his words in Aramaic, the language of the brothers. The divine language ability to speak Tamil had left him.

Still, Sadhu Vanaraj alone heard the demonic and unintelligible words coming from this false holy man. The very sound of the words ignited him. He, Vanaraj, was the hand of the divine. Of a god. And it was not the incarnation of the Goddess. He was mighty Lord Murugan, the protector of the Tamil people.

Vanaraj raised his trident, the first time he had ever done so against another human being. As he did so, from all the directions, his brothers, also taken with the spirit of the Lord Murugan, rushed in. Sadhu Vanaraj struck down hard on the demon, driving the trident deep into its chest. His three other companions fulfilled their roles and did likewise from the cardinal directions.

Thomas, his hands still raised, felt the metal run deep into his chest and being. He coughed and tried to catch his breath. There was no need to speak. Only joy was upon his face.

Exaltation! Sadhu Vanaraj and Apostle Thomas locked eyes on each other in religious fervor, as each experienced the power of their God. They both sensed the presence of the divine, tremendous ecstasy, and release from their burdens.

Moksha was still his. Joy!

Thomas had at last found his twin, the brother he loved, Isa. Joy!

Chapter 28

*Our ability to reach unity in diversity will be the beauty
and test of our civilization.*

—*Mahatma Gandhi*

NATARAJAN WAS SITTING in the garden in deep meditation when the news from Mylapore arrived. A young student carried the news.

"Pandit," said the man, slightly out of breath as he bowed respectfully to his elder. "Sadhu Thomas is dead. Several of the Shaivites killed him in Mylapore."

The news shocked the Brahmin. Natarajan rarely betrayed emotion, but he genuinely liked the apostle, despite their religious differences. It pained him to hear this news.

"How did this happen?" he asked somberly. "When did this happen? It was not so long ago that our Thomas was safely here with us."

"Yes," responded the student. "I remember listening in when you and Sadhu Thomas would meet for chai. But I was in Mylapore ten days ago when this terrible news arrived. I was visiting my family and was planning to return to Muziris in a few weeks, anyway.

However, when I heard this news and confirmed the matter, I knew you would want to know right away. I came right back to you. But I don't think there is anything one can do, either."

"Did they tell you what happened, exactly?" inquired Natarajan further. His tone was solemn, betraying the sadness he felt. "He had some strange beliefs, but he did not represent a real threat to any of us. I am so sorry this happened." He frowned and shook his head as he spoke.

"I don't know all the details of how he was killed, Pandit. It is my understanding that several sadhus attacked him with their tridents. They ran him through with their tridents," he repeated. "Sadhu Thomas was living on a hill in front of the entrance to a cave the Shaivites also use. They were followers of Lord Murugan too. There is one sadhu who is famous for his fearlessness. It may have been him, but I don't know his name. I have heard about him."

"Thank you, my son." Natarajan nodded gratefully, but he was still unable to hide the pain reflected in his face. "I appreciate you coming to tell me so quickly. I will have to reach out to the seven communities here. They will want to know right away, too."

"Pandit, there is one more thing," the young man added before leaving. "There is a story that the raja ordered his death. I don't have any proof of that, but it does make sense. We all know that our king here did not like Thomas. The king could have easily told the raja, who likely would have the same mind on this matter. He would not have wanted to hear the message of Thomas, particularly the message about denial of relationships with women."

Natarajan nodded his head in thanks. The same thought had occurred to him. *This killing was not random and was more likely brought on by action by one of the kings or princes in the area. It did not make sense. It is the right of kings,* reflected the pandit. *They kill who they want. They let live who they want.* There was nothing more to do. He thanked the young man again and bid him farewell.

As the student left, Natarajan called for his nephew with instructions to go to the seven communities in Cranganore and ask them to immediately send representatives. The leaders, deacons of the seven communities, were quick to arrive. Rumors were already circulating in the community, so Natarajan wasted no time and got right to the point, conveying the bad news.

"Thomas, your beloved, is dead. I am so sorry to have to tell you," pronounced the pandit, his tone clear but gentle.

At this news, the seven deacons all cried out in anguish. One elder deacon inquired, "What happened exactly, Pandit? How could this have happened?" There was a strain in his voice.

"My news is that four sadhus, followers of Lord Shiva, killed him. I don't have all the information yet. I will share more when I know more," clarified the pandit.

"This is not right, Natarajan," said the elder, shaking his head and momentarily forgetting to address the pandit by his title. "How could this happen? We will need to seek out justice for our apostle."

Natarajan took a deep breath and raised his palms in an effort to calm down the seven deacons. "I don't think there will be justice of that kind, my friends," he said gently. "At least not that way. Justice will be found in karma. In the divine. You will have to accept that." The pandit said this last firmly.

The senior deacon was seasoned enough to finally realize that some authority, if not the raja himself, must have had a hand in the killing of their man of God.

As the elders turned to go, Natarajan stopped them for a moment. "There is something more you can do, my friends. We all knew and loved our apostle, Thomas. Send a delegation to Mylapore to recover his body or his remains. Do not go to Mylapore for revenge. Do not send a team to find out more facts about what happened. Leave that to me. But send a delegation of young men to recover what you can and bring him back here. We can then perform the proper rites for burial. You are the apostle's family. Go to Mylapore as family, recovering a loved one."

The deacons thanked Natarajan for that advice and then filed out.

⊹⊨◉ ◉⊨⊹

Abbanes learned of the death of Thomas two years later, on his return journey to Muziris. The Jewish community was the first to tell him what had transpired. Abbanes listened to the story in shock and sadness.

He then paid a call on Pandit Natarajan to learn more about his friend's death. The Pandit graciously accepted the visit by Abbanes, and the two elder men talked for a long time, reflecting on the life of their friend.

"I am struck by how often I now encounter members of this new religion, this 'cult' of Judaism, of my religion," commented Abbanes. "This religion is growing. They are calling it 'Christianity,' now, after Christ, after Isa. When I talk to other 'Christians,' I am struck by the similarity of themes that our friend Thomas pursued. They hold many of the same tenets of my faith too. Yet, I fear our apostle, far and distant from the other practitioners of his faith, took some things to the extreme. This was always a worry of ours. You and I did not discuss this at the time, but I think I understood you were concerned too."

Natarajan smiled lightly and nodded in agreement. He then motioned to his nephew to bring forth a simple wooden box. The box was about one meter long and was held together by bright red cotton ropes, tightly wound.

"The deacons of the seven communities recovered the remains of our beloved apostle two years ago. There was no agreement among them as to what to do with our friend's remains. Should it be a burial of some kind, or what does one of your religion do?" Natarajan asked. "We were not sure, and we did want to honor him. I decided to hold his remains until such time as I could talk to you about it. May I entrust them to you for proper burial or rites? The apostle was one of your people, after all."

Abbanes was shocked. He stared at the funerary box for a moment, and then, considering what he should do, silently nodded his assent. After two years, Abbanes wondered what could possibly remain of his friend but realized that it was likely just his bones. He knew from visiting stupas and other holy places that this part of the world was accustomed to the proper handling of funerary objects. Thomas' remains, once recovered, were probably well taken care of, he thought.

While Abbanes was contemplating the funerary box of Thomas, Natarajan broke the moment and posed a new question. "What is the legacy of our Thomas, Abbanes?" he asked. "What is the legacy of all these Christians as you call them? What will it be? You travel the world, and they seem to come from your people. Have you considered this? I suppose I will call our seven communities 'The Thomas Christians,' now. He has planted a seed in India, and I am sure it will grow. His heart was good. I will do my small part to protect the legacy of our friend."

Abbanes listened to the pandit carefully. Nodding in agreement, he spoke slowly. "The question of the legacy of Thomas is difficult to know, and only time will tell. It's a difficult question," responded Abbanes. "In many ways, like the followers of my God, they are strong, moral leaders. The teachings of Isa are remarkable and beneficial to many. At times, they seem to be able to tap into the very power of God as they conduct healings. I have seen this with my very own eyes. I am still astonished when I think of how a prince was raised from the dead. I was there. I am sure all of that will be one of the great legacies of these Christians." Nodding his head, he affirmed, "I like calling your community 'Thomas Christians.' Yes, a great legacy of our friend. Perhaps his church will grow."

After pausing for a moment, he continued thoughtfully. "But I also think our beloved apostle lost his way on some matters. He would have benefitted if Isa had stayed with him longer. I know Thomas was always frantically looking for Isa on his long journey, but Isa never returned after we left Andrapolis. At least not physically. Perhaps in death, he finally found the brother he loved."

The pandit nodded his head affirmatively. Abbanes continued, "Thomas would have also benefited if some of his brother apostles had been with him too. I fear his legacy and insistence of being 'married to God' will have consequences down the ages. In other places I have traveled, this idea that man is 'married' to God persists. However, among the other Christians I encountered this practice seems to be limited to priests. I understand there are even Christian nuns, women priests, too. What will be the legacy of all this? I don't know, but I think our Thomas would have done well to have changed some of his thinking. I was initially hoping that he would adopt some of the moderating ideas and philosophy of the Middle Path of Buddhism. It might have influenced and changed his practices. Pandit Natarajan, even some of your tolerant, inclusive views would have helped." Abbanes let his voice and tone drop. "But he did not."

Natarajan nodded in agreement. "Yes, even just among our priests—Buddhist, Hindu, or Jain—this total denial of needs can result in wrong thinking and expose human weakness. Men and women are strongest together, not apart. Their union is divine."

"Yes," concurred the Hebrew. "God made a man and a woman. Two parts of one." Abbanes carefully lifted the remains of the apostle in the funerary box. He found the box surprisingly light. "I will carry this back to Jerusalem."

~Epilogue~

LIEUTENANT ORNA KIRETZ looked out from the side of the El Al Boeing 777 as it made its final approach into Tel Aviv International Airport from Mumbai. Orna was still mulling over all she had learned in Kerala. Apostle Thomas, her own Jewish distant ancestor, even? She smiled at the thought. What an amazing impact he had. Millions of Thomas Christians in the world identified with him, now. Maybe there really was hope for Israel. Christians, Jews, and Hindus had once come together to make that happen. Who would have believed it? That might be the real legacy of Apostle Thomas. Why not Jews and Arabs today?

She had loved her Indian holiday, but now it was time to get back to work. Isaac looked up from his magazine and smiled at her. He was still reading an article about divisive American politics and had earlier remarked that the situation over there was almost as bad as Israeli politics these days.

The baggage terminal was the usual jammed, chaotic mess. The carousel was packed with bags, lined with travelers jostling for advantage. Recovering their bags, Isaac managed to flag down a taxi. The drive was quick, much to the relief of Orna. Finally, home, the young couple unpacked and lounged about their apartment.

The phone rang. It was Eddy.

"Orna, ah . . . sorry, Lieutenant," he corrected himself playfully. Eddy loved to dish it out to the lieutenant. "Where have you guys been? Missing in action?"

Before Orna could respond, Eddy continued. "Yeah, yeah, I know. The beach. I have been there. Nice spas and good food there." Turning serious, he continued. "Listen, Bibi is sending us down to Haifa. Some guard duty or something. You'd better come in. They're looking for you. The Indian Navy is going to be visiting, and they're sending the INS Kochi along with a few other warships. I think the Kochi is the one that carries the Barak 8 missile?" Eddy was never too sure of these things. He didn't deal with missiles. Eddy was a real fighter.

Orna again was about to respond when Eddy continued. "They want to make a show of it. Nothing can go wrong, so we have to go down there and help those girls with security." Eddy purposely used the word "girls" just to make a final dig at his commander.

Orna sighed. Ignoring Eddy's commentary, she said resignedly, "Tell them I will swing by in two hours. I just flew in."

"Roger, Boss," responded the young man cheerfully, delighted that Orna was back in town and back in action.

Orna hung up the phone. She had been amused when Eddy said the name of the visiting warship—The Kochi—recognizing the name from the signs she saw in Cochin as another name for her holiday destination. *Just completed holiday,* she thought wistfully.

Cochin was still on her mind as she climbed into the shower. *We're making a full circle with that country. Jews, Christians, Hindus, a few shared religions, and we even donated an apostle 2000 years ago! And now we're sharing missiles.* The thought filled her with hope and also with concern. Hope that the two countries could get along because they were able to coordinate a visit of a foreign navy at peace. Concern that it was weapons and a naval vessel, a vessel of war, that was bringing them together.

What is next? Her mind was too active. She shook her head, determined to clear her head. *If only we could all get along. If only.*

The shower door opened. It was Isaac.

The Legacy of the Apostle Thomas and his consequential journey to India: Today, some 6 million Thomas Christians live in South India and link their heritage to the arrival of the Apostle Thomas at Muziris in modern-day Kerala.

Acknowledgments

I OWE A debt of gratitude to many who helped me write this book. Thanks so much to Angelika Chin, Gary Bagley, Cecilia Op de Beke, Adeeti Joshi, and Greg Garland for suffering through early versions of this book and providing me with very helpful feedback. Any errors in this book are mine to own.

My story largely follows the Acts of Thomas. I tried to be true to the "Acts" as much as I could, although in some places I had to fill in blanks or refer to other research. I utilized a number of translations of the "Acts," including two listed below. I also collected a large body of information in India on Apostle Thomas and did my best to sort through lots of contradictions. I don't know the truth of Thomas' journey to India, but I do believe that my account might not be that far from the truth. Perhaps the author of the Acts of Thomas did not get everything right. However, surely a few nuggets of truth found their way into the 21st Century.

I realize that for some, the very idea that Christ had a brother who could pass as his twin will be shocking and sacrilegious. However, I did not create that part of the story—the basic outlines surrounding Thomas' identity already existed, beginning with his very name. I am also drawing attention to the many historical documents that exist but are not part of any version of the Bible.

I wrote this book in part to highlight the dangers of intolerant thinking—a growing problem in our wonderful world. We all need to learn tolerance and to accept each other. As Orna says, "Can't we all just get along?" It's a great world out there. Let's try.

Paul Folmsbee, Ambassador (ret)

Selected Sources

The Acts of Thomas; Translated by M.R. James; The Apocryphal New Testament; Oxford: Clarendon Press, 1924

The Acts of Thomas; Translated by J.K. Elliott, The Apocryphal New Testament; Oxford: Clarendon Press, 1993.

Lost Scriptures; Bart Ehrman; Oxford University Press, 2003

The Hymn of the Pearl; Translated by J.K. Elliot, The Apocryphal New Testament; Oxford: Clarendon Press. 1993

The Bible

The Coptic Gospel of Thomas, various translations

The Talmud; Berachot 55; various translations

The Dhammapada; various translations

The Bhagavad Gita; various translations

Glossary

Abbanes: The senior Hebrew trader from Gandhara and companion of Apostle Thomas.

Acts of Thomas: A New Testament Apocrypha which recounts the story of Apostle Thomas' journey to India.

Adi Parashakti: A female deity and a Supreme Being of Hinduism.

Ahura Mazdai: The creator God of Zoroastrianism.

Alexandria: The mighty port city of Egypt on the Mediterranean Sea and Nile River.

Andrapolis: A port city on the Asian mainland described in the Acts of Thomas.

Aramaic: A language commonly spoken in Syria, Judea, and surrounding lands during the time of Christ. Related to Hebrew.

Arhat: A Buddhist term referring to one who has gained insight and achieved Nirvana but has not yet achieved the status of Buddha.

Bharuch: An ancient port city located in Gujarat, India.

Bhikkhu: An ordained Buddhist monk.

Bodhisattva: Someone who has resolved to become a Buddha.

Buddha: Gautama Buddha, the founder of Buddhism.

Coptos; A port city on the Nile. Also known as Qift and Gebtu.

Cranganore: A town located on the Periyar River; part of the larger municipality of Muziris.

Dharamarajika: The great Stupa of Taxila which houses funerary objects of the Buddha.

Didymus: An ancient Greek term for twin.

Four Noble Truths: The primary and first teachings of the Buddha: the truth of suffering, the truth of the origin of suffering, the truth of the ending of suffering, and the truth of the path to the ending of suffering.

Gad: Brother of King Gondophores, as described in the Acts of Thomas.

Ganesha: The popular elephant-headed God of Hinduism. Son of Shiva.

Ganapati: An alternative name for Lord Ganesha.

Gandhara: An ancient region and empire stretching from northern India into modern-day Afghanistan.

Gandhari: Language of the Gandhara region.

Gondophores: King of Gandhara during the time of Thomas. Gondophores was originally only known in the Acts of Thomas. However, coins bearing his likeness and name were discovered in the 20th century during excavations at Taxila.

Gospel of Thomas: Also known as the Coptic Gospel of Thomas. Non-canonical gospel of 114 saying of Jesus.

Hinayana: An early school of Buddhism.

Hymn of the Pearl: A hymn recorded in the Acts of Thomas which Apostle Thomas sings while praying with fellow prisoners.

Indra: An important deity in Hinduism and often referred to as the King of the Gods. Indra is frequently included in the Silappathikaram story.

Isa: The eastern form of the name Jesus.

Jainism: An ancient Indian religion. Mahavira was a savior and spiritual teacher of Jainism as well as a near contemporary of Lord Buddha.

Jerusalem: The timeless city.

Judas Thomas: An apostle and brother of Jesus Christ.

Kajula Kadphises: A Kushan Prince who founded the Kushan Empire around the time Apostle Thomas was in Taxila.

Kanchi Matha: An ancient Hindu Monastery located in South India.

Kannagi: Loyal wife and one of the main characters in the story of the Silappathikaram an ancient Tamil story and poem of love and betrayal.

Kovalan: Cheating husband and one of the main characters in the story of the Silappathikaram, an ancient Tamil story and poem of love and betrayal.

Kutch: Dry desert and tribal region of Gujarat, Northwest India.

Laksmi: Hindu Goddess of good fortune and fertility.

Maadhavi: Dancer, courtesan, and one of the main characters in the story of the Silappathikaram, an ancient Tamil story and poem of love and betrayal.

Mahadeva: A Chola king of South India.

Mahavira: A Jain ascetic and spiritual teacher who preached in India. He is a near contemporary of Lord Buddha.

Mei Kalochi: The Queen Mother of the satrop in Andrapolis.

Mithra: A Zoroastrian deity with many qualities similar to Christ.

Moksha: The concept of release, freedom, and liberation in Hinduism. The term and concept are also used in Jainism, Buddhism, and other religions.

Murugan: Popular deity in South India. Often depicted as the God of War and a son of Shiva.

Muziris: An important port on the Periyar River in South India.

Mylapore: A port city on the east coast of South India located in present-day Chennai. Apostle Thomas died on a hill in Mylapore.

Myos Hormos: A port city on the Red Sea at the terminus of the Wadi Hammamat. Also known as Quesir.

Nabateans: An Arabian people who became traders and controlled large tracts of the Middle East.

Nasrani: A common term referring to someone from Nazareth, as in a follower of the one from Nazareth.

Natan: A cup bearer and serving boy as described in the Acts of Thomas.

Natarajan: A tolerant Hindu scholar from Muziris. A devotee of the Goddess and of Shiva.

Nirodha: The cessation of cravings and desire in Buddhism.

Nirvana: A concept found in many eastern religions and often misunderstood to be the equivalent of heaven. In Buddhism, it refers to the release from the endless cycle of birth, death, and rebirth and the cessation of all suffering, one of the Noble Truths.

Noble Eightfold Path: The summary list of Buddhist practices, part of the Middle Path.

Pandit: A Hindu scholar.

Parvati: The wife of Shiva and an important Goddess in her own right.

Petra: The capital city of the Nabateans.

Quesir: A Red Sea port also known as Myos Hormos.

Raja: The South Asian term for king.

Ram: A young man and guide from Kutch in India.

Rinpoche: The senior Buddhist priest in Taxila, originally from Tibet.

Sadhu: An ascetic holy man who has renounced worldly existence. Often an advanced practitioner of yoga.

Samudaya: A term for the Second Noble Truth of Buddhism.

Sangha: A community of monks (bhikkhus).

Sarida: A Hebrew slave girl and flute player, as described in the Acts of Thomas.

Satrap: A provincial governor in Persia and northern India.

Shaivite: Follower or devotee of the God Shiva.

Shakti: The principal of divine female power and energy.

Sher: Lion.

Shigao: A devoted priest of the Hinayana School of Buddhism.

Shiva: One of the principal deities in all of Hinduism. Shiva is part of the Hindu trinity, which includes Brahma and Vishnu.

Silappathikaram: Ancient Tamil Poem that recounts a story of love and conflict between a loyal wife Kannagi, her husband Kovalan, and a courtesan.

Siphor: A captain, trader, and traveler from Muziris described in the Acts of Thomas.

Stupa: In Buddhism, a large round structure containing relics of the Buddha and often a place for meditation and worship.

Surya: The Hindu God of the Sun.

Tai: The satrap of Andrapolis.

Tamil: The South Indian language. Modern Tamil and Malayalam are derived from ancient Tamil.

Tamilakam: The region of South India inhabited by the Tamil-speaking peoples.

Tau'ma: An Aramaic word meaning twin. Alternate spellings include Toma, Tomas, Thomas.

Taxila: An important city in Asia and the onetime capital of Gandhara. Its location was pivotal at the junction of the subcontinent, Central Asia, the Indus River system, and the Silk Road.

Temple Mount: The place where Apostle Thomas died, located in present-day Chennai.

Vanaraj: A Shiva devotee and sadhu who has renounced worldly life. Vanaraj lived a spartan life dedicated to Shiva and Lord Murugan.

Wadi Hammamat: A dry riverbed and highway to the Red Sea from the Nile. Some believe that the Wadi Hammamat was the route that Moses took fleeing from the Pharaoh as described in the Book of Exodus.

Wild Asses: At the time of Christ, large herds were common in Northwest India and the Kutch. Wild asses are described in detail in the Acts of Thomas.

Xenophon: A companion of Thomas at Taxila as described in the Acts of Thomas.

Yahweh: The God of the Hebrews, whose name is too sacred to be uttered.

Yam Suph: A Hebrew term for the Red Sea.

About the Author

Ambassador Paul Folmsbee (ret) is a former US diplomat. His father was a missionary doctor, and so Paul grew up in India, Mexico, and places in between.

As a child, Paul visited all the primary sites in South India where Apostle Thomas was said to have visited, including the hill in modern-day Chennai where Christians believe Thomas was martyred. Later in life, he wandered the archeological site of Taxila, Pakistan, and walked the streets of Bharuch and Cochin, India. Those visits and many others inspired him to track down more of the story of Apostle Thomas, always wondering how difficult it must have been for a man from Nazareth to travel to South India in the 1st Century. He has collected works on Apostle Thomas for many years.

Ambassador Folmsbee focused his diplomatic career on the developing world and hardship assignments. He served in Mali as the United States Ambassador, where he spent three years encouraging the government and northern separatists to come together and implement the Algiers Accord. Other assignments included

Washington, Haiti, India, Afghanistan, Iraq, Pakistan, Switzerland, Kenya, Gabon, Sri Lanka, Bolivia, and Tanzania.

He is married to Angelika Chin, a former diplomat, and lives in Florida and Jamaica.